The Death Mage Volume 1
(Yondome ha Iya na Sizokusei Majutsi vol. 1)

© DENSUKE 2016
© BAN! 2016
© HIFUMISHOBO 2016
Originally published in Japan in 2016 by HIFUMISHOBO Co., LTD
English translation rights arranged through TOHAN CORPORATION, TOKYO.

ISBN: 978-1-64273-202-3

Written by Densuke
Illustrated by Ban!
English Edition Published by One Peace Books 2022

Printed in Canada
1 2 3 4 5 6 7 8 9 10

...ity New York 11101

Densuke

Resides in Saitama Prefecture. Has loved light novels since his childhood and has been writing them himself for close to twenty years. He was aiming to become an author of orthodox fantasy, but kept getting distracted along the way. After many twists and turns, he won an award during the Fourth Internet Novel Awards, and achieved his debut as an author. He likes pizza and chicken skin *senbei*, and works out every day. He likes undead heroines the best.

1

The Death Mage

Densuke

Illustrations by Ban!

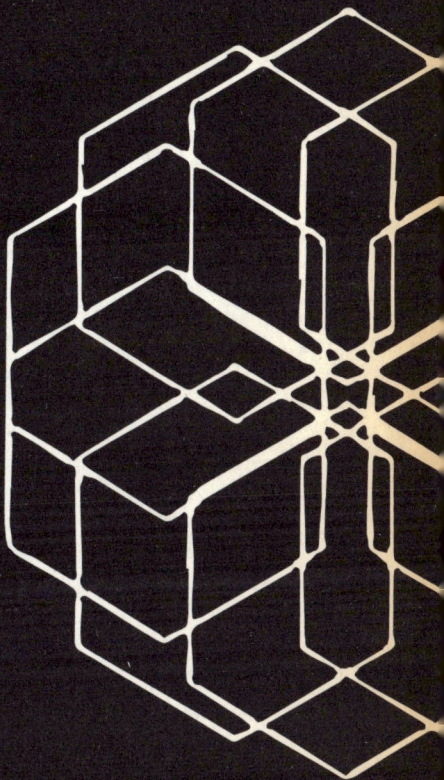

CONTENTS

The Death Mage

Written by Densuke   Illustration by BAN!

The Death Mage

PROLOGUE

THE FIRST AND SECOND LIVES

A terrorist bomb blew up and sunk a ferry full of students on a field trip from Prefectural Yasaka High School. Aside from the terrorists, this tragic attack led to the loss of 102 lives among the passengers and crew.

I wondered why all that cold salty water just vanished. We're all dead, huh? Hiroto Amamiya recognized his demise with a terrible feeling of loss. He was in a faintly illuminated place, crowded with people. There was no sign of the River Styx or fields of heavenly flowers, but this had to be the entrance to the afterlife.

The other dead folks reacted in all sorts of ways: weeping, consoling each other, some searching for friends and loved ones and reacting with relief when they weren't present.

Some of Hiroto's classmates were among the flailing deceased.

"No! I don't want to die!" This from a boy, Miyaji Konoe.

"Why? Why do we have to die like this?" This from a girl—probably Kanako Tsuchiya.

"Damn. I should have had a little more fun. Hey, there might still be time for us now?" came one hopeful voice.

"I know you," said Izumi Shimada, class president. "You're Aran Machida, from the next town over. Sorry, no time for that! Everyone! I know you feel like crying, but try to pull yourselves together!" She ignored the sleazy pickup line as she moved among the students, trying to calm them down. Hijiri Rikudo, the handsome president from another class, and a female ferry crewmember were helping out.

"Everyone!" shouted Asagi Minami, the class hothead, adding his voice to the cacophony. "Let's chill out! Crying, complaining—it's meaningless now! Try to calm down until we find out what happens next!"

Hiroto saw numerous other familiar faces among the crowd. It looked like very few kids from his class had survived.

Hmmm, what about teaching staff? Hiroto scanned around again. *Ah, there we go.* He spotted the class homeroom teacher, Junpei Murakami, sitting with his head in his hands.

"Dying didn't make things any easier," the teacher muttered, looking at Shimada and Rikudo with cold eyes. He clearly wasn't planning to extend his teaching contract beyond death. He had never been an especially passionate educator, so Hiroto wasn't surprised.

No one—not Shimada, Rikudo, or Asagi—gave Hiroto a glance. He was sitting quietly alone. They didn't feel the need to approach him.

Hiroto didn't want to be dead. He wanted to cry out and wail to that effect, but he simply didn't have the energy.

He sighed. *Looks like I died for nothing.*

This revelation came from spotting another of his classmates sitting nearby—Narumi Naruse, or "Naru" for short. She was—had been—the tone-setter for the class, and Hiroto died trying to save her. When the ferry tipped, about to capsize, Narumi had missed the railing and been about to fall over the side. Hiroto had grabbed her hand, in a flash, and placed it on the railing—leaving him to roll away down the deck, smashing his back into a wall and then falling over the side to drown. It had all been so quick, he hadn't even thought about it. Reflecting on it now, it had been reckless. He would have felt better about it if he had at least saved her life.

No. I did a good thing before I died. That's the only way to think about it. Hiroto didn't have anyone to grieve for his death. His parents had died when he was little, and he had no siblings. His uncle on his father's side had taken him in, but not without plenty of reminders. His uncle even told him that he'd have to leave as soon as he graduated high school. He had no friends, and certainly no girlfriend. Now his uncle would get all of Hiroto's parents' assets in addition to whatever sympathy gifts his own death would produce, so Hiroto figured that could serve as fair compensation for having taken him in. More than fair, even, considering the way Hiroto had been treated, especially when compared to his cousins.

Even his dreams for the future were nothing more than "to be happy." Maybe that could still come true, even if it had to be in heaven. At least his uncle wouldn't be there.

The reality, however, was equally unpleasant and unbelievable.

"You souls whose lives have now ended."

A new voice came from a mysterious new figure with a glowing light behind him, probably some kind of god.

"You have been selected. I will now give you special powers, special fates, and special fortunes. I want you to use these things to walk a new life on a different world from the Earth that you came from."

Rather than going to heaven, then, it sounded like reincarnation awaited them. Another world? That was surprising.

"Of course, you can decline my request. If so, you will follow the more standard procedure; your memories will be wiped, and you will be reborn somewhere on Earth. If this is your wish, speak now."

Hiroto didn't expect anyone to accept this offer, but one man did. Hiroto wasn't close enough to hear what he said, but then the god said, "you now return to the normal cycle" and the man vanished. Hiroto, meanwhile, was like everyone else—keen to accept the offer. Getting some kind of special power, being born to a new family in a new world, sounded great. He almost had hope for the future, for the first time in a long time.

"I will call your names. Come and stand before me when I do. Koya Endo. Mari Shihoin. Narumi Naruse. Kanata Kaito. Asagi Minami." The voice called out a string of names, each person receiving their special power, fate, and fortune from the god and then leaving the room. Narumi's name was called too. But even after more than half the people's names were called, Hiroto's turn still didn't come.

"Hiroto Amamiya? Amemiya." For a moment, Hiroto thought that was it. But no. It was just someone with a very similar name, standing up in front of the god.

"Amemiya?" Hiroto pondered. He didn't recall the name. Even if they were in different classes, if they attended the same school then Hiroto expected to know of someone with such a similar moniker. Probably another passenger, or member of the crew—just a coincidence. He looked in his late teens, and even had a similar height and build. If their faces had been similar then he could have been a doppelganger—or at least a long-lost brother.

Hiroto watched from the sidelines as Hiroto Amemiya

received not one, or two, or three special powers from the god, like the other people were. No, this Amemiya received no less than eight powers. All of them sounded pretty big, too. The god then forked over two fates and two fortunes as well. Like a grab sack of goodies. Hiroto was thinking the god must really have a thing for this guy. Then the divine one continued with his list of names. Eventually there was only Hiroto Amamiya left.

The god checked to make sure he had no special powers left, and then gave a big sigh. The kind of sigh someone gives who is finishing work for the day.

"Huh? Who are you?" The god finally noticed Hiroto.

"Hiroto Amamiya," Hiroto replied to the divine query. His name made the god start in surprise, which wasn't a good sign.

"Hiroto Amamiya? Amamiya, not Amemiya? That's Hiroto with one H and two Os, and Amamiya with a 'ma' not a 'me'?" As the god dissected the spelling of his name, Hiroto could only reply in the affirmative, his sense of dread growing. The god proceeded to groan.

"Wonderful. I got you mixed up with someone else. I thought you and Hiroto Amemiya were the same person, and I gave him all of your special powers. I even gave him the fate you were meant to receive and the fortune you were meant to be blessed with."

Quite the screw-up, then. That was why Hiroto thought he heard his name being called.

"But Hiroto Amemiya has gone," the god continued. "I can't get your powers back. We don't keep backups lying around either. Same with your fate and fortune."

"What does that mean? I get nothing? I'm the only one

starting from zero?" Hiroto asked, with some trepidation.

"Nope, you'll be starting in the negative. Coincidence and the whims of fate will never come to your aid. You will never be blessed with luck of any kind."

Not zero, but minus? That almost sounded like too much.

"No thanks, then. I'll take the normal resurrection that you gave the other guy," Hiroto said. If being reborn in a new world was going to only bring him suffering, best to just give up on that dream.

But the god was already shaking his head.

"The time for that decision has passed," he said.

"You're kidding?" Hiroto missed his chance, before he even realized he needed it. Hiroto was about to complain about all this red tape getting in the way of his fate and fortune, but a red light had already started to envelop his body. He felt his consciousness fading.

"The time for your resurrection has come," the god said.

Hang on! Hiroto thought. *How could I just receive nothing? That's ridiculous!*

"Unlike the other resurrected, this will leave your soul with a vast empty space. Rather than any special power, this empty space will fill your body with a massive volume of magical power. As you won't have any affinity for magic, however, you won't be able to learn the attributes of magic that exists in the world of Origin, to which you are being sent. So it's pearls before swine, in the end."

Is that supposed to make me feel better? Because it doesn't! He would have magical power but be unable to use magic? *That's worse than pearls or swine!*

"I really am sorry," the god said. "Without your powers,

your fate, and your fortune, you are sure to suffer. You will be raised in hardship. Being unable to use magic will severely restrict your future. You will be even lonelier than in your previous life, and more confined, and suffer so much. But please, don't let yourself hate others. Try to live a positive life."

That was easy for him to say! But Hiroto Amamiya didn't even get to shout that before he was plunged into the start of his second life.

The god—Reincarnation God Rodocolte—sent Hiroto and the others to a world called "Origin." It was a lot like Earth, but operated on a fusion of science and magic. The 100 heroes born into the world of Origin struggled with the differences from Earth and their new parents. But fortune served and saved them. They made use of their special powers, and fate conspired to bring them all back together. They achieved respect and fame. They kept the truth of their reincarnations just among themselves, but before long they become officially recognized as the "100 Heroes."

Without anyone knowing there should have been 101.

Rodocolte was the god of reincarnation for Earth, Origin, and multiple other worlds. People didn't believe in him directly, or become priests in his service, and he couldn't manifest in the world to make miracles happen or otherwise interfere with the course of events. All he could do was reincarnate souls and sometimes, very rarely, give something a nudge. But Rodocolte was by no means a nudger. The reincarnation system was well conceived and Rodocolte rarely had to make any tweaks at all.

A problem had started to present itself recently, however. One of the worlds he managed reincarnation for was falling behind the others in terms of progress.

While the other worlds flourished, this one world still struggled with all sorts of problems. Magic, warfare, literacy, science, engineering, art, cuisine. All sorts of fields saw an ebb and flow of development and degradation. The nations were the same, fighting endless wars, with no country managing to last a thousand years. Sometimes the emergence of a great hero would allow one nation to defeat its neighbors and become larger in size, but eventually it would fly apart at the seams and crumble back into smaller fragmented nations. Those that managed to achieve peace suffered attacks from powerful monsters, which caused more damage than even warfare.

There were other gods who managed this world directly and worked to lead the people. But when an insane demon king from another world arrived, those gods had been forced to summon heroes from a different world and fight alongside them to protect the stricken world. That fight had drained them of their powers. Some had fizzled out completely, while others clung to the barest fragments of their former divinity.

This world had to advance, somehow. It was simply stagnating at the moment, but that could lead to complete collapse at the drop of a hat. This was not a situation that Rodocolte could overlook. A reduction in the number of worlds he managed would mean a reduction in souls to reincarnate.

As he considered what action to take, Rodocolte had heard murmurings from the gods managing other worlds: that allowing souls to be reborn with their memories of their precious lives, what one might uncouthly called "cheating," had allowed their worlds to make prodigious, proactive advances in almost every field.

He found that somewhat hard to believe. Giving just one

person memories of their previous life surely couldn't have such a powerful effect. And yet it also seemed worth giving a try. The world in question already had numerous heroes from other worlds summoned to it in order to fight the demon king. This summoning involved taking living people directly into the separate world. It was an advantage that fell somewhat short of "cheating," but it was enough to defeat the demon king. While most of them had perished in the fighting, they had left numerous successes behind.

If he was going to give this a try, now was the perfect time, as the remaining evil gods subordinate to the demon king were not present. If the reincarnated didn't need to fight some kind of supernatural battle against god-killing beings, having them bring fully installed cheat-powers would surely result in even greater change and development in the world.

Luckily for him, his authority easily allowed him to send the souls of the dead to the problem world and have them reborn there. Letting them keep their previous memories wasn't difficult either. Producing cheat powers wasn't a problem, with all the divine energy he had saved up.

That said, just sending one person wasn't going to put his mind at ease. He decided to send 100, just to be on the safe side. And then, just as his preparations were completed, just over 100 people happened to die in a country called Japan, on a planet called Earth. According to rumor, these "cheat" souls had previously lived on an island nation with a unique culture, enjoying scientific and economic benefits. Japan fit the bill there perfectly.

Rodocolte didn't have anyone to call him out, so he plucked out the bad apples from those who died on the ferry and decided to use these Japanese souls in his reincarnation plan.

However, he decided not to send them to the problem world, but to a different one—to Origin. Rodocolte selected Origin as a testing ground, in order to allow the souls to gather experience and knowledge and be ready for anything. Once they had finished their second lives on Origin, he would make adjustments with new powers and fates, and then reincarnate them in the problem world. He had accounted for everything, and so he was sure it would work.

However, Rodocolte was himself inexperienced at things like this and so he made one small mistake. A mistake that even he, a god, could not foresee the impact of upon the entirety of his grand design.

As though foreshadowing all of this, one of the reincarnated souls appeared before him again, having already finished his second life. Even taking the order of reincarnations into account, this was too soon for the individual in question to have lived out a full life. Still, Rodocolte had actually expected this to be the first soul to return to him.

"You only managed a short life, Hiroto Amamiya," Rodocolte stated. The soul before him was that of Hiroto Amamiya. The 101st reincarnated, who had no powers, no magic, no fate, and no fortune. The soul of Hiroto Amamiya that appeared before Rodocolte had suffered horrific injuries and was wreathed in a dark and terrible magical power.

"I'll kill them!" he hissed. "I'll kill all of them! Send me back, I don't care! I won't forgive them! Or you either!" Hiroto didn't care that Rodocolte was a god, and came at him swinging
. . . .

In Origin, Hiroto Amamiya had been born into a military nation not too different from European countries on Earth. Just as Rodocolte warned him, he met misfortune from the moment of his birth. His mother was a prostitute, a woman his birth father discarded before Hiroto arrived. His mother found a new man, but did nothing to stop that new man from selling Hiroto for drinking money. Hiroto was purchased by a black site government laboratory performing illegal research. The experiments there revealed that Hiroto had far lower affinity for the magic of Origin than the average person—indeed, that he had no affinity for it at all.

Origin had a total of seven types of attribute magic: the standard earth, water, fire, and wind, and then light, life, and space. Any given individual would normally have an affinity for at least one of the seven attributes, but Hiroto went beyond a mere lack of affinity. He lacked even the basic aptitude for any of them. He was the exception proving the rule. The lowest of the low.

The researchers realized something else about Hiroto— that he possessed magical power far in excess of a normal person. He had no affinity for an attribute, but vast magical power. This was incredibly conflicting for the researchers. And then one of them realized something.

"Maybe it isn't that this subject lacks affinity for any attribute," the researcher posited, "but that his affinity lies with an unknown attribute that we haven't identified yet?" This hypothesis led their research in a new direction, and it was around this time that Hiroto regained his memories of his former life.

After years of human experimentation, the researchers did indeed discover an eighth attribute: death. They taught Hiroto the newly discovered death attribute magic, modifying every part of his body, even his brain, as they continued their experiments.

Hiroto's life was a living hell, nothing less. By the time he recovered his memories of his previous life, his captors had already planted a bomb in his body. The only people around him were researchers, who didn't see him as a person but rather as a test subject. He received some basic education, such as reading and writing—things he no longer felt he needed—but had zero freedom. At any sign of resistance, they shocked Hiroto with electricity, leaving him convulsing on the floor. The food was nutritious but worse than prison food. His days consisted of such meals and experiments, simply following the orders of the researchers.

Even after Hiroto awakened to his death attribute magic, he was unable to leave the laboratory. With the new death attribute magic, Hiroto had acquired incredible power. That had been made possible by Hiroto's hard work and the nature of the death attribute, only accessible by those with no affinity for any other attributes. He developed powerful magic, making a contribution to the laboratory, the researchers, and the nation they belonged to. But he was never rewarded for anything that he did.

Because, while the researchers acknowledged what he could do, they also feared him fighting back. The more useful and capable Hiroto proved himself to be, the more that fear grew.

They planted a bomb in his brain in addition to the one in his heart. They plugged GPS into him to prevent his escape and replaced his right eye with a mechanical eye containing a special camera. They fitted his ears and mouth with special listening devices that picked up every sound he heard or made. They restricted his meals to prevent him from becoming too strong. He had a tiny room and was only allowed out to participate in experiments. They modified and manipulated his body to allow him to make better use of death attribute magic, and further heighten his magical power.

In order to prevent him from finding friends and planning an escape or rebellion, and to prevent spies from other countries making contact with him, the guards and the operators giving him orders were all routinely switched around, keeping anyone from staying in his orbit for too long. In the end, the researchers resorted to truly inhuman measures, segmenting his consciousness from his body, turning him into nothing but a research puppet.

Hiroto still wasn't even 10 years old. From that day on, he lived unable to lift a finger on his own, a hell that lasted for over another decade.

The only reason he didn't lose his mind entirely was because of the souls of the dead that were drawn to him by his death attribute, and the hope that they might be able to save him from this hell.

But then, Hiroto died.

A new head researcher was desperate to prove himself over his predecessor and his extreme new experiments proved too much for Hiroto's exhausted body. Ironically enough, it was death that returned Hiroto's freedom to him. The power to control his magical power was returned to his soul upon his death.

"Power! Power rises!" he cried. "The joy of using my magic freely! The liberation of wielding my power without restraint!"

Spurred on by his hatred, Hiroto controlled his undead body and went on a rampage. He tore apart the scum who had toyed with his life, shredding the researchers like wet paper as they begged for their lives, beating the military personnel to death.

"So some of you are still alive, eh?" Almost completely out of his mind, he broke through the heavy doors to a separate room. But he didn't find more people to kill on the other side.

Instead, there were dozens of men and women, sleeping on filthy beds, locked in cages. More test subjects. Hiroto could tell what had been done to them.

"Right, there were other people here besides me."

The spirits that gathered around Hiroto were those of other test subjects. Apparently, the researchers had been trying to create a source of death attribute magic beyond just Hiroto.

"Ah."

Most of the subjects couldn't move, but a girl with black hair and pallid white skin looked up at Hiroto from her bed. His warped undead form was reflected back in her eyes, but she didn't seem scared at all. Maybe that was the reason why Hiroto proceeded to breathe death attribute magic into all of the test subjects, including the girl.

"This will let you move around. If you want to get out of here, come with me," he told them.

They would only slow Hiroto down if they couldn't even move. Blessed by death magic, the girl and then others recovered the power to move on their own, their modified and explosive-warped bodies coming back under their own control.

He did this out of sympathy, compassion, and gratitude for the reminder that he was more than just the enemy of the living.

"If you want to come with me, keep your distance. There might still be enemies ahead."

The magic and bullets used by the enemy soldiers wouldn't work on Hiroto, but they would tear these poor creatures apart. He didn't plan on leaving any enemies alive, so they would be safe if they stayed away from the frontline.

Determined, Hiroto continued down the empty corridors. He smashed through the sealed exit and came into the outside world for the first time since he recovered his memories of his previous life.

"No way!"

Dozens of people were forming a semicircle around him, as though waiting for his arrival, and Hiroto was happy to see them all. He recognized many of them, after all.

Some of them looked a little different, but they were his classmates from the same school in his previous life, along with the teaching staff. Junpei Murakami, Miyaji Konoe, Asagi Minami, Hijiri Rikudo, and Narumi Naruse! His friends. The others who had been reincarnated into Origin. Never giving up hope had paid off. Even without a fate from gods, he had been sure his friends would find him. That his friends would save him. That was all he had clung to, for twenty long years.

They took their time, sure, but he wasn't about to complain. He was overjoyed at this reunion. Now he had a second chance for his second life. He could fix things. Look how everyone had come to rescue him. Shaking with happiness and hope, Hiroto took a step toward them.

"Fire at will!"

At the command of a youth who seemed to be leading his "friends," attack magic hammered into Hiroto.

"Wait! Why are you attacking me? I'm one of you! I'm one of you!" Hiroto's cries were drowned out by the scorching fire, slashing air blades, stabbing ice, and crackling lightning that poured down onto him. Having dropped his guard completely, Hiroto was left exposed to everything they had, and collapsed to the ground.

"Pretty pathetic. All this talk of a dangerous undead, but there was no need to even use my powers," came a voice from above.

"Hah, we've got thirty of the 100 Heroes here! Nothing can stop us. Right, Mr. Murakami?"

"Drop the mister stuff. I'm not your teacher anymore."

Familiar voices chattered away, out of view. *One hundred? One hundred Heroes? No! There were 101 of us, 101 with me!* Hiroto wanted to shout, but his throat was gone. He couldn't make any sound. His right arm had been burned to a charcoal stump and his left ripped off completely. His feet were gone, and his left leg was just a lump of flesh. His face and torso weren't doing much better.

"We got off easy because this undead dropped his guard. Death attribute magic is truly terrifying."

Hiroto turned his one working eye toward this voice, to see Narumi Naruse standing there. She was older than in their previous life, now a woman rather than just a girl.

"Yeah. In the end, he's just another victim of this laboratory."

The youth who had given the attack order was standing next to her. From the distance between them, Hiroto could instinctually tell that the youth and Narumi had a close relationship.

"He must've wanted us to kill him."

"I'm sure you're right, Hiroto," Narumi said.

Hiroto? Hold on! Hiroto Amemiya? This guy is Hiroto Amemiya!?

"Let's eradicate him, so he can't feel any more pain."

"That's the only thing we can do for him now," Hiroto Amemiya agreed. "Narumi, with me."

Hiroto was raging inside at the injustice. The sheer nerve of his guy. He received the fate and fortune intended for Hiroto, and now he was playing the hero, about to kill him! Why did it have to be this guy, and not Hiroto himself? The terrible second life Hiroto had led was all because of this scumbag! The 100 Heroes leaving him out and then coming to kill him!

He tried to shout, to voice his anger, but then a brilliant light from the hands of Hiroto and Narumi reduced him to dust.

"This is all your fault!" Hiroto bellowed. "You call yourself a god? What kind of second life was that? You sent me into a hell far worse than my first life!"

Hiroto's fist was wreathed in what looked like black mist, but it didn't come close to hitting Rodocolte. That was the difference between a man and a god.

"I really am sorry for what I did to you." Rodocolte repeated the same platitudes, explaining to Hiroto's raging soul the situation he was currently in. The information, transmitted by the power of the gods, entered Hiroto's head in an instant.

"You're saying . . . there's a third time for me?" Hiroto said.

"That's right. This was the plan from before I first reincarnated you," Rodocolte said. "You have no recourse to turn this one down, and I cannot stop it from happening." It all seemed very unfair, but Hiroto also saw a glimmer of hope.

"Ah ha! In that case, in the next world I'll just kill them all! The ones who killed me, I'll kill every last one of them!" he cackled. "I was the first one to die, meaning I'll be the first one to start my second reincarnation. That'll give me the advantage! That'll let me kill the lot of them!"

He could become an adult first, build up his strength, and then find Hiroto Amemiya and the others when they were re-born later, while they were still children, and kill them! He could do that even without any special powers.

"Come on then. Adjust me, or whatever you need to do, your divine holiness! I'm getting fortune and fate this time, right? I'm the first one to die, meaning even you can't screw up again, surely?"

"I have nothing to give you." Rodocolte pushed forward with his palm, gently bumping Hiroto's soul away.

"What?"

That was all it took for Hiroto to start accelerating away, falling toward something or somewhere.

"At this point, I could give you something new. But for you, I can't."

"Why? I get nothing again? Just me? How can that be?"

"I can't have you killing the other resurrected," Rodocolte replied, falling into the distance. "I'm sorry, but if you kill them in revenge then you'll interfere with all my plans. Your death in Origin was an unfortunate set of circumstances. Bad luck. The fact that Hiroto Amemiya and the others didn't recognize you at the end was more of the same, although I doubt you will accept such an explanation."

After the boat explosion, Hiroto was sitting at the edge of the space where the souls gathered, meaning no one had seen him there. Only one person had declined to be resurrected. And the final blow—Hiroto had been resurrected last. So Hiroto Amemiya and the others either thought Hiroto had not died with them at all, somehow surviving the explosion, or that he had just declined the resurrection like the other person. To top it off, when they were reunited, Hiroto's face had been completed disfigured by all the human experiments, and even Narumi hadn't realized it was him.

"I brought all of this upon you," Rodocolte said. "I wanted you to never give up, to never hate, and to live a positive life, but that simply wasn't possible with the circumstances you were sent into. With the discovery of the death attribute and the development of new magic, you made a contribution to Origin, but received no reward for any of it. I hope you can forgive the fact that you now go into your third life, knowing it will probably be another life of misfortune."

The fact Hiroto most definitely could not forgive anything of the sort radiated from his soul as it fell farther away.

"All I can do is make you give up on your foolish revenge before you even attempt it, and prompt you to kill yourself."

With that, something like slime appeared in Rodocolte's hand. The next moment, it hit Hiroto.

Pain lanced into Hiroto as Rodocolte explained.

"That's a curse. A curse you'll never be able to break. That curse will stop you from obtaining any kind of power, even in this new world. But for your fourth reincarnation, I promise to wash away all of your painful memories and return you to the normal cycle of reincarnation."

Hiroto had no time to respond to this most awful of promises, and he blacked out.

The Death Mage

CHAPTER ONE
THE BEGINNING OF THE THIRD LIFE

H

Hiroto Amamiya was reborn in the world of Ramda!

Hiroto Amamiya was cursed by Reincarnation God Rodocolte!

Hiroto felt like these announcements rang out inside his head, but he couldn't really remember. His consciousness gradually returned from a semi-comatose state that couldn't be called awake, but also couldn't be called sleeping.

Where am I? What's going on? It does feel like I'm alive, at least.

But Hiroto still didn't really understand what was happening. Even with his eyes open, all he could see was darkness and he could barely move his arms or legs. Everything felt like a dream. His entire body was surrounded in a warm fluid, and he couldn't breathe. But it wasn't painful. It was almost like he'd become a fish.

I don't even want to guess, but maybe I've been reborn as something other than a human? It sounded possible. He has just been cursed. He might have some level of freedom as a human, but if he was born an animal or fish, he was going to be at a total loss.

Luckily, that wasn't one particular issue he had to deal with.

He heard a voice. Not a crying voice, or an angry voice, but a gentle singing voice. It was strangely muffled, and he couldn't pick out the words, but the emotion it carried came through loud and clear.

Love.

I see. I'm in the womb. I'm still a fetus.

The divine curse hadn't altered the destination of his resurrection, at least. Fragments of the information from Rodocolte that had flowed into him before he was resurrected told him that this world of Ramda was a world of swords and magic. He might end up an elf or a dwarf, but it would at least be some form of intelligent life.

Does this song sound a bit Japanese to me?

Then his awareness faded again.

When he came to, he was already born.

"You're such a good little boy, Vandal. I'm not complaining, but you can cry sometimes, if you like?" A woman was holding him, talking to him. He quietly looked up at her.

It sounds like "Vandal" is my new name, Hiroto thought. *Far better than the serial number I had in Origin. And this person is my third mother. Looks like I've done better than Origin on this score too.*

In that world, he had been sold off almost before he knew what was happening, so this seemed like a much more promising start. Not only was he lacking divine protection, but he was under a divine curse, so this seemed like a miracle.

So what environment was I born into? My mother looks like a dark elf.

The woman in front of him looked in her early 20s, with golden hair and brown skin. She was attractive, with a beautiful face, making him think he could hope to be handsome himself in the future. Her ears were clearly pointed. Vandal might have just been born into this world, but he could guess she was a dark-skinned dark elf—or a very tanned elf, maybe.

That might explain why we seem to be living in a cave, Hiroto thought. It wasn't a cave that looked like a house, either, but just a cave. There were doors, and furs down on the floor as a kind of carpet, but it was hardly the peak of civilization. The elves he had seen in fantasy on Earth lived alongside nature, though, so maybe this was normal. *The bigger problem is my body.*

The warm arms of his mother enveloped his small and fragile body. He looked at her smooth, chocolate-colored skin, and then at his own small, almost useless hands.

Hands that were as white as silk.

Why am I a different color? My ears do seem to be pointed.

His mother was a dark elf, but he was pale. Maybe he was something else. He knew nothing about the biology of dark elves. They might be white when they were born and become darker as they grew up. Or maybe he wasn't this woman's child by birth.

"Oh? You think the difference in our color is strange, do you? You're a smart one, Vandal, to spot that already. Don't worry, little one. You take after your father. I'm Dalshia, and I'm definitely your mother."

His mother—Dalshia—gave him a gentle smile, wiping Vandal's questions away. He was mixed race, born from parents from two different races. She might be lying, of course, but he saw no reason to suspect that. Rather than wasting his time and mental capacity on that, he just accepted this love without doubt, and allowed himself to relax.

I'm actually…pretty tired….

Then Dalshia put Vandal to bed.

Vandal was Dalshia's first child, but even at just 3 months old he was proving incredibly easy to handle.

When he was hungry, he would make a noise and tap on his own tummy, or even point at Dalshia's chest. When he needed a diaper change, he would make similar noises and pat at his bottom.

"Yes, dear, here you go. Here comes the milk for you. You really are a smart one, Vandal," Dalshia said, exposing her breast, lifting Vandal up, and letting him latch on. She was amazed again at how smart he seemed.

She also knew this wasn't normal. He wasn't just smart—he was too smart. But she couldn't feel bad about her own child. *He takes after his father. He's a lot like him.* The uncanny intellect of her child came from his father's bloodline, that was all. The strange flashes of magical power she has been sensing from Vandal recently only reinforced that thinking. His father was a far more magically inclined race than Dalshia and the dark elves.

I'm more concerned about how he never cries or laughs, Dalshia thought. *Maybe his father not being around is worrying him?* She more concerned about how Vandal never seemed to laugh or cry like a normal baby. Even when her beloved baby was hungry or when she tickled him, his expression remained as placid as that of a doll. At first, she thought that he was in a bad mood, but that didn't seem to be the case. He didn't seem to be lacking in emotions either. She had seen him cry, but just with that same blank expression, and without making a sound.

She cast some healing magic on him when that happened, worried he might be sick, but it turned out he had just been crying because of a bad dream. He could feel things too. He laughed when she tickled him. His expression didn't change, but his body shuddered.

But my biggest worry is when I feed him. I wonder if he doesn't like my milk. When feeding him, he didn't latch onto her nipple at once, but would freeze in place for a while, his eyes darting around. Eventually he would drink, but Dalshia couldn't help but worry that he didn't like her milk.

For Vandal, those acts that were only natural—and vital— for a baby, such as sucking on her mother's breasts and drinking her milk, filled him with embarrassment and feelings of guilt.

It ain't easy being a baby. Any kid should be happy and proud to have a young, pretty mother. But things became more complicated when the mind inside that kid was a guy who had lived for more than 37 years, once his past lives were totaled up. His mind was closer to that of an adult, but his body was that of a baby, making things really weird for him. He had zero experience with women, even back when he was in high school on Earth. That meant sucking on Dalshia's nipples made him uncomfortable. His body was a baby, so it wasn't physically turning him on, but he was embarrassed by the act itself.

I wonder what this was like for the others. My memories didn't return in Origin until about ten months after I was born. The other resurrected in Origin might have been struggling with their mothers changing their diapers too. *But I can't keep on worrying my mom like this. I need to suck it up—literally.*

Vandal was quick to start thinking of Dalshia, his third mother, as his "one and true mother." That was easy to do because it marked his first experience in three lifetimes of motherly love. It would have been harder to reject her than it was to accept her.

With that in mind, he started out trying to act like a normal baby. But it quickly proved an impossible task. He had the brain of a teenager, so he was completely unable to act like a baby. To top it off, for some reason he was unable to cry or laugh. He couldn't move his expression at all. It was like his muscles were paralyzed, but his mouth and eyelids still worked normally. It was just that nothing moved naturally. The only way to change his expression was to intently focus on it. Maybe this was another effect of the curse.

I can talk with my mom about my face once I can actually talk, Vandal thought. *There are some problems, but I've learned a lot as well.*

Dalshia didn't expect Vandal to be able to understand what she was saying, of course, so she didn't go into detail about their circumstances. But after living together for a month, Vandal had picked up most of what he needed to know.

Firstly, he learned that Dalshia's husband was from a race that her own father was terribly afraid of. That meant Vandal, being half that race himself, was subject to discrimination and dislike. That explained why Dalshia was living in seclusion out here in the forest, dwelling in a cave dug out by elemental magic, and why Vandal hadn't seen a single person other than his mother.

I've also learned that I'm in the Milg Shield Kingdom, a nation belonging to the Amidd Empire and located in the northwest of the Vangaia Continent, and that once I've grown a little more she plans to return to the dark elf village. I haven't been born with a silver spoon in my mouth, but this is more encouraging than my last life.

There was hope so long as he could make it back to the dark elf village, and so he decided to work toward that as his initial goal.

With that in mind, Vandal started his magical training before he could even crawl. He had achieved full control of death magic in his previous life. With these powers, he might even be able to help his mother. That was the plan, but Vandal found himself completely unable to use magic.

Because I'm still a baby? Or is this the curse too? That was a puzzle, but giving up just because it didn't seem to be working was not an option. Death magic was the only weapon Vandal had in his possession, having again been passed over for cheat abilities and affinities for other types of magic.

"It would help if I could see your status, Vandal," Dalshia commented, almost to herself, one day another six weeks after Vandal was born.

Status? Unable to activate death magic, Vandal started to work on holding his own neck up straight, but that one word from his mother surprised him. He wasn't expecting to hear a game term like that here—but then, to his surprise, he saw his own status displayed inside his head.

Name: Vandal
Race: Dhampir (Dark Elf)
Age: 0 years old
Alias: None
Job: None
Level: 0
Job History: None
—Status
Vitality: 12
Magical Power: 100,000,000
Strength: 10

Agility: 1
Stamina: 25
Intellect: 20
—Passive Skills
[Brute Strength: Level 1]
[Rapid Healing: Level 1]
—Active Skills
[None]
—Curses
[Unable to carry over experience from previous lives]
[Unable to enter existing jobs]
[Unable to personally acquire experience]

Wow, I've got some serious magical power, thought Vandal. *Looks like my dad is a vampire. And three curses? I guess that god really wants me to off myself.*

The content of his stats provided lots of surprises. His race was indicated as "dhampir." If his knowledge from Earth held true here in Ramda, that meant he was half-vampire. That definitely explained why his mother was hiding him away. He had no idea what the religious situation was like in Ramda, but he doubted half-vampire children were generally welcome additions to the family. In fact, they might be hunted like monsters. That definitely sounded like it might pose a risk to his continued existence—and like he probably had a lot of dhampir-related discrimination coming his way. This life was sounding tougher than he expected already.

Next, there was his magical power. Considering its location in the list, and the fact that no other separate MP item was displayed, he had to presume this was the MP for Ramda—and it was big, sitting at a cool 100 million. He didn't know what the average was for any of these stats, but it sounded like a massive outlier to him. This had to be the magical power that Rodocolte had talked about, filling the "empty space" left by the lack of the cheat-code fate and fortune he had been supposed to receive. In Origin he had lacked any kind of status screen, meaning he only had the assessment from his captors to go on, something like "thousands of times higher than the most powerful wizard." Now he could see the number for himself, it was more like tens of thousands.

But I'm still just a helpless baby. Having all the MP in the world didn't matter if he couldn't use magic. That was another reason why he needed to hurry up and relearn his death attribute magic.

"Strength" and "agility" look self-explanatory, as does "stamina." "Intellect" is probably more than just being smart. It probably affects learning magic, the effects of magic, using multiple spells at once, chanting time, stuff like that. It might affect mental strength too.

Based on these considerations, he could accept his agility being lower than the other stats. He was only 6 weeks old. His head still wobbled around like a broken doll. Crawling wasn't the issue—he couldn't even turn himself over. He was a baby. There was nothing agile about a baby.

Flipping that thought over, however, and putting his magical power aside for a moment, his other stats seemed pretty good for a level 0 baby. That had to be a benefit of being a dhampir.

Next, his skills. Vandal's gaming knowledge told him that passive skills were skills that were always in effect, even if he didn't think about them. Active skills had to be used to have any effect.

I've got Brute Strength and Rapid Healing. Sounds like more dhampir-based stuff—race specific skills, in game terms. But I don't see any death attribute magic skills.

You wouldn't expect a baby to have many skills, either, but Vandal had lived more than 37 years between Earth and Origin. It would have made sense for him to have some other skills—in particular relating to death attribute magic, as he had started down that path himself in his previous life.

The absence of such skills could maybe be explained by the three curses in the next section. *This "unable to carry over experience from previous lives" curse, that has to be the one. It means I can't bring over my experience from my previous life in the form of skills. The other two look rough as well. I'm going to have trouble taking jobs or levelling up like this.*

These were curses handpicked by Rodocolte to make him want to kill himself. They had to be the worst of the worst, Vandal was annoyingly assured.

But now I've been reborn, I'm not going to just lie down and die again! I need to become strong enough to survive—and that starts with getting my death attribute magic back…ah…nope, too tired….

Vandal had been holding out quite well, but he was still a baby and couldn't fend off the sleepies forever.

✦

Acquired death attribute magic skills!

An announcement rang out inside his brain. It was around the time his head finally stopped lolling around that Vandal managed to learn death attribute magic once again. Considering he had learned it for himself in his previous life, he hadn't expected it to take so long to do it again.

Two months of trying to turn my magical power into magic and failing. My hard work has finally paid off.

That said, his abilities were limited to Death to Bacteria, which killed all microbes within a certain radius, and Death to Bugs, which was the same thing but for insects. He also had Magic Absorption Barrier, which could create a barrier that absorbed any magic that touched it.

Unfortunately, these skills lacked a discernable, visible effect. He wanted to let Dalshia know he could use magic, but that was difficult with his current tool set. Absorbing her magic right in front of her eyes might have made an impact, but she never used elemental magic in front of him. She might have been using elemental magic to create some sparks when starting the cook fire, but that was about it.

I can barely sit up for myself, Vandal thought. *I still can't even see the whole room.* Sitting on the bed, Vandal sighed at his current lot in life. His mother chuckled, commenting that he looked like a frumpy old man, but that didn't bother him. *At least she's taking me outside a little now. I'm so bored in here, boredom might be the thing that kills me.*

When the weather was nice, Dalshia had started to take Vandal out with her on walks. She wanted to give him a little more stimulation than what the cave could provide. She was also a little worried about their food stores and wanted to top off their supplies. Vandal recalled how incredibly cautious she had been when they went out for the first time. All Dalshia had done was to open the cave door a crack and let Vandal touch the delicate shaft of light streaking in with his fingertips.

"I'm so glad! That's one vampire weakness you didn't in-herit!"

Her reaction reminded Vandal again that his father was a vampire. It sounded like an unlucky dhampir could end up having to avoid sunlight for their entire life. Vandal thanked goodness he didn't take too much after his father.

"This means we can go outside together."

Once Dalshia got him outside, Vandal was so moved he was at a loss for words—not that he could speak yet anyway.

Wow! The world…all this nature…it's so big! There was a forest outside the cave, and the air was pure and clear. The sun was bright, the sky a piercing blue, the clouds pure white, and the woods a verdant green. It was a forest, nothing more, but before Hiroto Amemiya and the others finished him off in Origin, he had been locked up like cattle for the better part of twenty years and then died as soon as he got free. His eyes sparkled at every twig and tree around himself.

"You seem to like it outside," his mother said with a chuckle.

He was still unable to operate his facial expressions, but Dalshia could tell how captivated he was by everything around him, so she set out for a walk and some light gathering. Of course, while carrying little Vandal along, she didn't do anything as dangerous as hunt animals with a bow or elemental magic. Rather, she gathered edible plants, nuts, and mushrooms, and set up some traps to catch animals. Dalshia ate most of the gathered food, but took a small portion to feed to Vandal.

What a strange feeling. Now he had a young and attractive dark elf spoon-feeding him. Once a day, and only a small amount, but still. That also meant his number of breast feedings was re-duced. If he was going to survive that meant leaving the region so dangerous to dhampir and heading for the dark elf village, and that meant he needed to be on solid food, but growing up wasn't easy to do.

It didn't help that the milk tasted better than the spoon-fed alternative.

Death attribute magic skill reached level 2! Acquired new skills Resist Maladies, Resist Magic, Night Vision, and Suck Blood!

About five months after Vandal was born, Dalshia started to leave her son for a few hours at a time and go into the forest to gather supplies.

"Just a little longer and we'll head for my homeland," she said. "I need to prepare carefully for the trip. I know you're lonely when I'm gone, but hang in there."

With that she would go off to hunt beasts, or slip into a village to pick up supplies by pretending to be a wandering adventurer. Sometimes she didn't come back for half the day, but this was also required for their survival, so Vandal knew she didn't have a choice. On Earth, people would have called child services on a mother leaving a baby alone for so long, but Vandal didn't have a problem with it. She was doing all of this to protect him, after all. She really was raising her baby—a half-vampire baby, no less—all alone, without any help from anyone else.

Recognizing that he still hadn't seen his father, it seemed they couldn't expect any help from that branch of the family. There were often stories in which vampires despised and denigrated mixed-blood children even more than humans did. Even in Japan, which was supposed to have a highly developed concept of human rights, half-Japanese were discriminated against.

So in Ramda, the issue surely applied to mixed-race children.

I might never get to meet my father, Vandal thought. Maybe his father was already dead.

Taking all of that into account, and putting emotion aside and thinking logically, Dalshia would have been better off casting Vandal aside. It would have been smarter, and she would have had an easier life. Nothing tying her down. Fewer burdens to carry. It might be hard for a while, and there might be guilt or suffering, but she'd get over it. Go back to a normal life. If she wanted children, she could go to another country, or back to the dark elf village, find a new man, and do it right this time.

The reason she couldn't abandon her son, in the face of all the risks, had to be the love she had for his father—and for him.

Hardly the ideal situation, but it's nice to be loved. That happiness helped fuel Vandal's continued hard work. When he was awake, he trained with his magic, moved his arms and legs to build his muscles, and practiced making vocal sounds. This all resulted in his death attribute magic level increasing, which in turn finally allowed him to perform magic that Dalshia could see.

"Wow! You're still a baby but you can use magic? You must be a genius, Vandal!"

He was so happy to be praised for his hard work. So happy that it made her happy. He learned some other skills as well, but they seemed to be the result of just growing up rather than his hard work.

Resist Maladies came from his vampire father, a skill that allowed him to resist everything from poison and sickness to lack of sleep and starvation, as well as the variety of ailments and status conditions that magic might bestow. The Resist Magic skill, meanwhile, came from his dark elf side, mitigating the damage from attack spells. Night Vision came from both sides, allowing him to see as clear as day, even on the most starless night. Suck Blood went without saying. His canine teeth—his fangs—had grown in much faster than his other teeth, and once he had a set above and below he was able to practice.

"I thought you might get those," his mother said, noticing that her son had fangs. "I don't think this is such a good idea, but okay." Dalshia took a rabbit she had captured and chopped off its head with her knife. Then she collected the blood in a wooden saucer. "Here. Drink this."

Mother, are you crazy? Vandal looked at her with narrowed eyes, the iron smell of blood filling his nose from the saucer in front of him.

There were dishes on Earth that mixed blood into their sauces, and people had been known to mix viper or turtle blood with alcohol and drink it. But those things seemed different from giving rabbit blood to a baby.

That was Vandal's take on things, but it didn't look like she was going to change her mind. *I guess I can give it a try.* He was sure it wasn't going to taste good, but he still extended his tongue and lapped a little up with the tip of his tongue. He was surprised when it actually tasted okay.

Hey. I can drink this. It tastes a bit metallic, but it smells okay… in fact, it's actually good! It wasn't mixed in a cocktail or drowned out by spices, but the rabbit's blood was as easy for him to drink as his mother's milk had been. That definitely surprised him. Dalshia stroked his thickening hair as she explained.

"You can drink blood, Vandal, the same as your father. But you don't have to do it to survive, so please only do it when you're hungry but I'm not around, okay?"

That made sense. He was half vampire. Another reason people hated dhampirs. For now, though, it gave him another alternative to milk.

✸

Around six months after Vandal had been born, and around the time he started to crawl. Dalshia had left her son alone again, taking a trip into a nearby town.

I'm lucky she's being so positive about what a smart baby I am. Everything that was odd about Vandal, including his use of magic, was simply "amazing" to his mother. She didn't suspect or read anything more into it than that.

"Dhampir really are amazing," she would say, suggesting that was where she pinned the cause of everything strange about Vandal. He was happy she didn't take things any further than that. He was a 6-month-old baby, after all, without the power of speech. He was continuing his vocal training but couldn't get words out yet. Otherwise he would have explained everything.

About Rodocolte, about my past lives, and about Hiroto Amemiya.

In the light novels and manga that Vandal had encountered on Earth, characters often kept secret the fact they had been reborn from another world. But he planned on trashing that trope completely. He needed to share this information with Dalshia, at least, as quickly as possible. She was his mother, after all.

If this was your run-of-the-mill reincarnation, or just a daytrip to another world, I might choose to keep quiet, Vandal thought. *But that's not the case. One hundred other people are going to also be reborn into this world, and with cheat codes loaded and ready to go.* Hiroto Amemiya and the gang, his "friends" who had never searched for him on Origin, leaving him to die. Once they died in Origin themselves, they would also be reborn here in Ramda. He had no idea when that would be. When Vandal died in his previous life, they had looked to be around 20. It might take fifty years for them to get here, unless they got into accidents or the like. Of course, that was presuming the passage of time was the same in Origin and Ramda. One day in Ramda could be a year in Origin.

While that extreme was unlikely, they were coming to here to Ramda eventually. Even Rodocolte didn't have the means to prevent that, as Vandal knew all too well.

What if Rodocolte says something before they are reborn? That could be a problem. I shouted at him that I wanted to kill them all. If they're going to be reborn before I die here, he's sure to warn them. After all, Rodocolte's plan was to have them advance this world. He didn't want them to die before they could do that, and so he was sure to warn them about Vandal.

That would put them on guard about him. They had all grown up in peaceful Japan in their first lives, so they might be willing to hear him out, or try to apologize for what happened on Origin. Amicable vigilance was understandable.

But he also couldn't write off that some of them might try to locate and kill him first. Just like how Hiroto had ended his life so tragically in Origin, he couldn't predict what might have happened to them. Even if they started out as heroes, warriors for justice, who knows what years of fighting twisted terrorists and criminal collaborators could do to them.

Heroes. They were a problem.

Just before I died, they said something about a report of undead. That's why they came to kill me. They must have been using their cheat abilities to be some kind of international band of superheroes. Like some American comic book.

Upon their arrival, they had met the evil undead who wiped out the entire lab staff. Not the best first impression.

Before he died on Origin, Vandal had saved some of the other test subjects. Hopefully that had cast him in a slightly better light—postmortem, of course.

I wonder what happened to all of them. I've been reborn into a completely different world, so worrying about them now doesn't really get me anywhere. I guess that's something I really do have to leave up to the heroes. He was worried about whether they all made it out safely or not, but there was little point in such thinking right now.

He was a half-vampire, a dhampir. If they still had that Japanese pacifism and humanitarianism, that respect for life, things might work out. But he was equally as worried that such values may get overwritten by the anti-vampire and anti-dhampir sentiments of Ramda. He wouldn't stand a chance against 100 enemies with all their cheats enabled.

This was what Dalshia had been dragged into. It was too dangerous, and too unfair to leave her in the dark. That was why Vandal wanted to tell her everything about himself.

If that makes her leave me, so be it. He had only known her for six months, but she was still the only mother he had ever known. No one in any of his lives had ever treated him with such tenderness.

I mean, if possible, I'd rather she didn't leave, Vandal thought. If giving up on his revenge was what it took to achieve that, well…he wasn't going to forgive or forget, not at this point, but maybe he could just keep out of the heroes' way.

That was how attached Vandal had become to Dalshia. His mental clarity since being reborn also played a role, but he cared so much for his mother that he was willing to give up on his revenge.

In which case, once he was a little older, he would tell Dalshia everything. If he could then use his knowledge from Earth and Origin, and his death attribute magic, they could probably live a relatively comfortable life. After that, he could sit back and watch the cheaters help improve this world. It almost sounded nice.

Vandal was crawling around, building his muscles as he thought things through. He realized he was hungry.

I guess I'll drink some blood.

He picked up one of the live rabbits in Dalshia's basket. He was only 6 months old, but he was a dhampir with a skill called Brute Strength, letting him catch it much easier than expected. Then he used Death to Bacteria and Death to Bugs to clean the struggling rabbit, before biting into it. *Blood tastes good, but mom's milk tastes better.* He mercilessly sucked down the twitching rabbit, appeasing his empty stomach, but thinking about his mother's bosom.

That day, however, Dalshia didn't come back at the normal time.

Name: Vandal
Race: Dhampir (Dark Elf)
Age: 6 months
Alias: None
Job: None
Level: 0
Job History: None
—Status
Vitality: 18
Magical Power: 100,000,600

Strength: 27
Agility: 2
Muscle: 33
Intellect: 25
—Passive Skills
[Brute Strength: Level 1] [Rapid Healing: Level 1]
[Death Attribute Magic: Level 2 (NEW)]
[Resist Maladies: Level 1 (NEW)] [Resist Magic:
Level 1 (NEW)] [Night Vision (NEW)]
—Active Skills
[Suck Blood: Level 1 (NEW)]
—Curses
[Unable to carry over experience from previous lives]
[Unable to enter existing jobs]
[Unable to personally acquire experience]

❖

Vandal awoke the next morning, but Dalshia still wasn't back.

This is strange. I don't like this. I need to go and find her.

A baby of 6 months normally wouldn't plan to go outside alone, but if Dalshia didn't return today, then Vandal would have to go out alone anyway. There was still one live rabbit, but he'd drink that dry today for sure. After that, he'd need to find food for himself, but his 6-month-old intestines couldn't handle much but his mother's milk and blood.

A baby eats more than you'd think. Five or six feedings a day. In my case I'm burning even more energy than normal on magic training and building muscles. That meant Vandal needed a lot more food than a normal baby. If he just sat here waiting like a normal baby might, he would starve to death in a matter of days, although he was a dhampir, not a human, so he couldn't be sure about that timeline. *I need to get ready.*

But much less than running off to find Dalshia, he couldn't even walk. He needed to prepare, and the first thing to prepare was a way to get around.

"First—rise."

Focusing his mind behind the command, the wild rabbit that he himself had drained of blood twitched and started to move.

It hadn't returned to life. He had used magic to make one of the spirits wafting around in the vicinity possess the body of the rabbit, turning it into an undead. Such was the art of making undead using death magic.

It worked, Vandal thought. *My death magic is only level 2 so I wasn't sure I could pull that off, but it looks like I can brute force it with MP. At such a low level, I can barely make more than an animated corpse, but at least it will get me around.* All the rabbit was good for was moving around, and with none of the agility it had boasted in life. He had planned an escape from the military facility on Origin using much the same tactic as this, but the security had been too heavy for pawns of this magnitude to help him out.

It had also taken a massive volume of magical power to turn a single rabbit into an undead, especially when compared to using Death to Bacteria and Death to Bugs. He checked his stats to see that his MP had decreased by 10,000. Death to Bacteria cost 1 MP. That was a big step up.

"But one rabbit isn't going to be enough. More of you, rise. You too, and you, rise! You there, rise for me!"

Some vines that Dalshia used as a rope started to writhe around like snakes. The small knife that she used for cooking rose into the air. The roughly made bed with its wooden frame started to clatter and shake. He could possess more than dead bodies with spirits. It was also possible to possess vines, wood, and even inorganic matter like metal. He got the idea by reflecting on some of the fantasy and occult properties he had encountered back on Earth, featuring elements like weapons possessed by evil spirits, cursed gemstones and jars, and poltergeists moving furniture around the house. One big caveat was that possessing inorganic matter cost significantly more magic power than creating undead.

All of that cost a cool million. My head is starting to throb…I'd better top myself off. He sucked the blood of the last remaining rabbit, drinking it dry to recover his MP, and then turned that into undead too before leaving the house riding on his bed.

"Come on, rise, rise, rise! Which way to town? Which way toward lots of people?"

All sorts of new additions had joined in on carrying Vandal's bed: a skeletal deer, a mummy bear wrapped in the tatters of its own fur, a boar missing a head and internal organs, and even a bleached human skeleton. Anyone who might have seen this sight, if not a stalwart adventurer or soldier, would have probably collapsed in terror. A white-haired baby, with one crimson and one violet eye, commanding a horde of undead. A terrible scene, for sure, but actually not as much of a threat as it may have appeared.

He had turned the animals into Living Dead and Living Bones. The undead tools and furnishings were considered

Cursed Tools. A hale farmer swinging a hoe could take any of them out one-on-one, and an adventurer would hardly even need to draw their sword. Vandal knew all of this, and so he kept making more of them even as he hurried onward.

She isn't in the forest.

He had turned winged bugs into undead to search the forest, but they found no sign of Dalshia. He asked spirits wandering the forest for help, but didn't get the answers he desired. It felt like the inside of his head was boiling and he felt dizzy. He had used millions of MP already, losing track of the expenditure in his haste. But his bad feelings about this situation were only getting worse.

I should have tried to make undead sooner! I should have sent them out with her! Then he would have at least known her location. If anything happened, he would have been able to sense it right away. If Dalshia had known what he could really do, she might have decided to leave the forest sooner and head back toward her hometown. But he hadn't pushed himself. Even after his skill level increased, he had just let time pass in the haze of Dalshia's affection.

Quickly! To the town!

He had about 50 million MP left. Night had fallen by the time the horde of undead led by Vandal reached Evbejia, the closest town to the forest. It was a smallish settlement that had grown up in-between the local villages, home to around 2,000 people and the territory of Baronet Bestello. The village had walls around to keep monsters out, with the only access from gates in the east, west, south, and north—unless you could fly in.

"All of you, stay here in the forest. Bone Monkey, carry

me on your back." Vandal grabbed onto the back of an un-dead made from the bones of a large monkey, whom he named "Bone Monkey," and crept up to the walls. It was only a small town of 2,000 people, placing it beneath the notice of powerful monsters or enemy nations, and the security looked more like a sieve than a dragnet. After all that time under heavy military security, a badly maintained wall in the boonies wasn't going to keep him out.

That said, the gates were closed at night and sentries were alert. A skeleton monkey the size of a man approaching was going to set off all sorts of alarms. So Vandal ignored the gates and headed to the walls. Then he used MP to force a nearby spirit into the stone of the wall.

"Open a hole large enough for us to pass through."

The section of the exterior "undead wall" was unable to disobey the orders of its master. It changed shaped with a soft rumbling sound, and then a hole appeared. He had 49 million MP left.

Death attribute magic skill has leveled up!

Vandal thought he heard something like that inside his head, but he still felt so dizzy. He had a headache like a hammer pounding relentlessly on his temple.

"Bone Monkey. Keep to the deserted backstreets."

Bone Monkey started forward again, its bones clacking as it went. Its movements were uneven, paying no heed to Vandal on his back, but it wasn't a problem. He didn't have the strength to walk on his own, but the strength of his arms was already higher than an average adult male. His baby body was so light, he could easily support himself by clinging to Bone Monkey's back with both hands.

They proceeded through the dim town. His Night Vision allowed him to see as though it were daytime.

"Search for my mother." He released undead bugs to search for information and talked to the spirits wandering the city. The spirits of regular folks, when not even turned into undead, would rapidly degrade after death unless they had superior mental fortitude, so he wasn't counting on them for anything.

"In the town square."

Getting a response surprised him so much, his heart almost stopped.

"The square!" Bone Monkey clattered toward the destination. It came into view, and there he saw Dalshia. Right there—*oh no*.

"Vandal…I'm sorry."

She was a spirit and looked ready to vanish any moment.

"Mom!"

"I'm sorry. I died. But I didn't tell them about you."

"What happened?" he asked.

Dalshia's spectral form showed whip marks all across it. She proceeded to explain what happened.

She had come to Evbejia to gather information required for their trip to the dark elf village, where she and Vandal would be safe.

"You have one red eye from your father, and one purple eye from me. Everyone knows you're a dhampir just by looking at your face," his mother said. So she needed to avoid the roads, but also take a safe route with fewer monsters. But someone had ratted her out. Her name and description had been passed to the Church of Divine Alda, informing them that it matched the description of a dark elf adventurer who sometimes came into town. Dalshia came to Evbejia again, without any idea, and walked into an ambush laid by Baronet Bestello's knights, monks of the church, and hired adventurers. She had resisted, but was captured.

"I fought as hard as I could, but they had adventurers who were better with the bow and elemental magic than me, and I couldn't win," she said. "The church whipped me, calling me a witch, and asking where my dhampir baby is."

The church's torture methods were terrible. They whipped her, crushed her fingers, and pressed hot brands into her flesh. That pain had actually damaged her soul, with the marks remaining on her body even after becoming a spirit.

"I stayed silent. I did well! I did it! But once they realized torture wasn't going to break me, they burned me at the stake."

The baronet and the church had put on a public execution, as a display of their power and to show the people what happened to those who succumb to the allure of a vampire.

"I was burnt alive. That's how I died. I wanted to turn into a ghost and find you, but High Priest Goldan poured holy water over my ashes. So managing to cling on here is the best I could do."

As Vandal listened to her words, despair and powerlessness started to fill him, as though his body was rotting away and his vision crumpling into nothing. If he had come looking for her yesterday, he might have made it in time. If he had gone sooner, he might have made it in time. When he was languidly napping, his mother's beautiful brown skin had been under the lash. When he was filling up on rabbit blood, she had been seared with burning brands. And when he was wandering the forest, she had been burning alive. The only remaining trace of her life was the pile of ashes and bones on the cobbles of the town square.

Acquired the skill Spirit Pollution!

"If only I had grown up faster! If I had honed my magic harder! If I had gathered more information sooner! If I had only been stronger, you wouldn't have had to die, Mom!" Insanity tore through Vandal's mind. His expression hardly changed, but his body shuddered with sadness, and regret and anger caused tears to flow endlessly from his eyes.

Spirit Pollution skill increased to level 2!

Dalshia watched him sadly. She hadn't wanted to share all of the details of her death with Vandal. But she couldn't stay quiet, either. She was a weak spirit, on the verge of vanishing, and so she had been unable to resist Vandal's request to tell him what happened. He possessed death magic, as well as vast magical power, after all. As she watched, the undead bugs all returned to Vandal. They had gathered information on what happened from across Evbejia, which now flowed into him in a jumble of voices.

"My lord, the public execution today was quite the show."

"Indeed. It might not have been the vampire, but taking care of the dark elf who opened her legs for him had merit enough. His Majesty and the church will take notice of this. I sense my promotion is soon to be handed down."

"Indeed, my lord. The 'et' will be removed from Baronet Bestello before you know it." An exchange between lord and servant, happily speculating on a rosy future.

Spirit Pollution skill increased to level 3!

"That witch didn't give the dhampir up."

"Hah! A monster playing at mother. She could've at least

begged for her life when burning at the stake. Unrepentant to the end! A real witch."

"Burning again for that now in the fires of hell, I'll abide. And what's for tomorrow? Dhampir hunting with the Five-Colored Blades?"

"Do we need worry about a babe? It won't last three days apart from its mother. It's probably dead already."

"Fool! Babe or not, it's still half vampire. We don't know what dark abilities it might have inherited. If the father was a subordinate species, all very well, but what if he was a noble species? Lord forbid, a progenitor species! Then what?"

"Yes, of course. My deepest apologies, High Priest Gold-an!"

"Not that we have the coin to keep the Blades around for much longer, and I don't like fueling tales of their deeds either. I doubt they want any more part of this anyway. Filthy adventurers! They are nothing like we disciples of Alda, God of Law and Life. For the hunt into the mountains, we'll have some trappers lead the way, and go with knights from the baronet."

"Yes, High Priest." In the church, the high priest and his holy knights discussed the downfall of the "witch," and talked of locating Vandal and killing him too.

Spirit Pollution skill increased to level 4!

"That was an easy day's pay today. That dark elf was pretty good with her bow and elemental magic, but good is still what, grade D? No match for us, Heinz!"

"Something wrong, Heinz? You don't seem yourself."

"No, it's nothing. I just don't like the aftertaste of this one."

"You're taking pity on that dark elf? You're the leader of the Five-Colored Blades, an alias-holding grade B adventurer!

Don't go soft on us now."

"I don't know if she fell for the allure of that vampire, or was after eternal life, but that dark elf brought this on herself. Don't pay her any more mind. And you're the one, Blue Burning Blade Heinz, who wanted to take this job, remember?"

"Yeah, after being introduced by the count. I didn't really have a choice."

"Whatever. Let's spend some of this windfall on food and drink! Just like eating the meat of a kill on the hunt. You'll feel better. Honor her death." The Five-Colored Blades, a group of adventurers hired to help capture Dalshia, were eating well off the payment for their aid and feasting in her memory.

Spirit Pollution skill increased to level 5!

"Cheers! Cheers to the baronet, and cheers to the high priest!"

"And cheers to your dark nature, Olby!" Much laughter.

"Hey! Who are you calling dark?!"

"You, you nutter, you! You're the one who got rejected by the hot dark elf coming to town and decided to try and teach her a lesson for shutting you down! Some hunting buddy I've got here!"

"That's why we found out she was the wanted witch, isn't it?"

"A real waste too. Burning such a beauty alive. At least we can make some more coin tomorrow, hunting down the dhampir. The knights will take all the glory, but we can make easy money pointing them in the right direction."

"We can do more than point! If we catch the dhampir ourselves, we'll be making bars of gold, not bags of pennies!"

"You never told them where the dark elf's hidden home was?"

"Well done, Olby! If we bag that dhampir they'll be lining up to buy it—the church, the magician's guild, slavers, we'll have our pick of the purchaser!" The trappers who sold Dalshia out, cackling to themselves are they planned to catch and sell him too.

Spiritual Pollution skill increased to level 6!

"If you aren't a good girl, you'll get burned at the stake like that witch."

"They still haven't found the dhampir. I'm worried. I hope they catch it soon."

"You think the vampire might come for some payback?"

"It'll be bad for business if our wine gets labeled as coming from a town with a vampire problem. They'd better wrap this up quickly." And then the regular folk of the town. The comments from those people just going about their daily lives. None of them had any sympathy for Dalshia either.

Spiritual Pollution skill increased to level 7!

This was all too much. Vandal had never once thought, in any of his three lives, that the world revolved around him, or that it was a place overflowing with goodness. But he had never considered it as evil, twisted, as bitter a place as this. Earth, Origin, and Ramda.

He had lived three lives now and hadn't been happy in any one of them. All he had done was lose, suffer, and withstand pain. He had done nothing wrong in any of them, and yet had everything taken away, and given nothing in its place. Even the god—who actually did exist—hadn't done anything to help him.

"I'm sorry, Vandal."

And now, right in front of his eyes, he was about to lose Dalshia again.

"I can't hold on any longer." She was already faint, and now she shuddered, her voice fading. Her spirit was no longer able to remain in this world.

"Wait! Mom, you can't go!"

She was heading into the afterlife, where she would encounter the Reincarnation God Rodocolte. He would surely get a chuckle from learning Vandal had lost his mother on Ramda too, reveling in the despair this would cause, and probably right in front of Dalshia's soul. Vandal couldn't accept that. He couldn't stand that thought.

"I'm sorry. I wanted to talk with you more, just like this. I wanted to see you grown, as a man. I wanted to see you married, with children, so happy."

Spiritual Pollution skill increased to level 8—9— reached capacity!

"It's okay, Mom."

He took his remaining MP, all 45 million, and poured them into Dalshia's spirit body. She made a puzzled sound, and then started to moan. Vandal continued to fill her fragile, flicking form with all the magic he could, just like when he was making undead. It was like pouring water into a bucket with a big hole, but if you poured enough water it could still be full for a moment.

"Now I just need something for your soul to possess…."

He couldn't just use a stone, tool, or bone. That would make it harder for Dalshia's personality to remain intact. The best thing would have been her own body, but that had been burnt to ash.

"There has to be something."

Vandal had Bone Monkey search the ashes, and found a

burnt piece of bone there. Just a small fragment, fitting into Vandal's own small hand.

"This will do. Mom, into this." Even with his vast magical power flowing into her, Dalshia still tried to resist the wishes of her child.

Because that was what was best for him.

It was sad, but she was dead. Even if she became undead, it wouldn't be like when she was alive. It wouldn't be good for her son to have her around like that. Indeed, it would only cause him harm. She wanted to be with him, but pushed down her tears and tried to break away....

Acquired the skill Death Attribute Allure!

Dalshia's head throbbed: *I want to be close to you, close to you, always close to you! I never want to leave your side!*

"Don't worry," Vandal said. "We'll always be together."

Vandal overwrote Dalshia's own thoughts and feelings, and she happily went into her own fragment of bone.

"Now you've got your spirit body back, at least. I'll make you a new body one day, you'll see."

He had provided the MP needed to maintain her spirit body, and something for her to possess, but ultimately it was just a bone fragment. Dalshia wasn't strong enough to move it herself. The only option was for her to go to sleep until Vandal woke her up again. He decided to hone his death attribute magic powers and create a body that would allow Dalshia to be just as she was during her life. He swore it.

"But first, I need revenge."

The baronet and his ministers, those in the church, the adventurers, the trappers, and the people in the town. Revenge on all of them. He was going to go crazy otherwise. They deserved punishment. It was too unfair for this to stand.

"But not…right now."

He was down to less than ten percent of his magic. His head was throbbing, his throat was dry, and he was hungry and tired. His body was only 6 months old. He had pushed too hard.

"I'm sorry, Mom. I'll avenge you…later. Bone Monkey, back the way we came."

Bone Monkey picked him up and clattered back through the streets of Evbejia. Once they passed through the hole in the walls, the stone wall returned to normal, and the waiting horde of undead obediently followed behind Bone Monkey.

The townspeople didn't have any idea that they had purchased the wrath of the one individual they shouldn't be shopping with.

Rapid Healing skill increased to level 2! Limit Break skill increased to level 2! Resist Maladies skill increased to level 2!

Name: Vandal
Race: Dhampir (Dark Elf)
Age: 6 months
Alias: None
Job: None
Level: 0
Job History: None
—Status
Vitality: 18
Magical Power: 100000600
Strength: 27

Agility: 2
Muscle: 33
Intellect: 25
—Passive Skills
[Brute Strength: Level 1] [Rapid Healing: Level 2]
[Death Attribute Magic: Level 2]
[Resist Maladies: Level 2] [Resist Magic: Level 1]
[Night Vision]
[Spiritual Pollution: Level 10 (NEW!)] [Death Attribute Allure: Level 1 (NEW!)]
—Active Skills
[Suck Blood: Level 1] [Limit Break: Level 2 (NEW!)]
—Curses
[Unable to carry over experience from previous lives]
[Unable to enter existing jobs]
[Unable to personally acquire experience]

Feeling as though he was about to pass out any moment, and clinging to the fragment of bone holding his mother's spirit, the living bones and dead carried Vandal back to his home in the forest. He felt like he was about to starve, but luckily one of Dalshia's traps had caught a boar. He drank its blood, and then collapsed.

When he woke up, it was already noontime.

"Good morning, Mom. Everyone." After waking up, he quietly looked around the room at all his new companions—although his voice came out as a bunch of baby sounds.

"The trappers aren't here yet?"

Bone Monkey, standing by his bed, shook his monkey head. Luckily they weren't here yet.

"So to go over everything I learned yesterday..."

—Today, knights in the employ of the ruler of Evbejia, Baronet Bestello, and knights following the God of Law and Life Alda and High Priest Goldan were going to start searching the forest for Vandal.

—The trapper Olby didn't tell them the location of this house, so they would probably be looking in the wrong place for a while.

—Meanwhile, trapper Olby and his buddies would be coming here to capture the rare dhampir baby for themselves.

"That being said, I think I've got the forces to deal with three trappers."

He had made a couple of hundred undead yesterday, but most of them were things like rats or bugs, small creatures. He only had around thirty like Bone Monkey, capable of maybe putting up a fight, but even then they were all pretty weak. Bone Monkey looked more like an orangutan than a chimpanzee, and had probably been able to snap a man's arm like a twig when it was alive. It didn't have that kind of strength now. In fact, when Vandal tested it out, he proved stronger himself—although perhaps that said more about Vandal than it did Bone Monkey. The skeleton ape wasn't as agile as a human either. All bone and dead flesh, it might have some resistance to arrows or knives, but getting hammered by clubs would break the skeleton up pretty quickly. The final blow came when Vandal somehow managed to access its status screen, to see it had nothing in the way or passive or active skills. All the undead under Vandal's command at the moment were rank 1. In Ramda, that meant a barely trained peasant would still be able to defeat them, one-on-one.

But he did have thirty of them. He just had to get a little creative.

"I'd better get the bugs out searching. Bone Monkey, four of you others, stay here to protect me. The rest of you…."

Vandal decided to start by dealing with Olby and the trappers. He had many questions for Dalshia, including about his father, but he couldn't afford to have the trappers show up while they were chatting. Best to deal with that problem first.

Olby was proceeding through the forest with the other two trappers he had been drinking with night before. The divine knights might be the cream of the crop, but they weren't going to find the dark elf's hideaway in this big old forest just like that. Olby and his friends could get the baby first. All three of them were sure of that.

"Hey, just so we're on the same page here…"

"I know. I'm not planning on getting eaten by bears or wolves before we get rich," Olby replied to his companion's concerns.

They were sure of their prize, but they were also professional hunters. The forest wasn't infested with monsters, but there were still dangerous bears and wolves and other beasts, and some weaker monsters like goblins. They proceeded with caution, alert for such hazards.

"This is strange. These look like tracks from some kind of big ape. And over there—bear?"

That caution led one of his friends to spot the tracks that Vandal had made with his undead when returning from Evbejia.

"You think so? They don't look heavy enough to be from such large animals."

Olby wasn't so sure. The heavier the one making the tracks, the deeper they should be pressed into the ground. But the animals that had made these seemed very light.

"They are strange shapes too. Smaller than I'd expect. This one doesn't have enough toes for a bear."

They couldn't know it, but this was because the tracks had been made by living bones, creatures with less than half the mass from when they were alive, and missing pieces to boot. If they had been adventurers, practiced at dealing with such oddities, they might have been more careful.

"It has to be tracks from multiple animals, all on top of each other. That's all."

Olby and his friends were trappers, sometimes taking on monsters to make a little extra coin, so they didn't give this anymore thought. Their knowledge of the lack of monsters in the forest helped them jump to the wrong conclusion, and they stopped worrying about how strange the tracks seemed.

"We're almost there. She carved a cave out of a small cliff and made a hideaway there."

"Okay. Let's capture the baby before it starves or something."

With that, the party of three reached Dalshia's house. The trees thinned out in front of the house, making some open space. There were signs of a cook fire and other indicators of everyday life.

"Hey, why is it so messy here?"

"You don't think the knights got here first after all?"

Olby and his friends looked around. The ground in front of the hideaway had been dug up in numerous places, and there were vines and animal bones scattered all over it.

"I hope not! Let's go inside."

Olby clicked his tongue in annoyance, closing in with the door to check on the baby. In that moment, there came a terrible moaning sound, and the ground started to rise upward!

"What? A golem?!"

"An earth golem!"

It had been waiting for them, lying on the ground, and now an earth-bodied earth golem rose up before them. Olby gave a yelp at what it revealed.

"There's undead underneath it!" The reanimated bones of wolves and bears, tucked out of sight. "Run for it!"

"Where? We're surrounded!"

The three of them had all moved too close to the doorway, placing them in the middle of the golem and living bones. They had bows and short knives—not the best weapons for fighting undead with, even low-ranking ones. Then Olby gave another shout.

"A snake! No, vines, moving vines!" The vines that had been scattered across the floor like debris started to move like snakes, wrapping about Olby and his friends. "Dammit! Get off me, let go!"

Olby tried to draw his blade and cut himself free, but the golem and undead closed in to pin him down, and then a pot came flying right at his head. There was no way to run from this. All three of them were quickly captured alive.

"It worked." Vandal gave a sigh of relief, looking down at Olby and his hunting buddies.

They were wrapped in the vines, unable to speak, rolling on the ground. He had possessed the ground in front of his house to create the earth golem, and then hidden the living bones beneath it. Neither the undead nor the golem needed to breathe, and the smell could be any patch of rotting earth in this forest, so they had only needed to stay still to fool the trappers. Same with the vines and the pots. They weren't going around worried that every piece of trash littering the ground was actually undead.

"Now I need to try and talk to them."

Olby and his friends looked up in surprise at Vandal, who was looking down at them from the back of Bone Monkey. They would never have suspected that the baby they had come to capture had undead at his beck and call. High Priest Goldan had chastised his men for underestimating the dhampir baby. These fools could have used a bit of that themselves.

"For that, I need a means of communication."

After all, Vandal could still only make baby noises. He couldn't talk with these men. He proceeded to create a sand golem from gravel and dirt.

"Gweeeeergh!"

The trappers writhed about in terror. They probably expected to be killed. But rather than hammer them with its heavy fists, the sand golem collapsed back into sand right in front of them. The grains formed letters on the ground.

Calm down. Keep quiet. Answer me.

Recalling how he turned part of Evbejia's walls into a golem to change its shape last night, he had guessed he could turn a sand golem into letters. It had worked even better than he might have hoped. He had to supply the golem with considerable MP, which took some serious focus. His only concern had been the language he was writing in, whether his native Japanese would get through to these woodsmen. In order to confirm this final point, he allowed the vines to move away from the mouths of his captives.

"What, what do you want to know? We'll tell you anything. Just spare our lives," Olby said.

"Yeah. Whatever you want to know," said another.

"We won't tell them about this place. Just let us go," the third pleaded. It seemed written and spoken Japanese worked here in Ramda.

That suits me, but why? From Rodocolte's knowledge, I did see that heroes were summoned here to Ramda from other worlds in the past. Maybe that's the reason. That was also something he could investigate later.

Vandal proceeded to write out his questions, trying to extract info from the trappers. They didn't seem especially well educated, and he had to choose his words with care. Sometimes spelling things out meant more sand golem letters, which put a bigger drain on his MP and his focus. Even with all that of, he didn't always get useful answers.

What are jobs?

"Huh? You want to know our jobs? Hunters, of course."

What's experience?

"I mean...experience is experience?"

And God of Law and Life Alda?

"Ah, god, that's a god."

He wanted to know more about what jobs exactly were here in Ramda, and what experience was, but their answers to just basic questions provided him with no insights. His questions were too simplistic for them. It was like asking "What's air?" or "What's water?" on Earth. Someone with an education and linguistic skill might offer a proper answer, but Olby and the gang were unable to fulfill such criteria.

I'll ask my mom about those things later. Dalshia would be able to provide an easy-to-understand breakdown of that stuff. She was a mother raising a child.

Tell me about Baronet Bestello and his knights, he wrote. Seeking a topic that they would be able to talk about, Vandal switched to seeking information on his other targets.

"The lord took up his title about ten years ago. He's a greedy one, but nothing much else to say. Just a noble, like the rest of them, and certainly not any better than those others."

"He has five of his own knights, and then hires decent fighters from among the regular folk to bolster his ranks. He even trains them a little."

"But they still aren't that strong. Why don't we go and take them out together? We can do it, if we team up."

Vandal ignored that suggestion. It sounded like Baronet Bestello didn't have much in terms of numbers or strength. This was likely a pretty peaceful place to live.

For those allowed to live here.

Just answer my questions, Vandal instructed with more sand. *Tell me what you know about High Priest Goldan and the divine knights.*

"The high priest and the knights weren't always in town.

They came in about six months ago, bringing notice of the dhampir and the witch who birthed him—that is, you and your fine mother. He is a clergyman famous for killing vampires, and his divine knights are well trained too, so they say."

"I heard he strong-armed his way to high priest, an odd way of going about it for a holy man," one of the others said. "He has slaughtered mercilessly—I mean, quite unjustly *laid to rest* numerous vampires and their followers. They say he even killed a vampire who was hundreds of years old—a terrible deed, just terrible. He might be rated grade B if he were an adventurer."

"But we know the lay of the land, see? With us helping out, you'll get the jump on him no problem. Please, let us serve you."

So the priest is a skilled vampire hunter. Next I need to know about the Five Hue Blades, but I'm starting to feel hungry. Vandal had the living bones bring one of the three hunters before him.

"What, what is? Do you want me to serve you? I can do good, I know I can! I've the best archer in Evbejia…hah! I really can help! I'll do whatever you want, just spare my life!"

Bone Monkey grabbed his head and pinned him to stop his neck from moving. His voice raised in pitch as he begged for his life, but Vandal wasn't listening.

He clamped down on the man's neck with his fangs, causing his begging to become a pure scream.

"Yohan!" Olby shouted his friend's name, their screaming voices blending together are Vandal nosily slurped Yohan's blood.

Tastes richer than rabbit blood. A bit saltier too. Of course, drinking from Dalshia's teat while being held in her arms had been much better. But this was his breakfast, so he wasn't going to complain. He continued to drink until Yohan finally stopped screaming.

Phew…hey, Bone Monkey, can you pat me on the back for a moment? That's the way. After getting his skeleton monkey to burp his baby body, he let Olby and his one remaining friend get a look at the pallid remains of Yohan.

Then he started using the sand again.

I told you to answer my questions.

The two remaining trappers looked at the dead, drained Yohan and then the placid-faced baby who had done him in, and almost nodded their heads right off. They might be dealing with a baby, but it had none of the bouncy cuteness of an infant. It was clear that if they resisted for even a moment, this baby would kill them without a second thought.

Now. What do you know about the Five Hue Blades and Blue Burning Blade Heinz?

From that point on things went much more smoothly. Setting an example with Yohan had worked wonderfully. The Five Hue Blades were a party of five adventurers, with Heinz as their leader. He was still in his teens, but already grade B and had an alias. The other members were grade C, and all pretty good fighters too.

Sounds like the same thing as High Priest Goldan—I can't win against them yet.

Next, he asked about the local terrain, the area around Baronet Bestello's lands, and where High Priest Goldan and his goons might be searching at the moment. This all helped out a lot. Vandal had asked the possessed animals, like Bone Monkey, for this same information, but hadn't gotten much out of them. The spirits were being friendlier with Vandal than they had been yesterday, sharing whatever they could, but ultimately they were still just animals and bugs. They couldn't give details about directions or distances like a human could. They might be able to lead him places, but they couldn't draw a map of the paths they would take.

I'm going to need water and supplies, Vandal thought. High Priest Goldan might be searching the wrong place at the moment, but the forest wasn't all that big. They could cover it all in ten days. That said, it would also be foolish to rush into an escape attempt. Vandal had his one crimson eye, the mark of a dhampir, meaning he couldn't hide his identity and go into a village or town. But without somewhere like his cave-house, somewhere safe to hide away, he would be left out in the dangerous wilds. That was too risky.

This baby body is still only 6 months old. I need sleep, lots of sleep. I'm getting tired already.

He might have a vampire daddy, higher than average stats for his age, and already collecting a selection of skills, but he was still a baby. Things were better than they had been at 1 month old, but he still got sleepy all the time, and definitely couldn't stay up all night. His Resist Maladies skill let him fend off the sleepies for a while, but he was a growing boy. He needed to sleep. Dalshia wouldn't want him pulling all-nighters.

Vandal therefore elected to stay hidden until the High Priest Goldan gave up on his search. He hadn't expected to become a shut-in at 6 months, but this was how he was going to survive.

"Hey, are we done? Anything else you want to know?" Olby asked.

"If we're done, please let us go!" begged his friend.

They were getting antsy again, but their role providing

information was over. Vandal wrapped them up in the vines once more.

"Wait, wait! Please, let me go! I have a…"

A what? Vandal wondered as the vines cut him off in mid-sentence. A fiancé? A wife? A young daughter? An old mother? What was he planning to say, this man who had ratted out a young mother with an infant baby? Whatever it was, it didn't matter. They only had one purpose now.

Vandal informed them of it with more sand.

You are my rations.

Two more muffled screams rang out.

Long, long ago, there was nothing in this world but two all-powerful gods: the Divine Darkness Diakmel, and the Divine Brilliance Alazan.

The two gods fought. They had no idea which was good and which was evil. There was nothing other than themselves, and so they fought.

The seemingly eternal battle between the gods ended with each defeating the other, two finishing blows landing in the same moment.

The black and white gods collapsed together, and from their remains new gods were born. Vida, goddess of life and love. Alda, god of light and law. Zantark, war god of fire and destruction. Pelia, goddess of water and knowledge. Shizarion, god of wind and the arts. Botin, mother goddess of the earth and talent. Rekrent, demon god of time and magic. Zurwan, god of space and creation. Alongside these eight attribute gods, there were also the dragon emperor god Marduke, the titan god Zeno, and the beast god Ganpapelio, creating the eleven founding gods.

These new gods didn't want to simply use their strength to fight each other, like the two before them, and so they worked together to create Ramda. The eight attribute gods made people in their own image and taught them of their ways. The dragon emperor god Marduke created dragons and the titan god Zeno created giants. To feed them, the beast god Ganpapelio created countless birds and beasts and filled the seas with fish.

War god Zantark and earth goddess Botin became the forebears of the dwarves, and goddess Pelia and god Shizarion the forebears of the elves. "Humans" became a term covering all forms of intelligent life, with the human race as one specific race among others.

The resulting world was one of peace. The people worshipped the gods. The dragons and giants were intelligent, with birds and beasts and fish to feed on without any need for dispute.

However, this peace shattered when the demon king Gudranis appeared from the abyss beyond the stars.

After his advent upon Ramda, he led his cadre of demonic and twisted gods to try and take over the world. His corrupted magical power created monsters like goblins and orcs, creatures Ramda had never seen before, and the demon king used these new minions to wage war on the gods.

The humans might have honed their martial prowess and hunted animals for food, but they knew nothing of real warfare, and they were thrown into chaos by this incursion. The gods were quickly cornered. War god Zantark, dragon emperor god Marduke, and titan god Zeno led their followers bravely into battle. Demon God Rekrent instructed the humans in the ways of magic, but they were unable to turn the tide. Beast god Ganpapelio also fought bravely, but ultimately perished in the fighting.

That was when Zurwan, god of space and creation, summoned seven heroes from another world to fight the forces of the demon king. The seven heroes taught the people how to fight and how to make powerful weapons, and stood on the frontlines themselves when the fighting started.

After a fierce battle, demon king Gudranis was finally defeated and sealed away, his physical form eradicated completely. The evil gods under his command also lost their strength, with some perishing, and others being sealed away in a fashion close enough to death.

However, those who remained were hardly celebrating a great victory.

War god Zantark was cursed by an evil god and fell into darkness. Pelia sank into the sea and Shizarion returned to the winds. Botin was sealed deep under the earth, and Rekrent and Zurwan also sank into slumber in order to recover their strength. Marduke was torn asunder, and Zeno's heart crushed. Their brethren lost their power and fell into decline, with more powerful dragons giving way to less powerful wyrms, and many giants become monsters worshipping dark and evil gods.

Four of the heroes perished. Humanity was reduced to humans, elves, and dwarves barely being able to form a single town together. There were insufficient numbers to support civilization or culture, and even after the demon king was defeated, the monsters he had created with his corrupted magic still roamed the lands, creating swathes of uninhabitable terrain where the surviving monsters swelled their ranks.

Of the two gods who remained, Alda chose to live with and lead the remaining heroes and people. But the goddess Vida thought that the fastest path to reviving Ramda was by creating new races to intermingle with the survivors. Vida was the goddess of life and love. Her powers were better suited to the creation of a new race than for fighting.

First, she paid a visit to the sun giant Talos, who had retained his strong spirit and goodness rather than becoming a monster. Together they created the race of giantlings, with hale and hardy bodies but of a size that could still dwell—barely—among other humans.

Next, she visited the most powerful of the remaining of Marduke's dragon brethren, Tiamat, and created the dragolings, humans with the strength of a dragon and horns on their heads.

She dallied with the kings of the birds and beasts left by Ganpapelio, creating varied beast races, as well as creating the merpeople with Pelia's right hand, the sea god Tristan. She also had relations with an elf youth who served her at the time, creating the dark elves—humans with the same magical power as elves, but stronger bodies.

Alda was displeased with these actions of the goddess, believing they would only push the world toward greater corruption and chaos. As the god of law, Alda was unable to accept Vida creating these new races one after the other. But Vida believed herself to be in the right, and so they were never able to understand the other's argument.

Vida eventually started consorting with monsters, creating the lamia, scylla, arachne, centaurs, harpies, and demonlings.

She used her life attribute power to bring back the corpse of one of the fallen heroes, Zakkato, as an undead, and make the vampires with him. The resulting vampire, the original source of the species, was almost as strong as a god in every aspect. He was also able to share that strength with humans by giving them his blood, making them into vampires too.

Vida's intercourse with monsters, and then the creation of vampires, finally pushed Alda over the edge. Alda and three remaining heroes set out to destroy Vida and the races she had created as the source of fresh chaos, going against the order that they were trying to establish for the world. Vida, of course, wanted to protect the new races she had created, and fought with the revived hero Zakkato against Alda and his forces. But she received a near-fatal wound, falling from her perch as goddess and vanishing into the demon barrens with the hero Zakkato.

Alda survived, but lacked the strength required to finish off the vampires and other remnants of the races Vida had created. With the loss of the God of Life, Alda was forced to take on that role from Vida, even in his exhausted state. Alda became the god of light, law, and life, with his followers calling him the God of Law and Life. But now, 100,000 years after the battle with Vida, the world remained in confusion and chaos.

"And that is the legend of Ramda."

"Thank you, Mom. That's a big help."

Having finished his preparations to hide underground, Vandal had been listening to the myths of Ramda's past from the spirit of his mother in her bone.

He had ordered the undead to bring his emergency

supplies into the house, including Olby, Olby's one remaining friend, and some animals that had been trapped alive. He had also made pots by changing the shape of stone golems, and then had them filled with plenty of water. Then he continued to make golems from the earth and stone of the cave. He told them to stand without moving as pillars to prevent collapses, and then moved the golems made from the back of the cave out toward the entrance. Once there, he turned them back into plain old stone, effectively sealing himself inside. After realizing that he could use MP to freely change the shape of his golems, within reason, he wondered if he could use them for a little construction work, and he had been right.

He had left the fragments of furniture and pots smashed by his remodeling in plain sight, making it look like their hideaway cave had collapsed. He just had to hope that High Priest Goldan didn't order his men to dig until they found a dhampir body.

He closed up the entrance, burying himself more than fifty meters deep into the cave. If he wanted to do anything on a larger scale, he would probably need to hire a good earth attribute magician. He had some fist-size holes secretively secured to provide him with air, and with the Night Vision skill he didn't need to worry about illumination. Thus, the preparations for his subterranean life were completed. With all the free time this gave him, he spent it talking to Dalshia.

"We are in the northwest of the Vangaia Continent, in a nation belonging to the Amidd Empire called the Milg Shield Kingdom. The empire and its composite nations believe in the God of Law and Life Alda. That's why it's so dangerous here."

Alda was the god who fought against the races created by

Vida, including vampires, because they disturbed the order of the world. No wonder nobody wanted anything to do with a vampire half-breed, apart from kill it, of course. The influence of the Alda Faith had to be powerful because adventurers' guilds in the nations of the Amidd Empire posted requests to hunt dhampir down like any other quest. And as proof of the kill, the adventurers would procure the crimson eye.

Now he understood why she was hiding in the forest.

The other races that Vida had created after the fight with the demon king—even those not created with monsters, such as the dark elves, beast races, and dragolings—were also subject to eradication. The Amidd Empire only saw mankind, elves, and dwarves as "humanity," and everything else—giantlings, dark elves, beast races, dragolings—were called "halfkind" and discriminated against. The starkest example was how humans were not allowed to be slaves, apart from if they were already criminals, but halfkind could be sold, purchased, owned, and used without restriction.

All of the races that Vida had created by consorting with monsters—including vampires—were treated as monsters themselves. That said, for every vampire or lamia that an Amidd Empire adventurer or soldier had killed and carved up, an equal number were killed themselves, with even commoners facing the violence.

Those following Alda saw this reality as a sign that their god was right to curse these creatures as violent monsters, while those following Vida blamed the lack of guidance by their goddess for their fall toward the side of monsters—in other words, Alda was to blame. This pointless back and forth had raged for tens of thousands of years.

"Next, tell me about my dad, and vampires, and dhampir," Vandal said.

"Sure. But it's time for your nap. When you wake up again."

"Okay!"

Golem Creation skill was acquired!

Name: Vandal
Race: Dhampir (Dark Elf)
Age: 6 months
Alias: None
Job: None
Level: 0
Job History: None
—Status
Vitality: 18
Magical Power: 100000600
Strength: 27
Agility: 2
Muscle: 33
Intellect: 25
—Passive Skills
[Brute Strength: Level 1] [Rapid Healing: Level 2] [Death Attribute Magic: Level 3]

[Resist Maladies: Level 2] [Resist Magic: Level 1] [Night Vision]

[Spiritual Pollution: Level 10] [Death Attribute Allure: Level 1]
—Active Skills
[Suck Blood: Level 1] [Limit Break: Level 2]

[Golem Creation: Level 1 (NEW!)]

—Curses

[Unable to carry over experience from previous lives]

[Unable to enter existing jobs]

[Unable to personally acquire experience]

The Death Mage

CHAPTER TWO
A GENTLE REVENGE

T he goblin collapsed with a dull sound, relieved of its head.

"Psht! All we're finding out here are goblins!"

Goldan, high priest of the God of Law and Life Alda, was using his beloved mace to take out his bad mood on these particular goblins.

"High Priest Goldan, shouldn't we assume by now that the dhampir has either been spirited away by its father, the vampire, or was buried alive and died in the cave collapse?" One of the divine knights accompanying him made this suggestion, but Goldan wasn't having it.

Bohmak Goldan was born a peasant, but with his rabid faith and incredible strength—not to mention his life and light attribute magic—he dragged himself up to the post of high priest at the age of just 30 years. He was most passionate about defeating the monsters that Vida had created, including vampires, lamia, and scylla.

"Our God of Law and Life Alda is the only divine presence with any strength left in our world of Ramda! It is the duty of the faithful to strike down all that our god has branded as evil!"

He thought the same way as any other devout follower. The hunt for this dhampir and his mother was simply another act of justice. Certainly nothing to be ashamed about. And so he was tearing the forest apart looking for the dhampir, but even this small patch of woodland was giving him more trouble than he had bargained for.

First, they had been unable to make contact again with the trappers who had turned the dark elf in. They hired other trappers and cooperated with the regional knights, but all they found so far were wolves, bears, boars, and other wild animals, while sometimes getting attacked by weak monsters like these goblins.

On the fifth day of the search, they found a collapsed cave, which looked like someone had been living there before it was buried, but they were unable to confirm the corpse of the dhampir. Goldan wanted to excavate the entire cave, but it was too unstable. Moving more than a few pebbles risked burying them all alive, so he was forced to give that idea up. If he had an engineer or dwarf miner on hand then there might have still been hope, but there was little need for large-scale construction work in this region, and no mines to speak of either. The only reason they nevertheless continued the search of the forest for a whole two months was because the trapper who initially turned the mother in had vanished, along with two of his friends.

Three veteran trappers, with intimate knowledge of the local terrain, all going missing at once. To make matters more suspicious, they still hadn't found a single body.

Goldan's gut was telling him that this wasn't a coincidence or accident—that someone had taken revenge on them.

The dhampir is still a baby, but it's not unfathomable. A 3-year-old once took out a party of rank D adventurers. There's precedent, when it comes to dhampir. Giving up now could curse them in the future. They needed to find the dhampir and turn it to ash, no matter the cost.

"High Priest Goldan, we can't search these woods any more intimately than we have already," one of his knights said. "Not with our numbers,"

"Baronet Bestello's knights have all been recalled," another added.

It was clear that not everyone understood Goldan's passion, or his sense of what was at stake here. The lord of the region, Baronet Bestello, had initially lent five of his knights and half his soldiers to the search, but now refused to let even his lowest man join them. He argued that the knights and soldiers who normally worked to preserve the peace of his domain couldn't waste their time searching the forest for a baby. He had even intimated that the high priest should find a better way to spend his own time.

"I am aware that the people of Evbejia are displeased," Golden admitted. This forest was an important place for hunting and gathering for the locals. They were not pleased that the high priest shut them out for a whole two months because of the dangers of a dhampir baby.

"It is more than just the people," his knight continued tactfully. "Many adventurers aren't pleased either—although mainly the grade F and E types, fair enough. They're saying that we're taking their work from them."

Goldan and his men were taking care of the goblins and other monsters that adventurers would normally be hired to defeat, greatly impacting the adventurer economy in the region. Evbejia was a hub for other villages and towns, meaning lots of merchants and wealthy folk passed through looking for guards to protect them. The local branch of the adventurers' guild was worried about too many adventurers accepting such work and leaving Evbejia behind.

Baronet Bestello wasn't happy about the prospect of losing adventurers, either. High Priest Goldan might be keeping the goblin population down at the moment, but he wasn't going to stay in the town forever. Once he left, the globin population would bounce back almost overnight without sufficient adventurers to keep their numbers in check.

"What do you expect me to say?" Goldan said, frustrated. "We should leave alive these goblins that come for our blood?!"

"High Priest, respectfully, just that maybe it is time to give up. I don't wish to sound like the lord, but we do have many other places that require our aid."

That gave Goldan pause. There were still many other vampires out there. Other of Vida's monsters were also still hurting people. *Is this blind search for a dhampir baby really the best use of my time?*

"Very well," he finally said. "We leave Evbejia the day after tomorrow."

The setting sun cast his bitter expression in a reddish light. Something still pricked at him—as though the oncoming night was filled with the mocking laughter of the dhampir.

The dhampir in question, on the afternoon after High Priest Goldan and his knights moved out, sat outside, basking in the sunlight.

"Sunlight…love…." He had started to talk a little, expressing his love of the light. Living underground proved a cruel ordeal. He had thought one month would be enough, but Goldan had clung on for two whole months, leaving him trapped in the dark earth and rock.

He had used his death attribute magic to keep Olby and his friend alive, but they had only lasted two weeks. After that, he had Bone Monkey and the undead gang make him some cold, semi-solid food by mashing up the wheat and dried meat left by Dalshia with some water. In the moments he couldn't stomach that, he desperately searched the earth for bugs.

When one such search led him to hit an underground spring, it almost drowned him, but in the end that actually worked out. He had been running low on water, and the subterranean spring provided water he could wash his linens with. Up until that point, he had disposed of his diapers by using earth golems to create a pit in the ground and then burying them. Having used all the ones left by Dalshia, he was forced to use the clothing from the backs of the trappers. He had been nearing the limits of that approach too. He could use Death to Bacteria death attribute magic to protect himself, but no one wanted to wear a dirty diaper. He was a human, not an animal.

For the last few days, he got by on worms and the sap from tree roots. He relearned the useful spell Detect Danger: Death, which let him detect things or events that were likely to cause his demise; that let him avoid anything that would kill him outright, and yet his Resist Maladies skill also leveled up. He probably ate something that wasn't poisonous enough to kill him, but would have given him some serious tummy trouble.

I'm never going back to a life where it's a miracle to catch a mole, Vandal thought. He was firm in that determination.

Vandal was a dhampir, able to see in the dark as though it were the middle of the day. But that didn't mean he didn't also need sunlight. He was half dark elf, after all. He had been worried about dying from a vitamin deficiency in the darkness.

High Priest Goldan and your friends. The Five Hue Blades, you band of adventurers. I wish you well on your travels.

Vandal wished in his heart for nothing to happen to High Priest Golden and his knights, as they set out from Baronet Bestello's domain that day, or the Five Hue Blades, who departed two months earlier. *Please, don't get yourselves killed before I can kill you.*

He didn't want anyone else killing them, or for them to get sick, or die in an accident. He wished it with all his heart.

They say a human can only go around ninety hours in darkness before they crack. I made it through pretty easily, all things considered.

He calmed down from his desperation for sunlight. He had Bone Monkey and the others fix some traps while he breathed a sigh of relief at his mental state remaining seemingly unchanged from two months ago.

He checked his stats and saw the nasty-sounding Spirit Pollution skill was up to level 10, but he chalked that up to having sworn his revenge. It seemed to provide some mental fortitude. He actually didn't mind it, and so he moved on.

Death Attribute Allure was probably a skill he had been using on Origin, just without knowing it. The researchers there had considered him nothing more than a guinea pig for their tests, but when one of them died from a stroke in the middle of that "testing," the man's spirit immediately started to weep and beg for forgiveness. Vandal felt a little uncomfortable, but without being able to talk to the spirits, he would have lost his mind long before his body on Origin. When the spirits of the trappers tried to suck up to him, though, it made Vandal feel so awful he almost threw up. He hadn't wanted to let them cross over, so he made their spirits possess the pillars supporting the cave.

I still need to stay hidden until I get a bit bigger. Teeth other than his fangs started to grow in during his time in the cave. His head was still big compared to his body, making walking risky, but he could do it. That said, he still needed lots of sleep, and he couldn't run, just waddle along. He wasn't going to be covering vast distances in a single day. He either needed time to be able to grow enough to set out on his own two feet, or to arrange some kind of means of transport. That meant putting off his revenge against Baronet Bestello, his knights, and the people of Evbejia. He already had a plan, and was confident he could pull it off, so he wasn't pleased at having to wait. But patience was required.

It's winter now, Vandal thought. *I haven't asked Mom about the more recent history of this world yet, either. First things first, though—something with blood I can catch?* Feeling the nip of the cold wind once again and the gnawing pain of hunger, Vandal gave a sigh at the harshness of this world.

In Ramda, vampires were broadly categorized into four types.

The first was the true ancestor, the original vampire created by Vida and the undead hero Zakkato. The true ancestor was already long dead, even his name lost to the passage of time.

Next came the progenitor species, those who had been blessed directly by the true ancestor and their relatives. Their bloodline thinned over the ensuing generations, resulting in the noble species. Finally, the subordinate species, created by receiving the blood of the progenitor or noble species. They didn't have any of the magical powers that vampires boasted, such as Alluring Gaze, leaving them with only physical abilities such as Brute Strength and Regeneration.

In principle, the more closely a vampire was related to the true ancestor, the stronger they were. But each vampire was also unique, allowing for some subordinate species to be even stronger than noble species. That was why the monster rank applied by the adventurer's guild was little more than a suggestion when it came to vampires.

Vampires shared a few common characteristics, of course: a weakness to sunlight and the anti-undead life attribute magic used by the faithful of Alda, and the need for blood to sustain their lives.

Vandal's father was a subordinate species who served a progenitor vampire. Not one of the exemplary ones stronger than a noble species, either. Just a subordinate created from a regular human being. His name was Varen, and he had started out as just a thug from the slums.

The only thing Varen had going for him was his resistance to sunlight. He could resist sunlight to the point of just being a normal person, which his progenitor master was very pleased with. His master ordered Varen to carry out all sorts of tasks and information during the day. That was how he met Dalshia.

It was love at first sight, like some old-fashioned love story.

However, modern vampires also fell into two main camps. The conservatives, who continued to believe in Vida even after her defeat by Alda, and the radicals, who had given up on her and joined the evil and demon gods. The latter far outnumbered the former.

If Varen's master had been a conservative, then his love for Dalshia wouldn't have been a problem, but his master was a radical. Dark elves might be another race created by Vida, but his master was still incensed by the idea of polluting the vampire blood with that of another race. Varen used his ability to move in sunlight to flee with the heavily pregnant Dalshia, but eventually he fell to their pursuers in order to protect her and the baby. Fleeing into this forest, Dalshia created the name for her new son from parts of her husband's and her own name.

"So that's where 'Vandal' came from."

"That's right. Do you like it?"

"Yes, I do. It's a great name," he assured her. Having finally got a meal of something other than bugs and sap, Vandal was asking Dalshia for the umpteenth time about his father and vampires in general.

"I'm glad. I know your father would be happy too. We decided on 'Vandal' for a boy and 'Valshia' for a girl. Now, where was I? Oh yes, about vampires…"

Dalshia sounded like she was smiling as she happily started the same story all over again. Her mind was already starting to break down.

After death, spirits deteriorated as long as they remained in this world. In some cases, a powerful grudge, attachment, or sheer mental capacity could allow a spirit to retain its personality for more than 100 years. But not only had Dalshia been on the verge of vanishing, but then her last wish to be reunited with her son had also come true. That meant even having her possess the bone wasn't helping her spirit energy recover.

But she'll last 100 years if I keep supplying her with MP. Vandal decided to use those 100 years to find his mother a new body. Her memory might have been getting a bit foggy, but Dalshia remembered many facts from her life, and shared with Vandal whatever she could.

Time in general worked on Ramda as on Earth, with a day lasting twenty-four hours and a year lasting twelve months for a total of 360 days. Everyone spoke Japanese because the language spoken by the heroes spread among the remaining humans after the defeat of the demon king. Japanese had basically become the common language by now, but understanding of the Chinese *kanji* in Japanese was limited to the educated nobles and merchants.

"Experience" was a numerical representation of a person's life experiences. The people of Ramda gradually earned experience in the course of their everyday lives. Of course, they could also defeat monsters to earn experience. However, the experience earned, and the volume of it, depended on their "job."

These official jobs were known as blessings from the gods that had existed even before the appearance of the demon king. They were intended to give humans, so much weaker than gods, the potential to match their divine masters. When someone took a job, they received modifiers to their stat growth and skill acquisition, and could change to another job once they reached level 100. For example, if an Apprentice Warrior reached level 100, they could job change to a Warrior. In addition to jobs like Warrior and Magician, there were also jobs like Farmer and Craftsman. Combat jobs earned the most experience from battle with monsters, while Farmers earned the most from farming and agricultural research, and Craftsmen the most from making things.

I guess an adventurer in a Warrior job shouldn't be earning loads of experience from farming, and a Craftsman shouldn't be improving his crafting skills by defeating monsters, thought Vandal. *That means a Farmer should stick to farming and a Warrior stick to...warring?* Monsters, meanwhile, had no job but they did have a level. Reaching level 100 allowed them to evolve or rank-up into a promoted species of monster.

That meant Vandal's father, Varen, might have been able to rank up into something higher than a subordinate species—if he had survived for long enough. Then he could have survived for even longer.

Now I know just how nasty the other two curses from Rodocolte are: "unable to enter existing jobs" and "unable to personally acquire experience."

Unable to enter existing jobs—if a curse rendered him unable to take any jobs that had existed in the past, then it was a real nuisance. Unless he could find some totally new job to inhabit, he could never have a job at all.

Being unable to personally acquire experience, meanwhile, was even more serious. While the people around him continued to level up, Vandal would be unable to acquire a single point of experience, no matter how hard he trained or the battles he fought.

It's been eight months since I was born. I've had a harder time than most babies, putting myself through lots of magical training and usage, and I even captured the trappers, but I haven't leveled up at all.

At this rate he could still be level 0 by the time he grew up. Being a dhampir gave him above-average stats, but he definitely couldn't make it as an adventurer or soldier. That said, he wasn't going to make much of a Farmer or Craftsman either. He couldn't take a job, so he had no modifiers for acquiring skills. That meant he would need to work countless times harder than other Craftsmen to achieve the same results.

Vandal was also painfully aware of how poor his

interpersonal communication skills were. He had little real experience talking to others and had been born a crippling introvert.

The more I think about it, the darker my future is looking. I need to stop thinking.

It was time for bed. Growing boys needed their sleep.

That evening, he had turned some firewood into wood golems, making them rub together to start the fire. He got Bone Monkey to put that fire out, put some undead on watch, and then settled down to sleep in his furs. The lullaby Dalshia's spirit was singing rang comfortably in his ears, but he would have preferred some real human warmth.

Vandal had asked about one more topic: dhampir. But Dalshia had never encountered one outside of Vandal, and dhampir were themselves very rare, so she didn't have much to share about them.

Name: Vandal
Race: Dhampir (Dark Elf)
Age: 8 months
Alias: None
Job: None
Level: 0
Job History: None
—Status
Vitality: 21
Magical Power: 100001200
Strength: 28
Agility: 4
Muscle: 30

Intellect: 27

—Passive Skills

[Brute Strength: Level 1] [Rapid Healing: Level 2] [Death Attribute Magic: Level 3]

[Resist Maladies: Level 3 (UP!)] [Resist Magic: Level 1] [Night Vision]

[Spirit Pollution: Level 10] [Death Attribute Allure: Level 1]

—Active Skills

[Suck Blood: Level 2 (UP!)] [Limit Break: Level 2]

[Golem Creation: Level 2 (UP!)]

—Curses

[Unable to carry over experience from previous lives]

[Unable to enter existing jobs]

[Unable to personally acquire experience]

⬙

"Time to train."

Vandal had all of his undead minions line up outside the cave and he sent that thought to them. Knowing that Rodocolte's curses meant he couldn't level up or job change himself had led him to the idea of simply making his minions stronger instead. Having powerful undead at his command would greatly expand what he could do.

I won't be able to just walk into town, but Mom told me about adventurers with jobs like Tamer, Beast Master, and Summoner that control monsters. I'm sure it can work out.

He wanted them to be strong enough to take down other monsters safely in the future, but for now, simply being able to run fast while carrying him would allow him to leave the forest and strike out to safety. *They can't even beat wolves and bears at the moment, let alone real monsters*, Vandal thought. *A goblin destroyed one of my skeleton goblins already.*

Undead were very weak after just being created. They started at rank 1 undead, of course, so that made sense. He thought about trying to make monsters that started out stronger, but Vandal didn't know how to make undead that started at rank 2 or higher.

In his previous life—the one in which he first learned death attribute magic—he had almost no experience of turning anyone into undead other than himself. *The researchers in that facility weren't going to give me the chance to obtain pawns I could use against them. My body and my magic were hardly mine to control. If not for that, I would have access to all the research they did—their immortal soldiers project, everything. Although I believe that one failed.* He shook off such thoughts and got back to checking out his current strength. All the undead he could hope to count on in combat were lined up in front of him, excepting the scouts like the bugs.

The ones with any promise were Bone Monkey, a bone wolf, bear, and bird, and a human skeleton. He had others—boars, rabbits, and goblins—but they all had severe bone damage or just entirely missing bones. These five were the only ones with almost complete, almost undamaged skeletons.

"Let's start training right away. Which brings me to my next question—how to train you?" Vandal realized he had absolutely no idea what to do with Bone Monkey and other boney prospects to make them stronger.

Anyone could think of at least a few ideas for how to make a human stronger. Run laps for endurance, work out with weights for strength. Practice form with fighting techniques and weapons, or spar with actual opponents. All sorts of ideas. But Vandal had no idea what kind of training would be effective for the boney undead he saw before him.

Running laps was pointless. They had no hearts or lungs, and endurance wasn't the problem here anyway. Weight training would surely be pointless too, as they had no muscles. He imagined them doing pushups and crunches—all that would achieve would be wear on their bones.

Practicing form with fighting techniques and weapons sounded great, except Vandal didn't know any of that stuff himself. No dice. As for sparring, the undead were too dumb to do anything but hit the other party until it collapsed or they did. They'd just destroy each other.

Vandal himself had never been trained in combat. He had been relatively athletic on Earth, he at least liked to think, and had learned some judo in junior high and high school, but he wasn't ready to actually fight anyone. On Origin, of course, things had been no better.

What about the spirits of the trappers? Nope, no good. They knew how to use bows. The undead weren't up to the task of anything so complex yet.

I guess I'll start by checking their stats.

Dalshia had complained about not being able to check Vandal's stats, but he found himself capable of checking the stats of his own undead. Dalshia hadn't known much about the kind skills Beast Masters and Tamers had, so he couldn't be sure, but he assumed it was because the undead served him.

He took a good look at their stats.

Name: Bone Monkey, Bone Wolf, Skeleton, Bone Bear, Bone Bird
Rank: 1
Race: Living Bones
Level: 0
—Passive Skills
[Night Vision]
—Active Skills
[None]

Weak! Too weak!

The undead were all lumped together as the same race, regardless of the varied bones comprising them, and their stats were identical too. Living Bones. Animated skeletons. That was their only characteristic. They could move, but being nothing but bone made them slow, and their strength was far below that of a regular man. They could only move slowly, no running. They retained none of the abilities or skills that the owners of the bones had boasted in life. The bones were hard, but attacking their joints defeated them pretty easily. They had no intellect or instincts and were probably best suited as punching bags for newbie adventurers.

In summation, these undead weren't going to be any help in a real scrap.

But how can I make them stronger? Vandal thought. *It's been two months since I made them and they are still level 0. Which means I haven't done anything for them that would count as experience.* So what would? If a Swordsman got experience from fighting and training with a sword, a Farmer from farming, and a Blacksmith from smithing, what would undead do to earn experience? What did monsters do to earn experience?

Kill people?

That was his first thought—kill people, like all good monsters. If that was the right answer, he was going to have difficulty putting that into practice. Vandal could wipe out every soul in Evbejia and he wouldn't care, but if killing people got him marked by the adventurers' guild, then he would be either heading back underground or getting killed pretty quickly. He could use the undead as decoys and escape, but it was hard to find full animal skeletons like that of proud Bone Monkey. These weren't fire-and-forget pieces he could just pawn off.

In that case, I'll try having them kill other living things, like rabbits and rats.

As Vandal needed fresh blood to replace his lost mother's milk, he had been having the undead keep the animals alive even after trapping them. Then he bit them with his fangs and drained their blood. Maybe they could earn some experience by actually killing things.

The next day, the undead managed to catch a goblin alive. High Priest Goldan and his goons had significantly reduced the goblin population, but some were still clinging on. There was a reason the adventurers' guild had a permanent posting for hunting them down.

The goblin gnashed its teeth and screeched. Vandal couldn't be sure if it was just warning him off or speaking in some goblin language, but it certainly made a racket as the undead pinned it down.

So this is a goblin.

Vandal's expression didn't change, but inside he was quite impressed. This world just doubled down on typical fantasy.

Goblins: typically one step up from "slime" in a bevy of fantasy properties, the same seemed to apply here in Ramda. Goblins were low-ranking monsters found in normal forests and fields, as well as on the demon barrens where most of the monsters lived. It had muddy green skin and a height up to the chest of a human adult, with pointy elf-like ears but a disgustingly ugly face. In terms of strength, they were a little weaker than humans, and not especially agile. They had the intelligence of a human 3-year-old. Even the very best of them wore animal furs and were armed with sticks.

This one was rank 1, making it stronger than a single Living Bones, but still weak enough for a Farmer to beat to death with a hoe. There were multiple enhanced species, however, so one still had to be careful.

The most troubling things about goblins were their breeding power and general resilience. A goblin gave birth to at least three and as many as eight more goblins, and the children became adults in just six months. Those goblins could then spread out to any kind of terrain, from burning deserts to frozen tundra.

Just like in fantasy, it looks like they try to take human women too. Maybe not as bad as orcs. Judging from what Dalshia told him, this one probably hadn't done anything like that. It simply didn't look strong enough.

Okay then. Guys, finish him.

The time to be impressed by this living fantasy cliché was over. Now it was time to see if the undead could earn experience by killing it.

The goblin screamed out as Bone Monkey and Skeleton punched and kicked it in the head, with Bone Bear and Bone

Wolf biting into it and Bone Bird pecking at it. It wasn't pretty, but a single Living Bones wasn't powerful enough to kill the goblin in a single attack.

Still, after less than a minute, the goblin stopped moving. Vandal checked on the stats of Bone Monkey and the other bone chumps again.

Name: Skeleton Monkey (Bone Monkey), Bone Wolf, Skeleton, Bone Bear, Bone Bird
Rank: 1
Race: Living Bones
Level: 2
—Passive Skills
[Night Vision]
—Active Skills
[None]

They had increased from level 0 to level 2.

Wow, they leveled up, Vandal thought. *That solves it—the undead can gain experience by killing living things.* So even undead created using death attribute magic could level up. Vandal felt both relieved and elated. Now he had some hope of living as an adventurer, away from the influence of the Amidd Empire and Divine Alda. It felt good.

Hmmm. Something feels a little too good. Status!

Now he checked his own stats.

Name: Vandal
Race: Dhampir (Dark Elf)
Age: 8 months

Alias: None
Job: None
Level: 3 (UP!)
Job History: None
—Status
Vitality: 21
Magical Power: 100001203
Strength: 29
Agility: 4
Stamina: 31
Intellect: 29
—Passive Skills
[Brute Strength: Level 1] [Rapid Healing: Level 2]
[Death Attribute Magic: Level 3]
[Resist Maladies: Level 3] [Resist Magic: Level 1]
[Night Vision]
[Spiritual Pollution: Level 10] [Death Attribute Allure:
Level 1]
—Active Skills
[Suck Blood: Level 2] [Limit Break: Level 2]
[Golem Creation: Level 2]
—Curses
[Unable to carry over experience from previous lives]
[Unable to enter existing jobs]
[Unable to personally acquire experience]

Another surprising change had taken place.

I've gone from level 0 to level 3?! But the curse is still there! Why?

It had been eight months since he was born into Ramda.
Nothing he had done so far had allowed him to level up. Not

the death attribute magic training, not sucking a rabbit dry, not even killing Olby and the others. He checked his stats again, but there was no mistake. He double-checked the list, but the "unable to personally acquire experience" curse was still in place. Vandal thought for a moment longer, and something came to him.

Could it be—when Bone Monkey and the gang earn experience, some of it is carried over to me?

There were videogames on Earth where some of the experience obtained by monsters or the main character's clones then got added to the main character's own experience. Maybe this was the same thing.

The effects of the curse mean I can't earn experience for myself, but my undead servants can earn it for me. That's a big loophole for a curse created by a god.

Rodocolte cursed Vandal to make him despair and eventually kill himself, but with his death attribute magic he could still use undead to earn experience. It was such a simple workaround that he wondered if it wasn't a trap. Surely a god wouldn't overlook the fact Vandal could create undead. The evidence was mounting up that Rodocolte was just a moron.

He's not really a hands-on kinda god, now I think about it. He's given power and opportunity to us—well, everyone other than me—but hasn't provided any detailed follow-ups or further instructions. So maybe he would overlook something like that.

Rodocolte was probably looking down on Vandal, Hiroto Amemiya, and the others from above. It wasn't the difference between a nobleman and a peasant. It was like someone playing a simulation game and the characters inside the screen. That's how big the gap between them was.

That was why he wiped away everything he did to Vandal with a "Sorry about that," and then tried to get him to give up on his revenge and kill himself, without as much as batting an eyelid. That was why Rodocolte didn't give Vandal any serious thought. For Rodocolte, Vandal was just one of 100 characters he was watching over.

That explains this curse. I might be able to sort out the job problem too.

Vandal was still happy and relieved, but thinking things over again, he also felt a fresh surge of anger at Rodocolte. He had already sworn countless times that he wouldn't kill himself, but he vowed it anew now.

Vandal then had the undead bury the goblin's body. Goblin blood tasted bad, there were no materials to carve from it, and only adventurers could sell the bounty parts. He considered turning the corpse into an undead, but it would just make another monster he needed to raise, so he didn't bother with that, either.

The sun had set in the forest, and a fire was burning in front of the cave.

This flickering red fire was circled by five undead, each with pale blue fire dancing in their own vacant eye sockets. And then an infant, still small enough to be called a baby, shocking white skin illuminated by the flames. Then, beside the child, another figure appeared—the spirit of a dark elf, with terrible scars and wounds lingering on her beautiful body. The kind of scene that would send any travelers running in fear if they happened across it.

The spirit of the dark elf opened her mouth and sang a tune.

The party stumbled across the notes. It was a birthday song, first sung long ago by the Heroes, and still sung in Ramda to this day. The boney undead joined in, clacking and clicking with their teeth and bones, clapping their hands, and stamping their feet to add percussion.

Congratulations on your first birthday, Vandal!

The child gave a sigh, and then spat two short words toward the fire.

"Steal Heat."

The MP-infused breath snatched heat away from the flames, and they went out. The surroundings plunged into darkness, but the hearts of everyone gathered were as bright as the sun.

Congratulations on your first birthday, Vandal, the spirit said again. *I'm so happy for you!*

"Thank you, Mom."

It was June in the Milg Shield Kingdom, drier than it would be in Japan in early summer. Today, Vandal turned 1 year old. They were celebrating, but with a party somewhat lacking compared to those seen in regular households on Earth or Origin. There was no birthday cake and no presents. The special meal was raccoon dog bones, chopped up meat, and herbs stewed to make a kind of soup, accompanied by raccoon dog blood. The meat was tough and smelly, and Vandal was eating it by sheer force of will, so it wasn't really a great meal. For the dhampir, the blood got him through it.

I'm sorry. If was I alive I could have made you a nice meal, his mother apologized.

But Vandal was happy.

"No need to apologize, Mother. I'm so happy right now."

Vandal had lived on Earth and on Origin, but this was the first time anyone had ever celebrated his birthday. None of the researchers on Origin felt like throwing a party for a guinea pig. A birthday meant nothing more than increasing the number in the age column by one.

On Earth, he had lived with his uncle, but who told him that celebrating his birthday or Christmas while he was kid would make him soft, so he didn't receive cakes and presents then either, or a single word of congratulation. His uncle and aunt had celebrated the birthdays of their own kids, of course. So this was his first birthday party.

Vandal...

"There are lots of happy things to celebrate today," he said, trying to cheer Dalshia up a little as her spirit eyes watered.

First, he could actually talk. That had proven to be more important than he expected: talking gave him access to magical incantations he hadn't been able to use before. He overcome that by burning excess MP to force the magic to happen, costing him many times the required MP for half the results. Vandal only managed to make it work because of his vast magical power.

All that silent spell casting had rewarded him with the skill Skip Incantation the moment he learned to speak, meaning he still didn't have to bother with them. It was a very rare skill, surprising even Dalshia, but the irony of the timing took the edge off the achievement a little.

Another thing to celebrate was Bone Monkey and the other primary undead all reaching level 100, bringing them up to rank 2. Their only skills remained Night Vision, but the blessings from leveling up were substantial. They had become Bone Animals, with their stats rising to probably around what they had been in life. They had also regained some beastly intelligence, making them capable of doing more than just following Vandal's orders.

The Bone Man was the only one to become a different race, proceeding to become Skeleton. With strength and agility equal to that of a man, the Skeleton was still an easy kill for an adventurer, but represented a big step up for Vandal. He put leather armor on it that he had stripped from the trappers, a short sword, and a wooden shield made from a wood golem. Now he had a skeletal knight to fight for him. It was even learning to use a bow.

Vandal also reached level 100 himself. However, he still didn't have a job, so his skills hadn't really reaped any rewards. He now met the conditions for a job change, but he didn't have access to a facility that could do the task—generally a special room in each guild or a temple—and so it still felt pointless.

He had some fighting strength, then, but Vandal still thought it was too soon to try to take his revenge on Evbejia. He wasn't strong enough. He might be able to execute and complete his revenge, but he wasn't sure he could then make it safely out of Evbejia and the Milg Shield Kingdom to reach somewhere a dhampir could live a normal life. He couldn't be satisfied with just revenge on Evbejia. He had to bolster his strength and supplies before he made his move.

"Tomorrow, I'm going to go hunting bandits," he said.

Bandits. Not monsters, but criminals, living in the mountains, equipped with weapons and stealing from soft targets. In other words, humans.

If he was aiming to further increase his strength and supplies, he was going to have to kill humans at some point.

"My skeletons have stopped getting any real experience from killing bunnies and raccoons, and the strongest monsters in this forest are goblins. But Evbejia is at the hub of different roads, so I should be able to find some bandits without too much trouble. Killing them will provide experience for Bone Monkey and the others, and me with all of their own supplies. Two birds with one stone."

Even better, killing bandits and taking the things they had stolen wasn't against the law in this world. On Earth or Origin, killing a criminal and taking their ill-gotten goods made you a criminal too. But in Ramda, bandits were fair game, and no one would lose any sleep over someone killing them. People might even offer praise for it, but they would never call such a person a murderer or accuse them of disregarding human rights. Taking their belongings was the right of the one who killed them. If the original owners wanted them back, they would have to negotiate with the new owner.

Hunting bandits is dangerous. That's normally a job for rank D adventurers, Dalshia said, obviously worried about Vandal.

He gave her a reassuring smile. "I'll take them by surprise, don't worry. I've got a good idea where to find some of them."

And so the next day, the 1-year-old Vandal started out on a quest normally given to rank D adventurers.

Name: Vandal
Race: Dhampir (Dark Elf)
Age: 1 year old
Alias: None

Job: None
Level: 100 (UP!)
Job History: None
—Status
Vitality: 34
Magical Power: 100001223
Strength: 32
Agility: 7
Stamina: 33
Intellect: 45
—Passive Skills
[Brute Strength: Level 1] [Rapid Healing: Level 2] [Death Attribute Magic: Level 3]

[Resist Maladies: Level 3] [Resist Magic: Level 1] [Night Vision]

[Spiritual Pollution: Level 10] [Death Attribute Allure: Level 2 (UP!)]

[Skip Incantation: Level 1 (NEW!)]

—Active Skills
[Suck Blood: Level 3 (UP!)] [Limit Break: Level 2]

[Golem Creation: Level 2]

—Curses
[Unable to carry over experience from previous lives]

[Unable to enter existing jobs]

[Unable to personally acquire experience]

❇

Seven bandits were lounging in their simple hideout, drinking wine they had pillaged from their targets for today.

"We did pretty well today," one said.

"Sure did. Everyone in the village will be happy with this haul," another agreed.

They almost looked like farmers who had just finished bringing in the harvest, sharing a drink over the deeds of the day, but they were bandits for sure. The proof lay in the wine they drank, which they had stolen from a merchant who hadn't wanted to pay adventurers for protection—stolen along with his life. They only had old gear: damaged leather armor, handmade spears and bows, and axes meant for chopping wood. Bandits on the bottom rung. They had never received any formal combat training, either, and were more brawlers than skilled fighters, to put it politely. More crudely, they were a bunch of desperate guys wildly swinging weapons around.

With no combat training at all, most of them had Farmer as their job. They were playing at bandits in the mountains because they were poor, no other reason. There were all sorts of reasons why young people in poor, failing villages turned to crime. It happened a lot here in Ramda.

"Let's get the sentry set up and grab some sleep," one suggested.

The bandits' hideout was located in the middle of a plain of tall grass. They had cut some of it down to make an open area and set up a few simple tents. They did have a lookout tower, but they didn't make much use of it.

There was nothing out here on the plains other than the occasional wild animal, after all, so a stoked fire was all they needed. The sentries mainly watched for the goblins that did, very rarely, attack. But those approached so nosily that watching for them hardly seemed required. Often the bandits didn't bother with a sentry at all.

And that was why they had no way of detecting enemies who might approach more quietly.

"I think I've had too much to drink…" the drunk sentry slurred with a hiccup, and then yelped as he was grabbed and snatched away by the paw of the Bone Bear reaching out from the wall of grass.

Nasty crunching sounds rang out, but no one emerged from the tents. In the sentry's stead, Skeleton, Bone Monkey, and the Bone Wolf with the Bone Bird on its back all stepped out from the grass. Vandal came up the rear.

"There's six more. Be quick with it."

Bones scraped and cracked.

The bandits never did make it back to their village.

For Vandal, the nastier the group of bandits, the easier it was for him to find their hideout because the spirits of those they killed could provide him with all the information he needed. These victims who had not only lost their possessions but their lives. That regret and hatred was powerful, making it easy for the bug undead to locate them.

Once he found a spirit, he used the Summon Spirit spell to bring it to him from any location, and then asked it for information. Then he fed what he learned to the bug undead, which located the bandit's hideout within days.

Vandal had already used this method to find four groups of bandits working in the domain of Baronet Bestello. Once located, he continued his reconnaissance, determining their numbers and armaments. The former villagers he attacked today had been the smallest group of bandits, with the worst weapons.

"A successful practice run. Well done, everyone," Vandal said as he confirmed the bandits had been wiped out.

His expression didn't change, but inside he was pleased with the undead. His boney minions couldn't express themselves with smiles, but the blue flames in their eyes did happily wobble around.

The Bone Bear proved himself the MVP of this battle, taking out the sentry with a bear hug and then another of the bandits with its claws. Skeleton killed two with its short sword, and then Bone Monkey and Bone Wolf took out one each by strangling and biting.

"Hey. Buck up, bird head. You'll learn to fly eventually."

The Bone Bird had the hardest time, finally managing to peck one to death after Vandal buried the man up to his neck by transforming the ground into a golem. Bone Bird wasn't helping with the team yet, but there was a good reason—it couldn't fly.

It made sense. Bone Bird was all bones and no feathers.

"Earn more experience, rank up, and I bet you'll be able to fly. Believe in yourself," Vandal said.

The bird flapped its boney wings cheerfully at Vandal's support. It seemed to understand. Vandal watched it happily, then stroked it on the skull before checking out the bandits' treasure.

The first thing he saw was a wagon with three large barrels: the remainder of the wine opened by the bandits. Evbejia was a wine-producing town, so it was probably high quality.

"Anything else?" Wine was worthless for a baby and for his

boney companions. He might be able to cook something with it. He probably *could* drink it, taking his level 3 Resist Maladies skill into account. That would likely allow him to drink all the wine he liked without consequence, even with his infant body.

Naughty boy! If you start drinking as a baby, you'll be a complete drunk by the time you grow up!

Vandal decided not to drink alcohol without permission from his mother.

"But I guess taking one barrel can't hurt. There's a wagon and everything. Now, what else?"

Vandal searched around the wagon and inside the tents, but putting it politely, the place was a dump. He found a bag with copper and silver coins taken from merchants, and sacks of millet, oats, other grains, and cheap wheat that might be used as pet or cattle feed on Earth. Some dried fish, and everyday items used by bandits. Perhaps the best thing was a big pot full of some ten pounds of salt.

Hardly much "treasure," but that was to be expected. These bandits were just Farmers, and there had only been seven of them. Big targets—like wagons protected by adventurers—would have been beyond these losers.

But for Vandal, it was still far better than nothing.

"This is great. I was getting sick of eating nothing but meat and blood, and the salt Mom stored up ran out a while back. This cloth will be useful too."

Vandal survived by hunting animals in the forest. His mom had stocked up goods like wheat, cheese, vegetables, and salt, but those ran out pretty quickly after she was killed. She had only been storing what she could carry on the road by herself to begin with.

As Vandal was growing, he was starting to need more food. Getting enough blood to support all of his needs was too hard, and he couldn't risk turning too vampire and becoming susceptible to sunlight.

He wanted to survive on regular food. But blood-drained meat didn't taste great after being cooked, and sometimes he could only get meat that didn't taste good in the first place, like raccoon dog and fox. Both of those were still better than when he only found goblins.

For clothes, all he had were badly wrapped furs. He looked like some kind of barbarian child.

"I've probably got materials now to make clothes. After that, there's just money…I guess I might be able to use that."

The Amidd Empire and its nations used the "Amidd" as their currency. One Amidd was worth about 100 yen on Earth. It came in the smaller copper half Amidd coin, the copper 1 Amidd, the copper 10 Amidd, the silver 100 Amidd, the gold 1,000 Amidd, and the white-gold 10,000 Amidd. There were also paper bills, but only merchants and the highest class of nobles used those, with notes for 100,000 Amidd and even a million. Those were closer to government bonds than bills.

The bandits only had a couple thousand Amidd in cash, maybe double the monthly earnings of a laborer in the city. If Vandal went into town, guards or adventurers would quickly kill him, so he might not get much chance to use it. But when he finally did get to another country, he might be able to change it for a different currency, so he decided to hold onto it.

"Huh? What's this bag?"

He noticed a smaller leather bag beneath the coin sack. It was light and made small clicking sounds when he moved it around. He undid the strings and looked inside, to see two colored, slightly translucent stones. They might be gemstones, although they didn't look all that pretty.

"Mom, do you know what these are?"

Yes, Dalshia responded. *Magic stones. You can get these from monsters. From the size and color, I think these are goblin ones. They sell for about 10 Amidd, I think.*

Magic stones formed when the MP inside a monster crystalized upon their death. They were used in all sorts of magic items and spirit medicine, like potions, and provided the power for magical items that regular folk without much MP could use. When used as a power source, they were throwaway items, draining the MP they contained, which turned them into regular stones. But an alchemist could process them into magic crystals that a magician could then recharge.

Magic stones from low-ranking monsters like goblins, however, were not worth the trouble of processing like that, and were generally sold for very little and then simply depleted and discarded.

When you defeat low-rank monsters, his mother continued, *they usually don't drop magic stones at all. Rank 1 monsters might drop one for every 100 you defeat, if that. Higher-ranking monsters will almost always drop magic stones, however. Once you get to rank 5 and above, you should get some pretty much every time.*

The reason Dalshia hadn't talked about magic stones yet was because Vandal had only been defeating a few rank 1 goblins, so she hadn't thought there was any need.

She added that some monsters gave magic stones more easily even at low ranks, and others that gave higher-quality stones than their ranks suggested. Vandal was busy hunting bandits at the moment, not monsters, so this was interesting but not especially useful at the moment. He wanted to register with an adventurers' guild and become an adventurer as quickly as possible.

"I'll check my minions' stats again…wow, Skeleton killed two weak bandits and got almost thirty levels. Same for the bear. Bone Monkey and the others took out one each, but they're still up ten levels."

It was a surprise attack on untrained farmer-bandits and yet their levels rocketed up. There was no comparing this to the experience obtained from goblins and forest animals. If this experience gap held true with other types of monsters, it implied humans were a good source of experience. That would explain why monsters were so aggressive toward humans.

"In that case, I'm going to hunt down all the bandits around here and get all the levels we can."

After seeing these kinds of boosts, he couldn't go back to hunting animals for scraps. The Baronet Bestello domain still had one group around the same size as the one he took out today, another with ten bandits, and then a third with around twenty. If he wiped them all, out he should be able to push all his undead to rank 3.

If you killed us, the guys to the south will be easy for you, one of the bandit spirits said.

The ones to the west are from three villages over from us. You won't have any trouble with them, even if they have numbers.

But the ones to the north are professionals. Their chief was a soldier from some town or other, and they're all pretty tough. They extorted money from us too.

Vandal collected what information he could from the spirits of the bandits as he had an earth golem bury their bodies. Then he loaded up the wagon and left the slaughter behind.

One month passed since his first birthday. Now that it was summer, he was using Death to Bugs on mosquitoes every night. He also reached the point of planning his attack on the largest and most skilled band of bandits in Baronet Bestello's domain.

He was always careful of being spotted by travelers and guards on the move, honing his own skills and those of his skeletons in the woodlands and tall grass.

"These bandits are on another level," he told his skeletons. "The chief is a former soldier, and he'll have trained his men. Those weapons aren't just for show; they know how to use them." They knew how to use them for days like today.

The undead groaned, literal fires burning in their eyes. The experience from the bandits had ranked up his Skeleton to Skeleton Soldier, while Bone Monkey, Bone Bear, and Bone Wolf ranked up to Bone Beast. The undead learned the skill Brute Strength, as well as, perhaps because of all the creeping around and surprise attacks, Sneaking Steps. That meant the sound of rattling bones whenever they attacked was now a thing of the past. Skeleton Soldier also learned Sword Proficiency, Bow Proficiency, and Shield Proficiency skills. They were all skill level 1, but it could fight respectably after a month of training with golems.

There was one straggler. Bone Bird was still rank 2, but it was around level 90, so if this raid worked out it was sure to rank up.

"You'll need to fight carefully today. I have some spare bones, but make sure your skull doesn't get destroyed. If you see anyone who doesn't look like bandits—like people tied up or stuck in a cage—don't kill them. The operation starts when I cast support magic," Vandal explained.

His expression was as blank as ever and his tone light, keeping his internal tension from surfacing. Then he incanted the spells.

"First Lethality Enhancement on your weapons, fangs, and claws. Then Energy Steal on your armor and bones." Lethality Enhancement increased attack strength against living creatures and shaved off their life force when touching them, even through armor or shields. Energy Steal allowed all forms of energy to be absorbed—not just MP, but also heat, electricity, and even kinetic energy—which here in Ramda functioned as protection against both magic and physical attacks. These spells both had powerful effects, but they weren't that hard to control using death attribute magic.

With a moan, the Skeleton made the first move.

Wreathed in fresh magical power, it raised its bow—the one taken from Olby—and pointed it toward the sentry tower of the bandit hideout, which was itself a simple collection of huts surrounded by a fence. The target bandit also carried a bow and wore a quiver on his back, but didn't feel up to keeping watch.

"I can't believe this. It's the final night here and I drew watch."

After today, the bandits planned on taking their earnings and moving on. They'd collect the ransom for the prisoner they were holding, and then head to a different domain or country and continue their work there.

Bandits had been suddenly vanishing from the vicinity recently, with rumors spreading that the lord of the domain had put his best men to work on keeping the roads safe. It was time for them to move on. And so the bandits were having a bit of a party, eating all the excess supplies so that they could make a smooth getaway. The sentry was unlucky in that he didn't get to take part, and now that bad luck was also causing too much of a distraction.

The Skeleton's arrow flickered out of the night and plunged into his throat.

"Gya—!" Crying out in agony, he lost his balance and plunged off the tower.

The other bandits, reveling in drink, sobered up pretty quickly when their sentry friend dropped to the ground, an arrow in the throat.

"Enemy attack!"

"Men! Grab your weapons!"

In the moment the bandits went to take their axes, maces, and spears, Bone Bear and Bone Monkey tore the fence apart, the shattered wood scattering as they charged forward.

"Rooooooooah!" bellowed the skeletons.

"Undead! Monsters, monsters are attacking!"

"Keep calm, you fools! Axes and maces, forward! Those with swords and spears, change weapons! Bows too!" The bandit chief kept a cool head, giving directions as he selected a halberd for himself.

He had some experience fighting skeletons and zombies from when he was a soldier. He knew that, especially with the half-baked skills of his men, smashed and crushing weapons like maces and poles would do better than cutting or stabbing weapons like swords and spears.

"There's twenty of us! We can handle a couple of rank 1 or 2 monsters! Take them out!"

The death of their friend and the bold nature of the attack threatened to crush their morale, but their leader's orders and energy snapped them back. The bandits steeled themselves to take out the unruly undead that had interrupted their celebrations.

"GROOOOAH!"

That conviction didn't last long. Bone Bear, standing up on its hind legs, sent one man swinging an axe flying with its front paws. Bone Monkey crushed the head of another bandit like an egg. The fangs of Bone Wolf sunk into the legs of the bandits, and then tore out their throats where they fell.

The Skeleton Soldier groaned as it put down its bow, took up a long sword taken from the other bandits, and joined the fray.

"Hey! Aaargh!"

The undead versus the living. In a clash of untrained fighters, the undead quickly gained the advantage.

There was little difference between them in terms of skill and, if anything, the weapons being used by these bandits were of higher quality than the longsword held by the Soldier. In that area, the bandits had the advantage.

But a rank 3 Skeleton Soldier was stronger than the average human, and the Brute Strength skill in particular gave it a powerful edge. Humans didn't start out with any particular physical abilities or special powers, developing the martial arts and magic in order to combat monsters. But when monsters had equal abilities, they didn't stand a chance.

The Skeleton Soldier grunted and groaned, bones stained

red with blood, shuddering with the pleasure of obtaining experience by taking lives, and chopped into his next target in order to earn some more.

"Chief! These ain't rank 2!"

"We can't handle them! Help us, chief!"

The bandits were losing ground, losing friends, and losing their cool.

Worthless fools! I need to escape, on my own if I have to!

The bandit chief promptly decided to run for it. He didn't consider for a moment that he might fight these undead for the sake of his men. At his skill level, he wouldn't be able to beat a rank 3 or higher monster one-on-one anyway. Yes, he had been a soldier, and he had the Halberd Proficiency skill at level 2. The town guard he had served in crumbled, to begin with. If he was an adventurer, he might be grade E at best. Typically fighting rank 3 monsters in single combat required at least grade D. If he teamed up with his men, he might have been able to defeat one of these things—but there were four undead. No, five.

He wasn't sure what to make of Bone Bird, finishing off an already incapacitated bandit was a peck to the throat. That one was...unexpected.

But even if they could defeat it, it wouldn't matter when the rest finished them off. Striking a blow only felt good if you were alive to revel in it.

"We can do this! Don't give in, push forward!"

He shouted reckless orders at the remaining men, and then quietly backed away so they wouldn't notice what he was doing. He was going to run to the wagon they had taken from a merchant and ride away. If he ran away, he could start another group of bandits elsewhere.

"Rise."

The bandit's thoughts of escape were shattered when he bumped into the wall of earth that had suddenly risen up behind him.

"What? What's this? Alchemy?!"

From among the screams of his men and the groans of the undead, he picked out a high-pitched voice, like that of a young girl. That had to be the one responsible for this, and he looked around to find them.

It didn't take him long.

A child was standing a short distance away—more like a baby, almost—dressed in little more than rags.

This kid is doing this? The bandit shook his head, unable to believe it, but the child—Vandal—looked so bizarre, he knew he had to be right.

The child had white hair, with one hollow crimson eye and one purple one. Even on this bloody battlefield, it was like he was hardly there—a ghostly presence. If he hadn't spoken, the bandit probably wouldn't have seen him.

"You're the one controlling these undead? I surrender, then. I surrender! You can have all the treasure, and take me to adventurers' guild, whatever you want to do."

The bandit lowered his halberd and raised both hands above his head. If he couldn't win, then he'd run away. If he couldn't run away, then he'd surrender. He didn't have 1 Amidd of honor or pride left anywhere in his body.

"Surrender?" asked the child, his tone even.

"Yes. Happy to," the bandit replied with a grin. "There's a bounty on my head, and I've got info on the other bandits around here. You get half the money of anyone sold as a criminal slave. Keeping me alive sounds pretty good, don't you think?"

Everything he said was true. He was happy to sell out others in the same profession if it meant saving his own neck. Most bandits taken alive were sold as criminal slaves, although it would depend on the state of their wounds. Many ended up in the mines or as military grunts. The sale price for them was better than one might expect and, depending on the number, could exceed the value of the treasure they had stolen.

The reply, however, was an insult.

"Are you a moron?"

"What did you just say?!"

"As you can tell, I'm a dhampir," Vandal said. "If I turn you into the adventurers' guild, I'll be killed myself. In fact, I'll be dead long before you get sold as a slave."

In the Amidd Empire and its nations, where the people believed in the God of Law and Life Alda, dhampir weren't considered human, but just another monster. So even if he caught a whole bunch of bandits, soldiers and adventurers would kill him the moment he walked into town. The bandit boss chief wasn't an adventurer and didn't hear about the dhampir panic from last year, so it had taken him a while to notice Vandal was a dhampir.

"Then make me your underling! I can help out. Your undead are strong, but it can't hurt to have a human minion!"

He could think on his feet, Vandal had to admit, seeing this change of direction. Vandal had been painfully aware of exactly what this man was saying for a while now. He had skeletons who did everything he said, and the spirit of Dalshia, but that wasn't enough to cover everything he needed to get by.

But he wasn't thinking of using the man in front of him to resolve that problem.

"I do want a living ally, but I don't want a bandit who's just going to abandon his men and run away. I might let you join the party after you're dead."

The man's face had brightened to start with, but then sank into despair. Vandal gave Bone Bear the signal.

"Hold on! I don't want to die! Not like this!"

"Oh? And what about all the people you killed?"

What a hypocrite, Vandal thought. The moment he turned away, Bone Bear snapped the bandit's neck. The bear grunted, as though worried it has screwed up, but Vandal waved away its concerns, then gave a sigh.

"Phew, that was pretty nerve-wracking. I've never talked to anyone other than Mom before!"

He had been born with communication issues on all three worlds; he didn't need the added backdrop of a bloody battle-field when he had to talk to someone.

"The smell of blood is so thick it's making me hungry. But I don't want to drink bandit blood and move closer to becoming a vampire, so I need to resist. First, let's see if anyone is left alive. Detect Life."

Seeking distraction from the rich smell of blood in the air, he used some death attribute magic that would detect a living presence within the vicinity. Ignoring the bugs, grass, bacteria, mold, and other abundant but small sources, he searched for larger animals and humans or monsters with magical power.

He got three large animal responses from behind a large barn nearby. Horses, probably. There was one more response from beneath the barn—and this one was human. The information gleaned from spirits had told him there were twenty-one bandits, and he counted twenty-one bodies.

"Who is it beneath the barn? A new member?"

No, not one of us. A merchant we captured a few days back. The kid of a merchant from a town in Viscount Majjio's domain, the next one over. We were hoping for a ransom, so we kept him alive—ah, my neck, my….

Due to the shock and terror of the death blow, the bandit's neck was all twisted even as a spirit. Vandal frowned at the information.

Things just got more complicated.

Name: Bone Man
Rank: 3
Race: Skeleton Soldier
Level: 39
—Passive Skills
[Night Vision] [Brute Strength: Level 1 (NEW!)]
—Active Skills
[Sword Proficiency: Level 1 (NEW!)] [Shield Proficiency: Level 1 (NEW!)]
[Bow Proficiency: Level 1 (NEW!)] [Sneaking Steps: Level 1 (NEW!)]

Name: Bone Monkey, Bone Wolf, Bone Bear
Rank: 3
Race: Bone Beast
Level: 24 - 32
—Passive Skills
[Night Vision] [Brute Strength: Level 1 (NEW!)]

—Active Skills
[Sneaking Steps: Level 1 (NEW!)]

The merchant Rudi considered himself pretty blessed.

He had been born as the third son of the merchant in the direct service to Viscount Majjio. Due to being born third, he didn't have a hope of inheriting the family business, but his parents and two older brothers always treated him well. He received the same excellent education as his siblings, preparing him to strike out on his own, as he wouldn't be inheriting anything.

Once grown up, Rudi started by gaining experience as a merchant. He only received some help from his family when first starting up, and while he had been through some tough times, he did pretty well for himself in the end.

It was his third year as a merchant. Things had gone well enough that he could decide to buy a carriage with his savings and form up a trading caravan with other merchants, or instead settle down and open a store somewhere.

But when the bandits attacked him a few days ago, he thought his luck had run out. He had hired two grade E adventurers as protection, but they hadn't been able to hold off twenty armed bandits. It was too late now to wish he paid up a bit more for protection.

The bandits stole his products and gold, but when they were about to kill him, he shouted, "My family will pay to get me back!" The lowest form of begging for his life.

But it wasn't a merchant's job to die with pride. It would cause trouble for his family, but he needed to survive and keep his business going. If he made enough money, he could pay his family back.

The best result, of course, would have been for a band of adventurers or knights to swoop in, wipe out the bandits to save him, and then return everything he had lost, but the world wasn't made quite that way. As he pondered his predicament, bearing the discomfort of the damp underground cell, Rudi heard a sound.

Someone is coming down here?

Noticing the small sounds suggesting someone coming down the ladder, Rudi raised his head from the rough, slightly smelly blanket and looked outside the wooden bars, but it was too dark to see anything. If it was a bandit coming down, there should have been light from a candle or magic. He was probably imagining things, and then he heard footsteps pattering toward him.

The footsteps stopped in front of the cell. He still couldn't see anyone in the darkness.

"Who's there?" he shouted, his voice shaking with fear and uncertainty.

A reply came back from the ground. "Oh, I'm sorry. I didn't realize how dark it is down here. Wisp Fire." A blue, fist-sized ball of fire appeared, illuminating the cell.

"A ghost!" Rudi yelped. "A ghost!"

He saw a child, hair wild and white, skin pale as a corpse, and clothing barely better than tattered cloth. Rudi was sure it was the undead ghost of a child these bandits had killed and he clutched at his blanket as he screamed.

"No. I'm alive."

At first, Vandal thought maybe this guy could also see spirits, but then realized he was just terrified. Vandal's shoulders slumped. He had come to help this guy out, so he didn't appreciate such a reaction to his appearance, but he shook that off and continued.

"The bandits who captured you have been wiped out. As you can see, I'm not an adventurer, but a dhampir." Vandal kept things light and Rudi started to calm down—then paled considerably when he realized what those words might mean.

"A dhampir? Are you going to...kill me?" he asked.

A dhampir. In the country of his birth, this was a monster. Something to be eliminated. The priests of the God of Law and Life Alda were very specific about this kind of monster too. Unlike adventurers and knights, then, this creature had no reason to save him, and now that Rudi saw the dhampir's face, it was likely to kill him.

But the dhampir child shook his head.

"No. If you keep your mouth shut about me, I'm not planning on killing you," he replied.

"R-really?"

"Yes. You were captured by the bandits, but when they started fighting among themselves you managed to escape. That's the story I want you to tell. Please say nothing about me."

Rudi still didn't seem convinced. From his perspective, it was like he had just met a friendly demon. It didn't add up. Vandal knew it would be best to silence this young merchant. But he had a reason why he didn't want to kill Rudi, if possible.

Do the best you can, every day. For the sake of your future.

It was that simple. Killing bandits to protect himself wasn't a problem. No one in Ramda would question that. But killing a victim like Rudi to keep himself safe was going a step beyond. Vandal believed that acts of that kind had a negative effect on your character, even if no one else knew about it. His uncle on Earth, the terrorists who had blown themselves up with their own ferry bomb, and the scientists on Origin who had performed experiments on so many people—Vandal saw them all as scum who had fallen into darkness. He had no intention of joining them.

He hated them, so how could he let himself become like them? And beyond that, Vandal wanted to live a blessed, happy life here on Ramda—something he had never experienced on Earth or Origin. That was his dream. To be well-off, comfortable, surrounded by a warm circle of family and friends. If he built a life on madness and evil, how long would he be able to hold it together?

Furthermore, Hiroto Amemiya and the other cheaters would be reborn into this world in about fifty years. If he had fallen into darkness, then there was a chance they would purge him in the name of justice. They had cheat powers, so they could probably uncover his crimes even without evidence or witnesses. Some of them could probably read minds, see the past, or make people spill their darkest secrets, and they were all going to be highly skilled with magic. That was why, if possible, he wanted to avoid killing people like Rudi, who were just victims.

"If that's okay with you, that's okay with me. I'm not an adventurer either," Rudi replied.

Luckily, he wasn't a crazy religious Alda fanatic. He opted to take Vandal's conditions and live.

He was also smart in that he didn't underestimate Vandal based on his appearance. He felt scared of this tiny child from the bottom of his heart and acted appropriately. For Rudi, that was just a natural reaction. Vandal looked like a baby but spoke like an adult, and had a creepy atmosphere around himself. He wasn't a normal child.

With a metallic clank, Vandal used the bandit chief's keys to open the padlock on the cell. Rudi gave a relieved sigh at being free…

"Oh, and if you do tell anyone about me, I will unleash evil spirits on you, so please don't have a change of heart," Vandal said, just to make sure.

Rudi paled and shook his head vigorously.

Rudi climbed the ladder and came out above ground. He trembled at the sight of the corpses of the bandits and the blood-stained undead. Bone Bird was surrounded by a pale blue fire, squawking happily at having leveled up. Rudi swore to never speak of what he had seen here—even for a mountain of white-gold coins.

Morning came. Rudi took the edge off his fear by drinking the wine the bandits had been enjoying, and then Vandal returned to him everything the bandits had taken. Rudi also received the horses—Vandal had little use for live ones—and even the carriage, to which one of the horses had been attached. Then Rudi set out.

He was traveling alone, without any protection, but it wasn't like there were any bandits left nearby. Vandal had wiped them all out. Unless the young man was unlucky enough to ride into a horde of goblins, he should make it safely to his destination.

Receiving the unexpected horses had led him to the decision to form a trade caravan with other merchants, but Vandal didn't really care about that.

Vandal spent the night fixing up the undead, swapping out broken bones with replacement parts—that is, bones collected from animals and humans. He also spent some time with Bone Bird, which had ranked up to Phantom Bird and obtained spirit wings that allowed it to fly. Then he buried the bodies of the bandits.

The next morning, Vandal slept until close to noon. The undead had seen Rudi off. Rudi meant little to Vandal, but that might have been too much for the poor guy.

After waking, Vandal ate a lunch of the bandit's leftovers: salted meat, bread, and cheese. There were dried vegetables in place of a salad and some dried fish soup. For dessert, he ate fruit from the forest.

"These bandits lived a pretty good life." That thought made him feel pretty low, even as he ate. Attacking bandits and obtaining more supplies had freed him from needing to eat hard, smelly raccoon and fox meat, greatly improving his diet. But trying to cook with kitchen equipment he had turned into undead cursed tools was harder than he had expected. Cursed tools were magical implements that could move on their own once possessed by a spirit, but they didn't have any strength or dexterity. That made them poorly suited to cooking.

He could have had the Skeleton do it, but the spirit possessing those bones was the same as all the other undead—a former bug, mouse, or other small animal—so it didn't understand the concept of cookery. Ordering it to "cut vegetables" led to more of a butchering than a salad, with the chopping board itself getting chopped. It was impressive that it had managed to learn the sword and bow by this point.

And if Vandal tried to cook for himself....

No! You're only 1 year old; you can't cook! Dalshia protested. *What happens if you get burnt?*

"But Mom, eating dried meat and hard bread like this can't be good for my stomach, even with the strength I have compared to a normal baby."

No, no, I said no! What if you get burned?

"I'll use water and Steal Heat to cool off."

Death attribute magic was the opposite of life attribute, meaning it didn't heal very well. It wasn't completely without options, but they were hard to handle. Death magic could heal fatal wounds or serious sicknesses, but not light wounds that weren't life threatening. So he could heal full-body burns, but a keloid on his hand would be difficult for him to handle.

No! I say no!

"Okay, Mom."

When she was alive, she must have been strongly aware of keeping her child away from fire, and her death and transformation into a spirit only intensified it. That said, he had only just turned 1. His arms and legs were still short, and he could easily suffer an unexpected injury handling pots and pans, so Dalshia wasn't necessarily incorrect.

He made do by having wood golem branches rub together to make a fire. He boiled some water and stewed up bread and dried meat chopped up by the skeletons. That was his regular meal nowadays. It tasted...well, better than raccoon dog and fox meatballs.

"It's fine. Once I grow up I'll earn loads of money, hire skilled cooks, and eat delicious food every single day. Anyway, time to look over today's haul."

First, the bandits' weapons. The other bandits used handmade spears (a knife attached to a stick), clubs, and low-quality bows, but these ones had decent weapons worthy of the most powerful band of bandits in the region, for sure.

The metal was standard steel, but these hadn't been made by pouring metal into a mold. Real craftsmen made them. Some of the weapons got chipped or shattered by Bone Monkey and the gang, but since the undead killed many of the bandits in one strike, plenty of weapons survived unscathed. The armor was in the same condition: fixed and repaired in many places, but far better than anything used by the other bandits. They had certainly attacked an arms merchant before.

Then, there was the treasure from the carriage. He had let Rudi take all of his own stuff back, but there was plenty of money left. In cash, there was approximately 50,000 Amidd. There were also numerous accessories, the exact value of which he didn't know: a pile of fancy fabrics and two barrels of high-quality wine. Luxury sugar, expensive because of not being made in the Milg Shield Kingdom. On top of all that, there was also the bandits' backup weapons and food.

Including the carriages, it was all probably worth more than 200,000 Amidd. Converted, that was about 20 million yen—plenty of money, but hardly a fortune. That said, Evbejia was the only town in the area, so they had done well to steal this much. Although maybe he shouldn't praise the bandits, but blame the poor security instead.

"Well, none of this is very useful, apart from the food."

Vandal wasn't going to have many chances to spend cash. He already tried to make clothing for himself, and the results were the semi-rags he was wearing, so he couldn't make the best use of the treasure. Not yet.

Skeleton Soldier could use the weapons and armor, though, and he could split up some of the leather pieces to protect the bones of Bone Monkey and Bone Bear.

That said, even if he had bags of treasure, moving it all around became the problem. He had given all the horses to Rudi, so all he had left was the carriage. He wanted to have Bone Bear and the others pull it, but the wagon needed some modification.

For that, Vandal had an idea.

"Who gets to do it?" Vandal looked around at the spirits nearby.

There were a lot of recently dead bandits, but also a thin middle-aged man who surprisingly kept his form after death.

Please, allow me, Sam, to take on this task! I tended the horses and drove the coach for a noble during my life! I can handle any wagon better than anyone else!

It was a stroke of luck for Vandal that the spirit of this Sam fellow, apparently well-versed with horses in life, hadn't crossed over yet. The fact that he was retaining this form without any supply of magical power meant he had incredible mental strength. Sam's spirit might turn out to be the best thing he got out of this.

Master Vandal, you have avenged myself and my daughters! Taken vengeance for the terrible things they wrought upon my family! To repay you, my daughters and I will serve you for the rest of your life!

Vandal assumed that the two spirits bowing their heads behind him were his daughters. They were both burnt black, their bodies on the verge of falling apart, so he could tell little about them other than they had been female.

Maybe the bandits went a little too far, let things get out of hand, and ruined the "products." Unless these bandits didn't have connections with slavers? Something nasty had got the family killed, in any case.

He looked at the bandit spirits and they trembled. Looked like he was on the right track.

"You've got the job, Sam."

Deciding to consume the spirits of the bandits, he brought Sam's spirit into the horseless carriage.

"Rise."

Vandal poured in his magical power and gave the order, and the wagon gave a squealing sound.

"Forward."

On command, the wheels started to slowly turn, even though a seemingly key element—the horse—was still missing.

Vandal gave a satisfied nod. "That worked. Sam is now a Cursed Carriage. Now I've got a way to move around. Let's head back to the forest and run over some goblins on the way to level up."

Two days later, a local guard raided the bandit hideout on information from Rudi. They found the graves of the buried bandit bodies, and the beasts and goblins who dug them up to eat them.

Wagon tracks did lead away, but the soldiers assumed that they belonged to the faction that won this deadly squabble and didn't launch any particular investigation. The captain was a little surprised at the lack of hoof prints leading the carriage, but saw no reason to include that detail in his report.

✿

Baronet Bestello had been in a great mood for the better part of a year.

Everything had gone great since he captured that witch and burned her. Sure, the high priest and his goons took over the forest for two months, and three good trappers went missing, but those were minor details. They hadn't found a body, but the dhampir was considered dead, and the baronet received a medal from the King of the Milg Shield Kingdom. The lords of surrounding domains had also taken notice, starting to chip away at his reputation as ruling over nothing but vineyards.

The grapes for the wine this year had also been of remarkable quality and his bandit crisis, which had caused so much trouble over the last couple of years, had also somehow been resolved. Neither the local security, his own knights, nor even a band of adventurers defeated them, which he wasn't especially pleased about, but those bandits had been a real issue. Even if they just gone and wiped each other out, that was plenty reason to celebrate.

Best of all, he received a court rank increase.

It wasn't official yet, but he had quietly received word that he would receive an invitation to the capital of the Amidd Empire before long. The first Baronet Bestello, his great-grandfather, always longed for the title of "baron." Now it was finally happening. With that under his belt, he wouldn't have cared if his glass held vinegar rather than wine—he would have still knocked it back.

One hot summer night, a shadow skulked outside the walls of Evbejia.

"Get in, get in."

Vandal had brought countless spirits along with him and placed them one by one inside the walls.

Even if anyone did see him, they wouldn't understand what he was doing. Only someone with death attribute magic affinity—maybe a medium—could see the spirits of people who hadn't been turned into undead monsters.

If sentries spotted him, they might have fired off an arrow, but their job was to stop monsters and bandits trying to get over the walls, not venture beyond the walls at night and actively hunt anything down. They focused on the gates. The chances of them noticing a baby moving around in the complete darkness along the barren walls were very slim.

An adventurer or storied knight with a skill to detect magical power might have noticed him. But what Vandal didn't know yet was that his death attribute magic MP was actually quite difficult for others to detect. He could use magic in front of people with the Detect Magical Power skill at level 1 or 2 and they still wouldn't notice. At level 3 or higher, they could spot him with a little concentration, but Evbejia didn't have demon barrens with powerful monsters nearby, and no dungeons to speak of. The strongest adventurers here were grade D, at best, and so no one had Detect Magical Power of level 3 or higher.

After walking halfway around the walls, Vandal let out a sigh.

"That's everything. It took two days, but I'm ready. One word and my revenge will be complete. But it can wait for tomorrow morning."

The following day, illuminated by the sunbeams of a morning just like the day before it, none of the people of Evbejia had the faintest inkling of what was about to happen.

They didn't know that the name of this town was about to ring out across not only the Milg Shield Kingdom, but all of the Amidd Empire. All because of the bizarre fate that was about to befall it.

"Collapse."

The five-meter-high wall that had stalwartly protected the town from monsters like goblins, dangerous animals, and bandits rumbled. The guards looked at each other in puzzlement—and suddenly the walls simply collapsed in a deep bellowing rumble.

That wasn't all. The rubble began to form into massive human shapes, one after the other, roaring with the voices of evil spirits to the uncaring sky.

Then the fragments of wall started to walk away.

"What's going on? What's happening?"

"Captain! The walls, the walls have turned into golems!"

"I have eyes. I can see that much!"

Even as the captain frothed at the mouth, part of the gate they had been defending also turned into a golem and walked away.

"Don't just stand there, stop the golems!"

"But Captain, they aren't attacking, just walking away. If they were coming toward us, then that would be one thing, but should we really go out and try to...?"

The captain's men weren't keen to obey. Few people would happily go and put themselves in front of a five-meter-tall stone giant. The iron spears held by the guards weren't going to be much use anyway. The men were likely questioning the sanity of their captain.

"You fools! Our walls are walking away! How are you planning on defending the town tonight without walls?!"

The captain saw the bigger crisis ahead. The boars, wolves, and bears that roamed the night would be free to come and attack produce, livestock, and even people without the walls. Goblins and bandits wouldn't be far behind. The town might have enough guards to protect the gates, but not enough to patrol the entire parameter.

Recognizing this problem, of course, was not the same as being able to do anything about it.

"B-but Captain..."

The men realized the issue better now, but they hadn't become better fighters in the last few minutes, either. All they could do was watch their new stone golem walls plod away from town.

The walls suddenly turned into golems and walked away. Everyone in Evbejia noticed this crazy occurrence, of course, but it was so sudden that nobody could do anything about it.

Baronet Bestello was stunned. The knights and soldiers panicked. The staff at the adventurers' guild rushed to get emergency jobs posted. The townsfolk were simply aghast.

But the walls were only the beginning.

"The earth! The earth is turning into golems!"

"Those are my fields! My grape vines!"

"Wait, my wheat field! Wait!"

The earth of the fields rose up, burgeoning produce still attached, and started off after the walls that had already left town.

The farmers ran desperately after their crops. The farmers were brave, trying to stop golems so much larger than themselves, even if they were made of soil. The very fact they were farmers explained why they couldn't allow those golems to just walk away. More so than the crops and trees clinging to the golems' backs, the very soil that comprised the creatures' bodies was their livelihood. Farmers needed soil. Growing crops required soil, and they had taken years of hard work, fertilizing, and hoeing to make this soil the best. If they lost it now, they would have to start that laborious process again, right from the beginning. On Earth and Origin, fertilizer was easy to obtain, but on Ramda, it took time and effort.

The vineyards were also losing their vines. Replacing those would be even more difficult, making the issue doubly damning for them.

And it wasn't only the fields.

"The lord's manor!" someone cried. "It's turning into golems from the top down!"

"The adventurers' guild too! I've got friends in there!"

The lord's manor and the adventurers' guild building both also turned into golems, one after the other, and started walking out of town.

The golems were slow, but also big, giving them long strides. The people of the town, the knights, the adventurers, rushed after the golems to try to reclaim the rubble.

Vandal cheerfully watched them all scrabbling around.

The walls, the fields, the adventurers' guild building, and the lord's manor. It hadn't been easy to place so many spirits inside so many locations and then have them wait. The walls alone took two days, while the other locations took a day each.

Kicking the whole thing off, however, only required a single word. It was like watching a complex domino setup starting to fall. Revenge really was sweet.

"Look, Mom," Vandal said. "All the scum who denigrated you have such pathetic looks on their faces."

The moment their walls and buildings turned into golems, Evbejia died. Even if they defeated the golems and took back the materials, everything needed to be repaired. Out of the wreckage, the soil was probably the only thing that could still easily be used.

Evbejia needed to repair those tall, thick walls. Without those, they would be unable to function as a town in Ramda, with all its dangerous monsters. Of course, they also needed guards while they performed the repairs. Reinforcements, payments to adventurers, orders for materials and the arrangements for stone masons and laborers—it was all going to take a massive amount of time and cost a massive amount of money. More money than Baronet Bestello could surely afford, even if he left his manor for later. He could go squealing to the Milg Shield Kingdom government, but that would spell the end of his promotion.

Vandal's reach even extended to the wine cellars. He had used the spell Befoul on the wine in the casks, ruining it all. Just to make sure, he also used Death to Bacteria to kill all the yeast at work inside the wine. No one had noticed yet, but the primary industry of Evbejia was already dead. Saying that it would take a decade for them to recover from this was no exaggeration.

Thank you, Vandal. It can't have been easy, setting up this gentle revenge all for me.

Dalshia's spirit looked down lovingly at her small, MP-infused child. Quite a few people in the near vicinity might take exception to her use of the word "gentle" there, but with the sheer volume of magical power at Vandal's command—and the magic he could perform with it—perhaps it wasn't so out of place.

He could have made the wall golems walk into town rather than away, killing countless villagers. Add in the golems from the lord's manor and the adventurers' guild, and he would have leveled the entire town. High Priest Goldan and the Five Hue Blades had long left this town behind, after all.

He could have used the spell "Virulent Poison" on the well, or simply used "Sickness" to spread a plague. If he wanted to, he could have wiped out the entire population of Evbejia. Doing none of that, and even waiting until morning to bring down the walls—that was why Dalshia called him "gentle."

"I'm only doing the same thing to them that they did to me," Vandal replied, without agreeing with or denying Dalshia's position.

He didn't consider this mercy for the townspeople. To Vandal, every single one of them had sinned. All of them had stood by and watched as Dalshia was killed.

So he simply returned the favor.

"However many years, however many decades it takes, I

will get you back, Mom," he swore. "I'm going to make a new body that will suit your spirit. And if the people here work hard for years, for decades to come, they might be able to get their old lives back too."

His actions didn't kill anyone, not directly. He had been careful with the order the golems were going to move in, to make sure no one would get crushed. Nothing had been destroyed that couldn't be replaced.

Yes. You've given them a chance. You are such a gentle boy, Vandal.

One could also argue that he cursed them with decades of labor just to get back to where they were yesterday, but why bandy semantics around? Dalshia was already under the effects of the Death Attribute Allure skills, so certainly not her.

Vandal's hand passed through Dalshia's as he tried to touch her again. He narrowed his gaze.

"Let's move. Bone Bird, that's your cue."

With a cry like someone getting strangled, the ranked-up Phantom Bird spread its wings. Vandal put the bone fragment containing his mother back inside his clothing and held onto Bone Bird with both legs. Its pale blue spirit wings flapped, and then it flew Vandal back to where the other skeletons waited with the Cursed Carriage.

Name: Vandal
Race: Dhampir (Dark Elf)
Age: 1 year old
Alias: None
Job: None
Level: 100
Job History: None
—Status
Vitality: 34
Magical Power: 100001247
Strength: 32
Agility: 7
Stamina: 33
Intellect: 45
—Passive Skills
[Brute Strength: Level 1] [Rapid Healing: Level 2] [Death Attribute Magic: Level 3]

[Resist Maladies: Level 3] [Resist Magic: Level 1] [Night Vision]

[Spiritual Pollution: Level 10] [Death Attribute Allure: Level 2] [Skip Incantation: Level 1]
—Active Skills
[Suck Blood: Level 3] [Limit Break: Level 2]

[Golem Creation: Level 3 (UP!)]

—Curses

[Unable to carry over experience from previous lives]

[Unable to enter existing jobs]

[Unable to personally acquire experience]

Name: Bone Bird

Rank: 3

Race: Phantom Bird

Level: 17

—Passive Skills

[Night Vision] [Spirit Body: Level 1 (NEW!)] [Brute Strength: Level 1 (NEW!)]

—Active Skills

[Sneaking Steps: Level 1 (NEW!)] [High-Speed Flight: Level 1 (NEW!)]

The Death Mage

CHAPTER THREE

LEVELING

The mysterious "walls turning into golems" incident sent Evbejia into a panic of massive public works. The adventurers' guild gathered grade E adventurers to patrol and protect the town and the Shield Kingdom government drummed up skilled magicians and adventurers to investigate the problem. Meanwhile, the perpetrator himself was enjoying a trip by carriage.

Vandal had cushioned the wagon bed with animal fur and listened to the calling of fall insects as he rumbled along.

"This is my first big trip," he pondered. He had been blown up on the ferry during his school trip, so that one didn't count. He also remembered the whole thing not being that much fun even before that happened. That wasn't a trip.

"A trip is about different places, new experiences, unique scenery, delicious food, and chatting with family and friends... no, that's something else. A full-blown holiday."

What's the difference between a trip and a holiday?

"A holiday is for pleasure. A trip is just to get somewhere. Maybe?" He couldn't be sure what dictionaries on Earth would say.

I see. You know more than I do about some things, Vandal. Dalshia gave a happy laugh.

Overhearing this, it might sound like nothing more than a mother and child enjoying some time together. But the mother was the spirit of a dark elf, with the scars of terrible torture still marking her faintly glowing spirit body, and the child was a 1-year-old dhampir, one crimson eye and one purple glowing in the carriage, and yet as hard to detect as a ghost.

The carriage they were riding was a rank 2 undead monster, a Cursed Carriage, the wheels turning even without a horse to pull it. High above, a rank 3 Phantom Bird circled, its glimmering white body of bones watching for trouble on the road. Meanwhile, the carriage was flanked on all four sides by the rank 3 Skeleton Soldier, and the bear, monkey, and wolf Bone Beasts.

The sight of this unnerving caravan moving through the dead of night looked like some kind of small-scale zombie parade. Any nearby adventures would have either attacked or run for the hills.

"I'm going to sleep. Find somewhere to hide when the sky starts to brighten."

Vandal understood the risks, which was why they were moving at night. He was aiming for the Olbaum Electorate Kingdom, a nation that had been at war with the Amidd Empire for hundreds of years. At first, he planned to go to the dark elf village where his mother had grown up, in accordance with Dalshia's original plan, but his mother had stopped that herself.

It might be better if you didn't go to my homeland, she told him. *Now I'm dead there's no proof you are my baby, and I'm not sure people would believe me like this.*

Vandal's skin was as pale as a corpse. He had pointed ears, but the color of his skin meant it didn't look like he had a dark elf parent. Dalshia told him that elves and dark elves didn't get on well in Ramda. Some of the elves were friendly toward dark elves, but only a small number. Most of them saw dark elves as corrupted creatures created by Vida. The feelings of the dark elves toward those who hated them went without saying.

If Dalshia had still been alive, the dark elves would have believed her, but she was dead. She still existed as a spirit, but apart from Vandal, only a small number of jobs could see her, such as Mediums.

I also don't know if they would forgive me for your father. He was the subordinate species of a vampire who worships evil gods.

The dark elves were a race created by the goddess Vida, and so many of them worshipped Vida and various spirits, engaging in exchange with the other races Vida created. That meant they were friendly toward vampires and dhampirs—so long as they didn't worship Alda or the evil gods.

There were also new races, like lamia and scylla, that had been created with monsters as one parent, but jobs like Tamer allowed for coexistence with monsters, and so they weren't seen as such a problem. However, the evil gods and demon gods, the brethren of the demon king, were still very much ongoing enemies. Those who worshipped them, even members of races created by Vida, were traitors.

"This is such a hard world, Mom."

I know. That's why you should head for the Olbaum Electorate Kingdom.

The Olbaum Electorate Kingdom was one of the two nations, along with the Amidd Empire, that divided the Vangaia Continent. The Vangaia Continent was shaped in what was called "Zantark's War Hammer"—basically a T shape. The haft section was said to be where the hero Zakkato met his second demise, mainly high mountains and demon barrens, an inhospitable place that even adventurers stayed away from. The hammer section was divided into the Amidd Empire in the west and the Olbaum Electorate Kingdom in the east, with the two fighting over control of the continent for hundreds of years.

The Olbaum Electorate Kingdom had its origins in an alliance of smaller eastern nations, formed around 500 years ago as the Amidd Empire began to emerge. As it was formed from multiple different nations, it adopted a system of electing the king, with the ruler decided by vote from the noble dukes of each participating nation. An elected king served for ten years and could be reelected only once. In most cases they were reelected, meaning each king generally ruled for twenty years.

The personality and initiatives of the elected king did change national policy, of course, but the Amidd Empire was still their enemy, meaning Amidd's religion—the God of Law and Life Alda—should be considerably weaker there.

Some dukes are beast men and giantlings, so even as a dhampir I'm sure you will be fine, Vandal, said Dalshia. She had never been to the Olbaum Electorate Kingdom herself, so she couldn't be sure, but if there were beast men and giantlings among the dukes—the candidates to be king—it meant they clearly treated races differently from the Amidd Empire.

Thus, they were heading for the Olbaum Electorate Kingdom. But they also couldn't take the fastest, most direct course. It was another case of poor timing. They obtained information that a fresh war between the Amidd Empire and Olbaum Electorate Kingdom was soon to kick off.

This was a secret, of course—a big special national secret, the spirit of a dead Amidd Empire agent had informed them a few months after his death.

Vandal hadn't been sure if he could be trusted, but if he ignored the news, reached the border, and got caught up in open warfare, he would be finished. The security would be impossibly tight and sneaking out of one country didn't necessarily mean he would be able to sneak into the other. Everyone would be on the lookout for enemy spies, and it would be hard to prove he wasn't one. From a soldier's perspective, they looked like a minor troupe of undead, and without anything like an obvious Monster Tamer along, "Let's see what they have to say" was a far less likely outcome than "Let's kill first and ask questions later."

"If I get lucky they might take me in, thinking I'm just a baby, but I've put a lot of time into these skeletons. I don't want them to just get smashed. I don't know what they might do if they found Mom too."

Vandal was still a 1-year-old baby, so unless they wiped out the entire wagon from a distance with attack magic, soldiers were more likely to treat him as someone to be protected rather than attacked. But that thinking certainly wouldn't extend to the undead. There wouldn't be any Medium soldiers, so they wouldn't find Dalshia herself, but if they took her bone from him and buried it, this time she really might cross over.

For that reason, instead of heading to the northeast of Milg, which was closest to Olbaum, they went to the southeast, in proximity to the southern mountains and demon barrens of the war hammer's haft.

"It won't be easy to cross the mountains and the demon barrens, but easier than trying to sneak past a load of warmongering humans." The scariest thing is a living human, as they often said on Earth. He felt the truth of that right now.

Vandal hadn't raised any golem or zombie monsters yet because he knew he needed to make this journey. Golems were slow, and if he made them big enough to provide cover they would even stand out at night. Zombies had the same problem—speed. Some films on Earth had started to show turbo zombies with crazy dashing abilities, but Vandal couldn't hope for such fiction from reality. This world was fantasy, but it was also realistic.

Another issue was that the only choices for zombies were the bandits or the trappers, and to be honest, he didn't want to see their faces around all the time. So his party was all bones.

Vandal's trip continued smoothly, apart from the fact they could only move at night.

During the daytime, they moved off the road and concealed themselves in the forest. They started moving once it was dark again. If there were merchants or adventurers moving at night, or if there were road patrol waystations or forts, then Vandal headed off the road. However smooth it went, they were traveling at less than half of their maximum speed, but it was the best they could do.

"I need to be able to use the roads like a normal person as soon as possible." Vandal hadn't done anything wrong (apart from taking a little revenge). What an unfair world this was.

Heading off-road carried concerns about attacks from beasts, monsters, and bandits, but that didn't happen often. When potential attackers saw the skeletons protecting the wagon, they tended to stay away. Wild animals like wolves and bears instinctually feared monsters, unless they were clearly far weaker. Bandits were the same way. Their targets were merchants and travelers, not monsters.

Of course, defeating monsters yielded materials and even magic stones. But those with the skills to defeat monsters made their money by becoming adventurers, not bandits. When it came to monsters, not many chose to attack their undead brethren unless given no choice. Monsters would mainly attack other monsters to eat them, and there was no meat on a skeleton. Other reasons included turf wars and self-defense, but so long as Vandal and his troupe didn't push too far into their lands, the other monsters would observe, but not attack.

Sometimes, of course, weak monsters would still give it a try.

"Gyaaaaarrrgh!"

Bone Wolf tossed a near-dead goblin, gurgling in pain, out in front of the wagon. With a cracking sound, the relentless carriage wheels rolled right over it.

"Goblins aren't really providing any levels anymore," Vandal observed, but then quickly forgot about the goblin. Goblin right ears were their bounty parts, but he didn't bother collecting those, or looking for magic stones. Dalshia had told him that rank 1 monsters were a hundred-to-one shot for finding magic stones, meaning higher-grade adventurers would often just leave goblins untouched even if they defeated them. It wasn't worth wasting time if they weren't going to be worth anything.

At that moment, Vandal was more concerned about leveling up his undead.

At rank 1, they got levels just by mobbing a goblin together, but now they couldn't get a single level even if they killed multiple goblins one-on-one. The rank 2 carriage still leveled up by crushing enough of them, but the rank 3 skeletons got nothing at all.

"I guess it has to be bandits. I'd like the carriage to be rank 3 before we have to cross the mountains."

Vandal, rank 3 is pretty strong for normal people, Dalshia said. *Even at rank 2 it takes multiple normal people to defeat just one of them.*

Rank 3 monsters were powerful enough to overwhelm a group of ordinary people. Certainly more than the guards in Evbejia could handle, who might be good at beating up peasants but not much else.

"But Mom, there won't be any 'normal people' in the places we are going," Vandal said. "I can't become stronger myself at the moment, so I need my minions to be as strong as possible."

I see your point. But you can make golems too, if you need to. You'll be fine.

His mom was still an easy-going optimist, it turned out, even after she was dead.

※

The descendants of the hero Bellwood, who appeared in this world long ago at the behest of the gods, formed the Amidd Empire.

When the demon king's monsters threatened the world, the hero Bellwood rose to the front lines, bravely leading the fight. Ten days after arriving in Ramda, he defeated a dragon and rescued a princess, who became his first wife. Within a month, he defeated a force of giants with the warrior maiden who would become his second wife, and within six months he had fought and defeated the demon king's Dark Knights while protecting the high priest who would become his third wife. Ultimately, after ten years, he mourned the fall of the hero Zakkato while helping defeat the demon king and bring peace to the world, and then worked alongside the other remaining heroes to aid the people with his knowledge.

Much of the knowledge of the heroes had been lost in the time since, but some of it remained: the language, spoken and written, and Amidd, the village that eventually became the Amidd Empire. The empire, which appeared tens of thousands of years later, was headed by the first Emperor Balshumit, a direct descendant of Bellwood.

"It all sounds so fake. It makes me sick."

Vandal closed the book he had found among the bandit plunder and tossed it aside. There was no printing technology in Ramda, meaning every book was hand-copied. That made them expensive, luxury items. But the story of the illustrious deeds of the founders of the Amidd Empire, the hero Bellwood and the first Emperor Balshumit, wasn't worth a single copper coin for Vandal.

To start, there couldn't possibly be proof that the first emperor of the Amidd Empire was a direct descendent of the hero. The span of time involved was tens of thousands of years. The book called it fate, a prophetic dream, or a visit from the phantom of the hero himself, but that was all just theatrics.

Next, it made him so jealous that he felt sick. The hero Bellwood—his name had probably been "Suzuki" in Japanese, which would literally be "bell" and "wood"—arrived in Ramda and immediately got some crazy cheat powers. He defeated a dragon in just ten days and became a dragon-slaying hero while also saving a princess. After one month, six months, he continued to prove himself in battle, becoming a mighty hero in the span of ten years.

Vandal couldn't help but compare himself to that.

He had been alive for one year and three months. The only woman he had ever talked to was his mother. He couldn't hope to become a hero, even in ten long years. He was sure Suzuki had struggled and suffered, in his own way, and he had survived a fight for his life. But the difference between receiving blessings from the gods and receiving curses felt so painfully large.

"This is all Rodocolte's fault."

That's true. The god Rodocolte. But I'm a little grateful to him too. He's the one who make you my baby, Vandal.

"Mom…"

Her words soothed his bristling heart. He had to admit, making Dalshia his mother was maybe the one thing he could thank Rodocolte for.

However, without Rodocolte's curses, Vandal would have been able to use death attribute magic just like he had before dying on Origin. He would have been able to control countless golems, countless spirits, turning whole lakes into poison and poison into pure water whenever he pleased. With these powers, Dalshia wouldn't have needed to die. That thought made his gratitude evaporate.

As he pondered these thoughts, the wagon suddenly stopped its stealthy progress.

"What now?"

His Detect Danger: Death magic told him that this wasn't an emergency situation, such as being surrounded by enemies or faced with powerful monsters. This magic could detect not only things like poisonous mushrooms and plants, but also the intent to kill radiating from monsters and humans.

So he knew this wasn't a dangerous situation, but…Vandal poked his head out from the wagon and saw a gate leading underground.

"A gate? A hideout used by more bandits? But it looks pretty well made. Some kind of ruins?" Vandal tilted his head.

The Cursed Carriage Sam told him what this was.

Master, I believe this is a dungeon.

"A dungeon?"

Yes. A dungeon.

Vandal couldn't see Sam because his spirit was possessing the carriage, but Vandal could hear his voice clearly.

A dungeon. They started out as special breeding facilities under the demon king, intended to increase the numbers of monsters and enhance their strength as quickly as possible. The secret arts of Rekrent, demon god of time and magic, later turned them into places for humans to train and acquire resources.

Places corrupted by magical power for a certain length of time have some probability of spawning a dungeon. The format, scale, and dangers they presented differed vastly depending on the dungeon in question, with no apparent rhyme or reason discovered even after tens of thousands of years since the first dungeon appeared. Some dungeons looked like caves, with a single floor and nothing but weak goblins, and others were 1,000-floor fortresses filled with monsters even grade A adventurers couldn't handle. Regardless, land corrupted by magical power was a fundamental requirement for dungeons, so most of the dungeons were found in the demon barrens.

"Are we in the demon barrens right now?" Vandal asked.

I don't think so, Dalshia said. *We would be seeing a lot more monsters if that was the case. I think this is a rare case of a dungeon occurring outside the barrens.*

Very rarely, dungeons spawned in normal forests or plains. Those kinds of dungeons tended to not be very dangerous, but if left unchecked, the monsters could overflow from inside and turn the vicinity into a kind of pseudo demon barren. Ramda even had the Demon Barren Continent, where that process repeated so many times that the entire landmass and the seas around it all turned into demon barrens.

"So this one is probably full of weak monsters. The grass around the entrance looks undisturbed, so I don't think any adventurers have found it, either. Sounds like a fun detour."

A dungeon. It had an exciting fantasy ring to it, the sense of impending adventure. Vandal was getting excited. Of course, it would be his skeletons who actually explored and did the fighting. But he didn't have any choices there, still being a 1-year-old baby.

While Vandal prepared to enter his first-ever dungeon, in the town of Tellow the guild master of the adventurers' guild, a man called Degan, was in a tough position.

Three adventurers stared each other down. They were the leaders of three well-known parties based out of Tellow. They were all grade D. There was Kash, leader of Tradewind, Bahn, the leader of Ironwing, and Miranda, the leader of White Star.

They were unknown, when considered on the scale of the entire Milg Shield Kingdom, and unlikely to get out of grade D. But there were no demon barrens nearby and Tellow was just a small commercial town, so these adventurers were the top dogs around.

Indeed, they had dealt with bandits numerous times and saved the town during the surge of kobolts. When it came to Tellow, they were heroes.

They had been working together to defeat a rogue ogre, searching the nearby forest—and had found a dungeon on their way back. Only those present, the lord and his aides, knew what was going on, but as this was a major event and a big chance for the town to grow, Degan was in high spirits.

A dungeon was dangerous, of course. Leaving it untamed could lead to monsters pouring out, swarming the town. But if adventurers went in periodically and cleared the monsters inside, it was an immortal goose laying infinite golden eggs. An endless supply of monsters meant an endless supply of the materials collected from them, not to mention rare plants and ores only found in dungeons, and powerful magic items found from treasure chests. A dungeon would also bring in more adventurers to the town, their purchases bringing more commerce, growing their town.

That was why dungeons were such an incredible resource, offering far more return than risk so long as it could be cleared. Of course, Ramda had its fair share of trash dungeons, with nothing but pitiful goblins and pitiful treasures, like an annoying pebble in the shoe of nearby settlements.

So was this a good dungeon or a bad one? A hit or a miss? Above all else, Degan needed to dispatch adventurers to investigate. It was an unspoken rule that those who discovered a dungeon got the first shot. If someone other than an adventurer found it, or the adventurers who did weren't strong enough to handle it, the right for first crack could be sold through the guild to a different party. When multiple parties found one together, they could use some cash to negotiate for first dibs, or all just go in together.

"Tradewind will be the party to explore the dungeon!"

"You're crazy! Ironwing are the only ones who can handle this job!"

"Leave the real work to White Star, thank you! You go collect goblin ears!"

The problem today was that none of them seemed willing to back down, or tackle the challenge together.

"This is a problem," Degan said. "I know you're generally competitors...."

These three parties had been squabbling over the top spot in the town for a while. But they understood the creed of their profession and were willing to work together when the town was really in danger, such as from the kobolts.

There was no sign that monsters had come out of the dungeon yet, so exploring it wasn't a pressing concern. Not yet. Dungeons that appeared outside the demon barrens tended to be low-risk and small scale. Each of these parties could probably handle it alone. In fact, if the initial search went well, then they would receive the goodwill of the guild, and maybe even rank up to grade C. It was their chance to finally rise above the other two parties.

"Tradewind has party members who specialize in removing traps!" said Kash. "Your parties can barely stay concealed long enough to launch a surprise attack! You aren't suited to tackling a dungeon!"

"How dare you, Kash!" shouted Bahn. "You don't even have a healer in your party! Trying to clear a dungeon using potions alone is ridiculous! Ironwing has not one but two Healing

Mages to handle any wounds or poison in a flash!"

"You're both wrong!" Miranda argued. "Balance is what matters. White Star has one Attacker, one Guardian, a Bow Master, a Thief, a Healing Mage, and an Attack Mage! We're the perfectly balanced party. The dungeon should be ours!"

They looked ready to start fighting to decide things. Guild Master Degan frowned.

"Everyone, please. This is the third day of this!" For a moment, he wondered if it might be easier if they did just settle this with a scrap, and it took him a while to convince himself otherwise.

❋

My name is Sam. I formerly tended to the horses and was the coachman for a noble.

A servant of a noble doesn't live in the kind of luxury that peasants (although I am one of those too) like to believe. That said, looking shabby would reflect badly on my master, and so he provided me with a proper uniform and proper meals every day. On those counts, I was indeed fortunate.

I also met my wife through my work—she was a maid in the big house—and, with the blessing of the master, we married and had two daughters. The eldest, Saria, was kind and gentle, while our youngest, Rita, was bright and full of energy. My daughters also found work with the same family. Those were happy days.

One winter, however, my wife caught the pest, and passed away within a few days. While still reeling from that loss, our master fumbled his footing on the stairs and fell to his death, leading to a change of leadership. The new noble family had their own servants, and the existing staff were told we were all to be let go, myself and my daughters included.

All I had done for my entire life was tend to horses and drive carriages, and so I thought maybe I could drive a big carriage in the city, and decided to strike out with my family. My daughters could hopefully get married and find work there too.

But on the way, we were attacked by bandits. Those animals defiled my daughters in front of my eyes, then killed us all. They burnt our bodies so as not to attract animals or monsters, and discarded us. The experience was so brutal, so hard for my girls, that they still appear in their burnt forms even after death.

I cursed the bandits. I vowed to remain in this world, remain until I witnessed their destruction with my own eyes. If there had been any demon barrens in the vicinity, I may have even drawn on that magical power to become an evil spirit myself. But as a ghost, all I could do was resent them, and I spent my days doing little else.

Until one day, my current master—Master Vandal and his minions, shall we say—attacked the bandit's hideout and quite killed the lot of them.

That was when I entered his employ, so to speak. I never expected to have a second life after death like this, I can tell you.

Even more incredibly, this simple carriage driver now finds himself in the midst of a dungeon.

Master, I spoke, *I've heard that dungeons contain monsters far stronger than those outside. If you feel this is becoming too dangerous, please let me know at once.*

My new body is a carriage that the bandits stole. It's reasonably high, wide, and sturdy, and covered with a canopy. However, since I am possessing and moving it directly, I'm capable of making it move backwards if I so desire. That means we can run away quickly if necessary.

"Okay. One thing that's been on my mind—this "master" business. Can we do something about that?"

Master Vandal speaks up from the wagon bed. I'm really not sure what it is he means.

Would "young master" suit you better, Master? It's true that he's only 1 year and 3 months old, so that might be more fitting.

"That's not exactly what I was getting at…."

Vandal is embarrassed. There aren't many spirits that talk to him like you do, Sam. It was Dalshia, Master Vandal's dear mother.

I see. Ah, yes, I see now.

She has a point. None of the others currently under the command of Master Vandal are able to speak as I can. This isn't a question of emotions or manners. They just can't speak.

The skeletons aren't made from human spirits, but those of small animals. Even if they have some feeling they want to impart, they can't do it with words.

"Gyaaah!"

Although no one other than Master Vandal can see them, he has countless spirits along with him, like my daughters. They might reply to Master Vandal if he spoke to them, but they never offer anything for themselves. After becoming a spirit, it's easy to lose yourself in a single powerful emotion and end up simply repeating the same thing over and over again. My daughters are no exception.

"Gehhhheee!"

But I'm one of your servants, young master, I replied, *and my respect for you is only natural. Do you really want me to act like your Skeleton?*

The Skeleton looks like mobile human bones, but it's just the spirit of a small animal inside, meaning it often comes over to be petted.

"Gyagagagaaaah!"

That might not be a problem for the young master, who has always been able to see spirits, but it's a big problem for me.

Do you want me, a 40-year-old middle-aged man with thinning hair, coming over to get petted?

"Yeah, fair enough. 'Young master' is fine." He doesn't sound especially happy about it, but he accepts my proposal.

"Gugeeeeh!"

The gurgling screams accompanying our travels are being produced by the Goblin Soldiers I'm currently running over.

Goblin Soldiers are rank 2 monsters, a little smarter than normal goblins and with slightly better weapon handling. Rank 1 goblins often have nothing better than a pole or club—if a randomly selected tree branch could called that. Even if such a goblin was lucky enough to get their hands on a real sword or spear, they wouldn't be able to swing it around any better than a stick.

A Goblin Soldier knows how to use a sword like a sword, a spear like a spear, and a club like a club. They're only slightly more skilled than an amateur, and an experienced adventurer or soldier with some skills would have no problem taking them out one-on-one. However, they look almost identical to normal goblins, meaning Farmers and Hunters that drop their guard to chase them off will find a painful surprise.

However, these Goblin Soldiers are no match for the Skeleton Soldier, assorted Bone Beasts, and Phantom Bird that have all already hit rank 3. Each one that pops up quickly gets its head split by a sword, or split open by fangs, or thrashed with spirit body feathers, and defeated in short order. The skeletons then toss any that still show signs of life under my wheels. That allows me to earn experience.

"Gagiii, gigigigeeeh!"

The sound of organs being crushed, and the breaking of bones, my wheels pulverizing them. Wonderful, truly wonderful.

I hate to admit it, but I could get hooked on this.

"Please don't," Vandal says. "A carriage looking to cause accidents is the last thing I need. Although feel free to run over any bandits we see."

Thank you, Young Master.

Crushing bandits with my wheels! Just imagining it makes my spirit heart soar. Bone Monkey and Bone Bear guard the rear of the wagon, checking to see if the goblins drop any magic stones. From rank 2, the probability is supposedly one stone for every five killed.

Still, with Goblin Soldiers and Goblin Archers on the first floor, this seems like a pretty dangerous dungeon, I said. Goblin Archers are also rank 2, and only differ from the Goblin Soldiers in that they use bows rather than melee weapons.

"It doesn't seem that dangerous to me," Young Master replied.

That's because your skeletons have been making short order of them, Dalshia says. *This many monsters appearing in the moment you enter a dungeon is a rare occurrence. Or so I think—this is my first time actually coming into a dungeon myself.*

Dalshia was an adventurer when she was alive, but had mainly worked alone and so had never experienced a dungeon.

There might be this many monsters because adventurers haven't tackled this dungeon yet, she continues.

Is that a thing? I ask.

Sometimes. If there's a war, adventurers can get hired as mercenaries, or a big scale emergency might take them away from dungeons. Other times the rewards from a dungeon just aren't worth the trouble.

"Well, if the monsters are just goblins then it's probably not worth the effort. Humans don't do anything without some kind of reward."

You are so smart, Young Master. You don't sound like an infant at all. Please be careful around other people.

He's right, Dalshia agrees. *You use such big words too. You said you never even made it to adulthood in your other lives. Who taught you to talk like that? Ah, that's all I've got for today. You take care of him from here, Sam. Goodnight, Vandal.*

Very well, ma'am.

"Goodnight, Mom."

Dalshia returns to sleep in her bone, and we continue to explore the dungeon.

Everything goes very smoothly—almost too smoothly, with no particular peaks in the fighting. The first floor looks like ruins, with the floor and walls made of stone, and only Goblin Soldiers and Archers present. There are dozens of them, but the only damage we sustain is a few notches on the skeleton's sword. We also collect a total of six rank 2 magic stones.

On the second floor, it looks more like a natural cave. The ceiling was faintly glowing on the first floor, but here we plunge into complete darkness.

Normal adventurers would have to use torches, lanterns, or light magic, but all of us—including the young master—have the Night Vision skill. This allows us to proceed through the darkness as though it were daylight, much more convenient than the flickering fire of a torch.

The monsters down here start to include things like giant bats, giant moles, giant worms, and giant spiders, massive animals and insect monsters over a meter in size, while the goblins vanish completely. All apart from the giant spiders are rank 1, and the monsters are easy to defeat so long as we avoid the rank 2 spider webs, so we don't have any trouble here, either. Unfortunately, these monsters provide almost no materials of note, and none of them are particularly edible either. The only real reward is one magic stone from a giant spider.

The third floor is a marsh. Young Master looked dumbfounded, but that doesn't help with the scenery and the stench of mud and water. Looking up, there's even a light like the sun in the "sky" above.

In shock and wondering if we could still be underground, Dalshia wakes up to let us know that dungeons are like this. Very well. I can accept that without further comment, but the young master still seems to be having trouble with the concept.

The monsters on the third floor are all rank 1 bug and animal marsh types, including giant slugs, jumbo frogs, giant leeches, and giant lizards. I initially assume this will be as easy as the second floor.

However, as we proceed, rank 2 monsters start to appear. The Acid Slug, a big and nasty acid-spitting piece of work. Another is the Poison Frog, capable of spreading a neurotoxin using its tongue. Then there is the Dagger Finch, a bird that darts about quickly to peck with its pointy beak. Even at rank 1 or rank 2, all of these are far more dangerous monsters than the Goblin Soldiers. However, they still prove no match for the rank 3 undead. The main damage suffered here is when the skeleton mistakes an acid slug for a regular one and ruins his sword.

Damaging our weapons on the Acid Slug feels wasteful, so the young master uses a mud golem to bury it alive and then we continue before it can escape. I run over everything else. Poison doesn't work on the bone-only undead, and the dagger finch can peck as many holes in their bones as it likes—we have plenty of replacements.

Of course, the same goes for me and my carriage body. A few small holes won't hurt me.

"But I'll be the one sewing those up later," Vandal quips.

My apologies, Young Master.

Our reward is seven rank 2 magic stones, giant frog and poison frog hind legs and offal, and some dagger finch beaks. These beaks could be used to make knife or spear tips. The hind legs of the two types of frogs are delicious, and the offal is an ingredient for medicines. Bone Monkey and Skeleton carve up the monsters. Some of the offal and beaks get trashed in the process, but it goes pretty well overall.

Young Master, are you going to make some medicine?

"Nope. I don't know how. I guess I'll use Maintain Freshness magic and save them for later."

Death attribute magic allows the delicate organs to be preserved for a number of years. Very convenient.

"Today I'll eat some salted frog legs. Let's get a fire started."

Young Master, you aren't going to use Wisp Fire magic?

"Unfortunately, Wisp Fire doesn't produce heat. In fact, it burns colds, stealing heat away."

So death attribute magic isn't all-powerful, I thought, *although that does sound nice in summertime.*

Bone Monkey cooks the salted legs, and while he burned one of them, the young master enjoys the others.

"Better than rabbit blood," is his judgment. Unfortunately, that doesn't really help me to understand.

The fourth floor is another cave. All the monsters there are undead. Not rank 1 Living Dead or Living Bones, but powerful rank 3 Skeleton Soldiers, Zombie Warriors, and Bone Beasts, the same as our own, plus Wraiths immune to physical attacks.

Oh my, I exclaimed. *What a terrifying horde of monsters.*

"Sam, you're undead too," Vandal says.

Good point. I'm about to suggest we fall back one floor and rethink our strategy, but then something surprising happens. The skeletons and zombies open the way forward.

"We can pass?" Vandal ventures.

The skeletons with blue fire in their sockets and muddy-eyed zombies moan, as though in affirmation, and even drop their weapons on the spot. The metal sound of weapons hitting the floor rings out, and then the undead fall silent.

"Sam, everyone, forward."

Are you sure? It could be a trap.

"I sense no intent to kill us. It should be fine."

The young master trusts in his Detect Danger: Death magic and we proceed down the path opened by the undead. They don't make a single move against us. The only movements they show is to slowly pick up their weapons after we pass.

I think they all like you, Vandal.

I'm impressed, young master.

"I think it's the effect of the Death Attribute Allure skill. I just didn't expect it work on undead spawning in a dungeon like this."

The fourth floor appears to only have undead, who bear the young master no ill will at all, and so we proceed without further trouble. Of course, this also means we cannot acquire any magic stones, but it's a welcome development compared to the risks of fighting rank 3 monsters.

Vandal, there's a treasure chest here, says Dalshia. *I guess dungeons really do have treasure chests.*

Indeed, I agree. *I wonder who puts them here.*

Nobody knows, Dalshia responds. *Some say they are traps by the demon king to lure humans into these dangerous places, and others say the Demon God Rekrent makes them appear in order to inspire humans to greater feats and reward them for their deeds.* It seems that treasure chests can appear on certain floors inside dungeons. It is unknown who places the chests in such places, but the contents are always of value, fueling adventurers to come and try their hand.

Of course, the chests are often locked, and in some cases are equipped with traps too. It falls to Thieves to deal with these issues, but we don't have one of those along with us.

"Let's get it open and see. Rise!"

But the young master doesn't need a Thief. He possesses the entire chest with a spirit, turning it into an undead and allowing the chest to unlock and disarm itself. It takes 10,000 MP to open a single chest this way, making it fortunate that the young master has so much magical power at his command.

"And inside…what's this? It almost looks like poison."

The chest contains a blue liquid in an expensive-looking glass bottle. It's a potion, and quite an expensive one!

Young master, that's not poison. It's a potion!

"A potion? Like an item for healing?"

That's right, Dalshia says. *Potions are important items for adventurers. You can drink them or pour them on wounds to heal right away. This looks like a high-grade one too.*

That's correct, Lady Dalshia. I've never seen one as nice as this, even when I was working for my noble family.

Potions have a number of possible grades. Grade 5 potions are the general ones doing the rounds. Those heal about 30 vitality. A well-off merchant or solider would probably have one or two of those on hand, and they were necessities for adventurers or mercenaries. Grade 4 or higher immediately get more expensive, with mid-tier nobles managing a grade 3 at best. Of course, those have effects that match their prices.

You can tell the quality of a potion by the color, Dalshia says. *The lighter the blue, the better the quality, and the darker the blue the worse. This one looks like maybe a grade 2.*

A grade 2 would require a visit to a big city, like the imperial capital of the Amidd Empire, or a direct request to a skilled Alchemist. One bottle like this could cost 10,000 Amidd, I explain.

"Ten thousand? And what does it do?"

Not anything so much as growing back a severed limb, but pouring it on a wound will cure pretty much anything else, Dalshia says.

Drinking it will recover any extent of exhaustion, and recover some MP too, I add. *Likely healing any poison and sicknesses in the process.*

"And how does it taste?"

The higher the quality, the worse it tastes, Dalshia reveals.

Indeed. A legendary adventurer who drank a high-grade potion long ago is said to have passed out due to how bad it tasted. Upon waking up, he claimed he would rather have died.

In that respect, the young master's original estimation of it being poison was not incorrect.

"They say good medicine tastes bad, but isn't that going too far?"

I have no experience with drinking potions, and I can't drink potions now, so I'm in the clear. The young master doesn't seem to consider it much of a drink either.

We find many more treasure chests thereafter and obtain their contents. All of them seem to be pretty pricey items, but I was only a carriage driver, so I can't be sure.

"This is…a magic item? And this…probably a magic item. Ah, this one looks like just a gemstone…nope, hold on. A magic item?"

You don't seem very sure, Young Master.

"Please don't expect much in the way of appraisal from a baby."

But with your previous lives, you have close to forty years.

A few days earlier, the young master and Dalshia explained their general situation to me and my daughters. It was all very surprising. He has incredible magical power in his tiny body, even for a dhampir, and is able to use unknown magic without having anyone teach him. So hearing the further details made my spirit-head spin.

Of course, he laid out the risks we face in serving the young master for us, but Dalshia and I have no intent to leave the young master's side. He is the one who saved my life. He is my master. Whenever my master needs me, it is my duty to be here for him. Even if I did leave, I would just become a random undead monster.

"That's true, but on Earth we didn't have magic," Vandal says. "There was magic on Origin but I didn't get to touch any magic items. Apart from the stuff they tested me with." So the young master hasn't had any opportunities to hone his appraisal skills or abilities to detect magical power.

We find a knife, a dagger, a broadsword, a silver accessory, and a ring set with gemstones, but are unable to appraise them other than to know they contain magical power, so we have no way of putting a price tag on them. Dalshia explains that junk treasure chests could contain normal knives or stone necklaces, so finding magic items was already pretty good. We proceed to the fifth floor and find this one to also be a nest of undead. The monsters groaned and wailed.

However, these are rank 4 undead, stronger than the rank 3 that appeared on the fourth floor.

A Red Skull Skeleton Warrior, red from all the blood it has been bathed in. An Orc Zombie, even stronger and more aggressive than it was in life. There is a magician zombie, a Lesser Lich, able to use magic even after becoming undead. And finally, Living Armor, possessed by the twisted grudge of the dead, able to move around without anyone even wearing it.

Ah. Thank you, excuse us.

Just as on the fourth floor, the rank 4 undead all move aside to the walls, opening the way for the young master.

"Wait, Skeleton, Bone Wolf," he calls. "I think there's a trap in the floor there."

The only impediments are the traps. But the young master's Detect Danger: Death allows him to detect and disarm them.

"I sense death from a wide section of the floor, so I think it might be a pit trap. I'll make a golem and place it over the floor and we should be fine."

The young master turns part of the wall into a golem, then places that over the floor to nullify the trap. He's the only one who could resolve this problem like this.

"Let's carry on."

We find even more chests on the fifth floor than on the fourth and obtain all sorts of treasures. After we open the largest door yet, we find a large room beyond it with a powerful monster waiting for us. It's a Skeleton General, his two-meter-tall frame covered with golden armor, carrying a massive axe that could probably chop a cow in half and a shield that looks almost like a ripped-off section of castle bulwark.

I feel a shudder down the spine I no longer have at the palpable strength of what should just be animated bones. Ten Living Armor surrounded the Skeleton General like knights protecting their commander.

This has to be the dungeon's boss. Dalshia is awake again and reveals that every dungeon always has a boss at the end. The boss on the lowest floor is always much stronger than any bosses that might appear along the way.

The boss grunts repeatedly.

"Why thank you very much," Vandal replies. "This is for me? That would be a big help, but are you sure?"

As it turns out, even boss monsters aren't immune to the effects of the young master's appeal. The boss not only moves aside, but also offers his impressive axe and shield to Vandal.

"I can't just take your weapon and shield away, though. Please take these." The young master takes a battle axe and large shield from the wagon and gives them to the Skeleton General. They're items taken from the bandits, so fairly good quality, but they also aren't magic items. Just lumps of metal. "But that still doesn't make us even."

With that, massive magical power swells up inside the young master. It takes all I've got to remain conscious in the face of this overwhelming strength. Bone Bird stops flapping and drops down to the ground.

Right in front of my eyes, the young master's magical power flows out into the battle axe, large shield, Skeleton General, and Living Armor. I can see the Skeleton General tremble with pure pleasure, groaning loudly as its white skill turns jet black. A swirling energy surrounds the Living Armor, something they didn't have moments ago.

Young master, they seem to have ranked up. What did you do?

"I just used Lethality Enhancement and Energy Steal, but with about 10,000 times the MP as normal. Who knows what happened? I guess they have good affinity with death attribute magic? They're undead, after all. I'll have to try it on my own skeletons."

Being able to rank up monsters by using 10,000 MP is good news for the young master and his 100 million MP.

"If I get some decent armor, I'll try making some Living Armor as well. The Skeleton can't equip metal armor."

With its bone body, the Skeleton can wear flexible leather armor but not metal armor. Metal is oversized without any flesh, getting in the way of its movements. That means keeping metal armor isn't worth it for us, apart from shields.

The Skeleton General dungeon boss standing nearby is wearing full plate armor made from metal, but that's probably because it's a high rank monster and has some kind of trick to make it work. But I'm more interested in the young master's plan to increase his cadre of undead.

Young Master, please try it on my daughters. If they receive bodies, hopefully they will become able to talk again. I don't want them to remain charred spirits forever. *Saria and Rita were simple maids, so they know nothing of handling weapons, but they can do chores and cook simple meals.* The young master thinks for a moment and then gives his approval.

"We'll have to wait until I find some armor that can work, though, so they might have to wait a little while. We can't just walk into town to buy some, and most bandits wear leather armor."

I understand. Thank you, young master. It might take months, or even years, but just the knowledge that the three of us might be able to talk again in the future gives me a burst of hope.

However, that hope becomes reality much sooner than expected. The door located behind the Skeleton General is a treasure room, and we find nearly the same volume of treasure again we've already collected in that one room—including the exact kind of "armor that could work."

Oh my, more magical items! I exclaim. Metal armor imbued with magical power. The designs are womanly too, with the rough edges smoothed into feminine curves and plenty of ornamentation. I can't say what kind of magic they contain, or what capabilities they hold, but they're beautiful pieces of armor. *Young master! Please allow my daughters to use this Living Armor.*

"Just to make sure, are you sure? This is the armor you want for them? Really?" The young master doesn't seem convinced.

When I tell him its fine, he looks at the armor and narrows his eyes.

"I know this is a fantasy world, but one-piece swimsuit and bikini armor seems like it's going too far."

One-piece swimsuit? Bikini? Is that what you call this armor on Earth?

"This isn't armor…it's more like a bathing suit on Earth. Well, whatever. It's worth worrying about, now I think about it." The young master proceeds to place Saria in the armor he calls the "one-piece" and Rita in the "bikini," and then supplies magical power to turn them into Living Armor.

The required magical power is ten times that of making a Stone Golem, but I couldn't be more grateful at my daughters receiving bodies again.

But at the back of the treasure trove, there are no more stairs leading farther down. The dungeon ends at the fifth floor.

That concludes our first dungeon excursion. The Skeleton General sees us off, and we head back the way we came. Crushing goblins on the way back allows me to achieve my original goal for coming in here—a rank up, allowing me to evolve to a rank 3 Ghost Carriage.

The hardest part of the entire expedition, to be honest, was going up and down the stairs. The young master turned the stairs into golems to create a slope for me, which still wasn't easy to navigate, even with Bone Bear and Bone Monkey pushing me. Now I have the Off-road Handling skill, which will allow me to handle more stairs with ease. But as is so often the case, you only learn skills after you most need them.

Name: Sam
Rank: 3
Race: Ghost Carriage
Level: 3
—Passive Skills
[Spirit Body: Level 1 (NEW!)] [Brute Strength: Level 1 (NEW!)]
[Off-road Handling: Level 1 (NEW!)] [Resist Impact: Level 1 (NEW!)]
[Precision Driving: Level 3]
—Active Skills
[Sneaking Steps: Level 1 (NEW!)] [Speed Driving: Level 1 (NEW!)]
[Charge: Level 1 (NEW!)]

The Death Mage

CHAPTER FOUR
GHOUL GROTTO

A week after Vandal left the dungeon, Kash, the leader of Tradewind, and his party approached, having finally won the rights from the Tellow adventurers' guild. They had fought tooth and nail for this opportunity, not for the fame or the chance to rank up, but because of the treasure the dungeon was likely to cough up.

The rank of the monsters and the quality and value of items obtained from a dungeon were generally fixed within a certain range. But that only applied to dungeons that had already been found and had adventurers going in and out on a regular basis. If a dungeon was left for a long time without anyone defeating the monsters, they would increase in number and fight among themselves, with the survivors leveling up as a result and even potentially ranking up. That increased the difficulty of completing the dungeon, but also increased the value of the items found inside. This went double for new dungeons. The first party inside faced high risks, but with potentially high returns. Kash and his allies prepared as best they could, and were ready to bring home the proverbial dungeon bacon.

However, the dungeon was proved anticlimactic. The first floor only had goblins, with a few Goblin Soldiers and Goblin Archers mixed in. The second floor was easy so long as they kept the lanterns lit and proceeded with caution, and the third floor was also easy so long as they were careful on the slippery floor.

"Almost all the monsters are rank 1. There are a few rank 2, but they're very small in number."

"This must be a low rank, grade F dungeon after all."

The adventurer's guild assigned grades to dungeons based on their difficulty, the idea being that adventurers of the same grade could form a party to tackle it. A grade F dungeon was the lowest ranking, used as training for newbie adventurers. For grade D adventurers like Kash, that meant such a dungeon was hardly worth the effort.

"Why aren't there stairs in here? Going up and down these slopes is the hardest thing in here."

"At least we're getting a little exercise."

The casual banter continued until the end of the third floor. Once they reached the fourth floor, they suddenly started to have to fight for their lives.

"Grrooooooar!"

"Diieieeeee!" came the terrible cries.

"Why are there suddenly rank 3 Zombie Soldiers and Wraiths?" Kash shouted.

"Kash! There are Skeleton Archers targeting us from the back!"

"Yelp! A stone golem too!"

Vandal and his own undead had wiped out the monsters up to the third floor, thinning out the rank 2 monsters. But starting on the fourth floor, they hadn't defeated a single enemy. In fact, the stone golem created by Vandal to avoid the pit trap had joined the enemy monsters. As Kash and the others didn't have the Death Attribute Allure skill, the undead were holding nothing back in their attacks.

Kash and Tradewind were aiming to rise to grade C, so they had fought rank 3 and even rank 4 monsters before. Once, they had combined all of their strength together and managed to take down a rank 5 monster. They were veterans who could defeat twice their numbers in rank 3 monsters if they had to. But they couldn't fight an endless stream of them.

"Blast! Fall back!"

Kash called for a tactical retreat before things got out of hand, and they returned to Tellow. They abandoned taking all the glory for themselves and teamed up with Ironwing and White Star before taking on the dungeon again. With fifteen veteran grade D adventurers, they passed the fourth floor with no problem, and also managed to get through the fifth, but then ran afoul of the boss monster, a rank 6 Black Skull General, and his ten rank 4 Cursed Armor minions.

In the end, they had to retreat again, and the adventurers' guild offered the "first run" at the dungeon to a party of grade C adventurers. But those grade C adventurers ended up disappointed.

"I was expected more from an unexplored dungeon!"

They defeated the Black Skull General, but there was no trove of treasure for them to find. From their perspective, the dungeon was just a waste of time.

The weapon and shield used by the Black Skull General possessed a tricky power, absorbing magical power during the fight. But when they defeated the boss, both items crumbled into dust.

Undead monsters were more likely to drop magic stones than other monsters, but most monsters over rank 4 dropped magic stones anyway.

The adventurers called the dungeon a lame duck and left it behind, never once imagining that an infant had beaten it before them. It was then designated a grade E dungeon and it was theorized that the powerful monsters from the fourth floor and lower appeared simply been because no adventurers had cleared it quickly enough.

From then on, new adventurers used it as a training ground.

✳

The armor was incredibly well made, with metal plates on top of monster skin, backed with soft monster fur to protect the wearer from chafing. The armor was also imbued with magical power, providing all sorts of resistances. So while it looked like skimpy beach wear, it actually offered better defense than low-grade full-plate armor.

The blue one-piece was cut in a bold V-shape, exposing not only the thighs but the vulnerable belly area. The top only covered about two thirds of the chest area, leaving the wearer naked on the back down to just above the butt.

The red bikini armor was no slacker in the skimpiness department either. It also covered only two thirds of the chest, and the bottoms had a thong, perhaps taking into account use by a race with a tail. But they also had solid shoulder armor, gauntlets, and greaves. This unbalanced appearance made them appear to trap the wearer inside a frame of sexy metal. A really stimulating sight—if the wearer had been a flesh and blood woman.

"I guess there was nothing to worry about after all," Vandal said, looking at the one-piece and bikini armor with a nod. Yes—just the armor.

To be specific, the spirt of Sam's eldest daughter Saria now inhabited the one-piece, and his second daughter Rita inhabited the bikini. According to Sam, both of them took after their mother, and had been very sweet in life, as they hovered there in silence.

At this moment, they looked like nothing but armor, even to Vandal, with his death attribute magic affinity. Their spirit bodies had been burnt black, apparently, so maybe he was happier not being able to see them.

He had voiced his reservations to Sam when he possessed the armor with their spirits. But even with them inhabiting this insanely exhibitionist armor, there wasn't a pinky finger of female skin on display. There really had been nothing to worry about. You could stare at the chest all you liked and see nothing but armor. No cheesecake here.

"Well, it'll be nice to have some more rank 3 allies. Let's test this out."

With that, Vandal started to pour excess magical power into Saria and Rita. The girls absorbed tens of millions of death attribute magical power, black energy pouring into them.

Creak…creak…

Their new armor bodies quivered, but even after Vandal continuing to supply MP, nothing else happened. Checking their stats showed no changes, either, neither rank nor level. They were still just Living One-Piece Swimsuit Armor and Living Bikini Armor. They did seem to be enjoying it, but that was all.

"I guess this isn't working."

Vandal tried it on the other skeletons too, but nothing changed. Their bones might have taken on a fresh luster, and some of the cracks healed up. Maybe. But the Skeleton General and Living Armor they had encountered in the dungeon had visibly increased in strength, right in front of their eyes.

Maybe they don't meet the requirements to rank up yet, Dalshia mused.

"Requirements?"

Yes. I don't know everything about monsters ranking up, but I think they can have requirements other than just leveling up, the same as for human jobs. She explained that job changes could have a variety of other requirements in addition to reaching the level cap. For example, even if an adventurer in the Pupil job reached level 100, they needed to meet a certain standard of magical skills—such as at least one skill at level 2 or higher—in order to rank up. There were also requirements besides skill-related ones. A knight needed to actually be knighted to become a Knight, and a Demon Swordfighter needed to obtain a demon blade. So certain rituals, titles, and possessions could also serve as requirements. Others came down to conditions of birth. It was impossible to job change to a Beast Warrior if you hadn't been born a beastman. Dalshia was suggesting that monster rank-ups might have similar additional conditions.

"Which means those Skeleton General and Living Armor had already reached the level cap, but didn't meet the requirements to rank up. So when I gave them that magical power, they met the requirements and ranked up?"

That might be it.

"I see."

There was a logic to it. Rather than a goblin simply ranking up and turning into a Goblin Mage that could use magic, it made more sense for a goblin that could already use magic to hone those skills and rank up accordingly. That also meant simply pouring his MP into them wasn't going to rank up his undead, as he had hoped it would.

"Okay," Vandal said. "If we get some undead to level 100 and they still don't rank up, I'll try it again. Saria, Rita, thanks for your help with this little experiment. Now you can all do some weapon training together."

Saria and Rita had been maids, so they didn't know how to handle weapons. That meant a lot of training in their future. In order to pick up the skills they needed, they had to start from scratch.

In the first step toward that, he decided to let them choose weapons. He thought, as beginners, they would go for sword or spears, but…Saria chose a halberd, and Rita a glaive.

Both of these weapons came from the dungeon treasure. Vandal didn't know their exact effects, but they were reasonably powerful magic items—and also not suited to absolute beginners.

"Are you sure?" Vandal asked, to which both Saria and Rita waved their weapons around happily in response.

The benefits of being Living Armor were apparent. The two waved around weapons they couldn't have hoped to lift in life as if they were twigs.

"I'm happy if you are, but change to a sword or spear if it's too much for you. We have clubs if you just want something heavy."

The two of them then happily (if Vandal had to guess)

started to polish their skills with the other undead. The undead knew from experience that continuing to use a skill would level it up, which worked well alongside the fact that they didn't need to sleep or take a break for anything. That said, none of Vandal's troupe had any real idea how to use a halberd or glaive, so they were likely just going to be waving it up and down, thrusting like a spear, and swinging it from side to side for now.

It wasn't as effective as actual fighting. And while the undead were happy to fight off goblins and bandits as they continued their journey, Vandal most certainly was not. He was very conflicted about the positive contribution he had already made to the security of the Milg Shield Kingdom.

"I'm going to use the walnuts we found yesterday," he said.

The sun was still high and Vandal wasn't sleepy yet. He could take a nap later. Lounging around on his own didn't calm his nerves, so he started to make some walnut sauce with the walnuts he had found yesterday. They still had plenty of supplies, but he was getting bored of everything being salted.

First, he took the pot of walnuts. They weren't quite ripe yet and still had flesh on the outside, so they were inedible for now. He spread them out on the ground.

"About one month should do it. Decay."

He used the death attribute magic Decay to accelerate their natural process by about one month. The green walnuts turned all black and mushy.

Next, he used some spring water drawn up by a golem to wash the rotted flesh away, revealing the seed that had the walnut inside. He didn't just smash them open, however, because that would lodge pieces of shell in the walnuts, reducing the eventual edible volume. He turned some firewood into a wood golem and had the sticks rub together to make a fire, and gently fired the walnuts using an earth golem. That made the shells split more easily.

Then, just let them cool and peel them with a knife. All of the instructions were coming from Dalshia. She was a forest-dwelling race, after all, and knew how to make the most of the blessings of the forest.

Vandal used Steal Heat to drain the heat from the walnuts and then split the shells with his nails. His mother told him to use a knife, but he had recently become able to extend his nails a short distance at will, and so he put that new ability to use now.

"Maybe I'll use this to fight in the future," he pondered. His father had apparently been an excellent fighter, skilled with the use of claws. Maybe that had been passed down to him.

That thought seemed to prompt Dalshia as she spoke up.

The future. What do you want to become, Vandal?

"In the future?" Vandal asked. "I'm going to make a name for myself as a high-grade adventurer and become a noble. Everyone will know my name."

The first part I can understand, for a child, but I'm not sure about the second part, Dalshia said.

"Fame, a secure place in society, is the thing I need the most," Vandal explained, his nails splitting the walnut shells as he spoke. "When Hiroto Amemiya and the others get resurrected here in the future, if I'm successful and well-known, then it won't matter what Rodocolte tells them, they won't be able to act against me."

Vandal recently realized something that he shared in common with Hiroto Amemiya and the others—they all had to live here until they died on Ramda. There was no going back to Earth. No matter what cheats they came preloaded with, Amemiya and the others wouldn't be able to make enemies of the entirety of Ramda. When they were born into this world, they would gain siblings and parents here. They would make friends as they grew up, and probably fall in love too.

Once Vandal had fame and renown, the others wouldn't be able to move against him so easily because of the heat it would bring on their other attachments in this world. Even better if Vandal became a noble.

"Mom, once I have power and fame, society itself will be my shield."

Hmmm, that's not quite what I was asking, Dalshia responded. *Once you deal with Amemiya and the others, what do you want to do then?*

"After that?"

Vandal understood what she was asking now. His dreams for the future—what job he wanted to become, what wishes he wanted fulfilled. On Earth, kids might say they wanted to be in the big leagues or star in movies. Innocent childhood dreams.

Unfortunately for her, Vandal was not some starry-eyed kid.

He felt like he remembered a time when he had wanted to be a pilot. But after he moved in with his uncle, he started wanting to get ripped. He had dreamed of arms like two big logs and six-pack abs—because he had believed that strength would allow him to escape from his uncle's control.

But that wasn't what Dalshia was asking either. He thought for a moment longer. On Origin he had only had one dream, and it had been a single word—freedom.

"I just want to be happy."

That was the simple answer that he came to, after all that thinking. He stared off into the distance as he placed the peeled walnuts onto a stone plate and crushed them. "I want to be happy, have a warm home life with lots of friends, and want for nothing."

It was a pretty vague and commonplace dream, but that was truly what Vandal wanted, the ideal he used to think about before dying on Earth.

That said, his idea of "wanting for nothing" wasn't about driving a Cadillac or Ferrari with a model in the passenger seat, or wearing luxury-brand clothing and an expensive watch, or building a mansion in the middle of the city.

Vandal had something of a complex about living in such luxury, buried so deep that he wasn't even aware of it himself. When he had been Hiroto Amamiya on Earth, his uncle had raised him strictly, ostensibly so he would be strong enough to strike out into the world alone. He wasn't spoiled in the slightest, and anything that might be considered spoiling him was completely prohibited. Removing Christmas and birthdays from his personal calendar was only the beginning.

Vandal's uncle on Earth had prohibited all luxury, in any form. Games and toys were a luxury, so he wasn't allowed to play with them even if he borrowed them from his friends. The latest trends were all luxuries. Maybe yo-yos were trending among other kids, or combat spinning tops, or just collecting funny-shaped erasers. All off the table. If he had any, his uncle made him throw them away.

Steak and cakes were also a luxury. Hamburgers were a luxury—too similar to steak. He wasn't allowed to eat them even if they were served at school. His uncle told him to spit them out. Even steak-flavored chips. Anything sweet, anything with no benefit, anything that sought to circumvent the system. No short-cuts.

Eating out was a luxury, meaning he could never eat fast food or a bowl of noodles. Travel was a luxury, so no school trips. He had to stay at home when the family took a trip and couldn't even ask for new clothes.

His uncle had banned all luxury to the point he sounded like he had some kind of luxury allergy. Even cup noodles or convenience store sweetbread was off the menu if it had "luxury" or "premium" in the name, or even the advertising. His uncle would slap him, yelling that he had no right to luxury without even having parents.

The worst time was when they watched a documentary on TV about poor children overseas. He suddenly got a thrashing, his uncle going off about how these poor children had nothing, while Vandal was living in the lap of luxury, even without any parents.

He had worn clothing passed down by his cousins. For every meal he could only eat white rice. This all made him quite the weirdo, so he hadn't been able to make friends. The teachers had been on edge around him. His life had been the pits.

Even worse, his uncle believed that punching was child abuse but slapping was discipline, and so he never apologized for or regretted what he did. Of course, his aunt and cousins didn't do anything to help. They were safe so long as his uncle was focused on Vandal.

If the family's poverty was the cause of all this, it might have made more sense. But they were well off. They had the assets left by Vandal's parents on Earth, their life insurance money, and damages from the parties responsible for the accident. Altogether, it should have been enough to send three children from cradle to college. And yet his uncle treated him like crap.

His uncle finally let him join the high school trip after he saved up the money working part time, but that had resulted in terrorists sinking the ferry and killing him. Wonderful. Especially when he had been set to inherit the remainder of his parent's assets when he finally left his uncle's house. In the end, they got all of it.

His second life on Origin, of course, had been that of a lab rat. He hadn't known freedom, let alone luxury, in that existence.

That was why finally, in his third life, Vandal wanted to live happily in the lap of luxury. He wanted to live in a society where he could spend his own money.

"I'll have to think about what exactly 'luxury' means once we reach the Olbaum Electorate Kingdom," he said.

Okay. If you become a high-grade adventurer, though, you'll be pretty well-off.

"Oh, and don't worry. I'm still going to kill High Priest Goldan and Heinz for you."

Yes, well, thank you. But no need to take any big risks.

"I won't," Vandal said. "I'm going to be become so strong I'll be able to squash them like bugs."

I'm not sure if that's reassuring. Please, no big risks.

Dalshia wasn't sure if she was really getting through to him, but she also knew that she couldn't change his mind if she tried, so she gave up.

If he did become a noble in the Olbaum Electorate

Kingdom, then there was good chance he could become adversaries with Goldan and Heinz anyway, as they were active in the enemy Amidd Empire. Dalshia believed that if Vandal thought they needed to be killed, then surely he was right.

Vandal added some herbs from the forest to the crushed walnuts. The mixture was complete. At this point, recipes usually called for fragrant oil, but they didn't have any of that, so Vandal moved on. His meal tonight was going to be delicious. That was enough for him.

"I wouldn't say no to some rice rather than bread," he complained. His uncle's luxury allergy had rarely applied to rice. He hadn't given it much thought when he lived on Earth, but now it had actually been more than twenty years since he last ate rice.

You want some rice? I've heard they grow it in the Olbaum Electorate Kingdom. "Amidd for bread, Olbaum for rice," so they say.

"Seriously?!"

Vandal was suddenly a lot more interested in the Olbaum Electorate Kingdom.

✳

October came, and Vandal turned 1 year and 4 months. Winter closed in on fall by the time they finally reached the eastern edge of the Milg Shield Kingdom.

Going any farther east would lead into demon barrens and nature. Vandal and his troupe had not only to cross that, but also the mountains beyond. Attempting to cross a mountain range in winter would be insane, so he planned to hide in the forests and raid bandits until spring. Just like they were currently doing, hiding in the forest close to the demon barrens, waiting for the sun to set.

Vandal let his thoughts wander. "You know, I've never been skiing. With my newfound physical abilities, I think I could get started right away."

Just based on his stats, Vandal's abilities had surpassed those of an average adult man, even including his agility. That said, an inexperienced infant probably shouldn't be taking to a natural ski slope.

Skiing? Is that something from Earth?

There was a faint white shape in the carriage seat, where Sam was seated—his spirit body since becoming a Ghost Carriage. He held the reins of their spirit body horse. He was difficult to see, like some bad photo of a ghost, but it was easier to talk to him now than when he had been invisible.

"Yeah, it's a sport. You slide down a slope of snow with skis—like planks on your feet. You don't do anything like that here?"

I've never heard of that. We do have sledding.

Talking with Sam and Dalshia, Vandal realized that there was pretty much nothing like Earth sports here on Ramda. To be more accurate, there were no sports enjoyed purely for fun or for competition. People competed with swords and bows, but those things were primarily used to hunt monsters or in wars with other people. The same went for athletics and horse riding.

The only exceptions were rich and bored nobles. They didn't have ball games, like baseball or soccer, nor leisure sports like surfing or skiing. The presence of monsters was one reason, strong and abundant exterior enemies that gave a lot less leeway for fun and games than on Earth. If people had the bodies and energy to be playing sports, they should probably be fighting monsters instead.

But even if not as a sport, Vandal figured that sledding would've evolved into skiing with 100,000 years of history. Maybe the reason why it hadn't happened had to do with the way Rodocolte treated this world as inferior in some way. Of course, Sam might also just not know about skiing himself, and in countries with more snow it could be a thing.

"Sam, let me explain skiing to you…"

Vandal started, but then stopped he heard a faint sound.

"Was that a woman screaming?"

It sounded like it to me.

The breeze then carried something else to Vandal: the tantalizing aroma of blood.

Based on the direction of the wind, there was a woman screaming as she bled. In other words, someone was being attacked.

What shall we do? Sam asked because the normal two choices of "go and help" or "avoid getting involved" didn't exactly apply to their little troupe of undead. After all, they were all monsters targeted for death in the Milg Shield Kingdom. Saving a poor woman in distress could then lead to that poor woman coming back with adventurers to hunt them down. Vandal could imagine that all too easily.

That all meant the most logical course, considering all the risks, was to ignore her and continue their own journey. That said, having learned more about Vandal, his personality, and his goals, Sam also knew Vandal was unlikely to just walk away from saving someone, even if that person was an unknown woman.

"Sam, head upwind. Bone Bird, you go on ahead. Skeleton, Saria, Rita, climb on the carriage."

Vandal decided to get this person out of danger if the situation was as bad as it seemed, and work the rest out later. He was keeping a hand in each jar, but it would be too late to decide to save her once she was dead, and if it was a mistake, they could always finish her off themselves. This seemed like the logical decision to Vandal.

With a squawk, Bone Bird flapped its spirit wings and launched up into the air, and the other undead stopped their training and climbed into the wagon.

As you wish, young master.

The spirit horse started forward. Sam was one of the few undead in Vandal's party who could speak, but while he might share his opinions, he ultimately never opposed Vandal's decisions.

Vandal used magic to add Bone Bird's perspective to his own vision. It let him look around as though he was flying up above himself.

Flying up and up, he saw a number of people on the border of the woodlands and the grassy demon barrens. Maybe the issue was Bone Bird having no eyeballs, or maybe it was because Vandal was still new to this, but its eyesight was considerably worse than that of a normal bird. He could at least get an idea about the people who were there: five, no, six of them. Three of them were standing up. One of them was on the ground, with another straddling her. All of them were men, apart from the one on the ground. The three standing were wearing golden armor. Another leather armor, and another robes. The one straddling the woman had golden armor too.

With this mix of gear, they were probably adventurers. They seemed to be on alert, but more focused on monsters appearing from the barrens than anything coming from the forest. Bone Bird was comprised of just bone and a spirit body of pale fire, so spotting it in the middle of the day—and so high in the sky—would be difficult. Vandal's scouting was unlikely to be noticed.

The woman on the ground had long hair, and strange, gray-brown-colored skin. She was half-naked and bleeding. The man straddling her reached for her breasts.

In the moment Vandal saw what was happening, blood rushed to his head. "Sam, use Sneaking Steps, but go at full speed. We're going to wipe out her attackers."

He calmly gave the order to execute the men. They might be adventurers, but they had to be low-ranking, little more than bandits. Finding others just like Blue Burning Blade Heinz told Vandal all he needed to know about the morals of adventurers in this country.

As you wish, young master. Sam snapped the reins and the cart speeded up.

However, the carriage remained stable, running unbelievably quietly. The Off-road Handling skill allowed Sam to traverse the rough grassy plains with ease, even while using the Speed Driving skill. The horse was a part of Sam's own spirit body, meaning the Sneaking Steps skill eliminated the sounds it would normally make. Even Sam's Resist Impact skill reduced the normal rough and tumble of riding a carriage.

Sam was the full package as a carriage, and something of a cheat code himself. Vandal sincerely hoped he could evolve into a luxury limo in the future.

Beside the carriage, Bone Bear, Bone Wolf, and Bone Monkey raced along at wild speeds.

"When I give the signal, Skeleton, use your bow to launch a preemptive attack on the guy in the leather armor. I think those ones are bandits, so we don't want them getting away. I'm sure Sam could catch up with them, but even so. The one in the robes is probably a Magician, so I'll shut him down. Everyone else, two of you take one of the gold armors each."

Skeleton was already notching an arrow to his bow as Vandal gave the orders.

"Now, let's save this poor girl!"

Now this had to be a good deed.

Name: Saria
Rank: 3
Race: Living One-Piece Swimsuit Armor
Level: 1
—Passive Skills
[Special Senses] [Physical Strength Enhancement: Level 2 (NEW!)]
[Resist Water Attribute: Level 2 (NEW!)] [Resist Physical Attacks: Level 2 (NEW!)]
—Active Skills
[Housework: Level 2]

Name: Rita
Rank: 3
Race: Living Bikini Armor
Level: 1
—Passive Skills

[Special Senses] [Physical Strength Enhancement: Level 2 (NEW!)]

[Resist Fire Attribute: Level 2 (NEW!)] [Resist Physical Attacks: Level 2 (NEW!)]

—Active Skills

[Housework: Level 1]

That day, Zadilis went out from their settlement with three of the young women.

"Well then," she said. "Today I'm going to be teaching you about grasses, mushrooms, and plants."

"But Elder, we know all about the plants we can eat, and the healing herbs. Why are we going so far from home, and so close to the edge of the demon barrens?"

This was Bildy, the youngest of the three, who often had an opinion to share. She wasn't wrong, though—Zadilis had already taught them everything about the flora growing around their home. They could make sufficient medicines and grew enough rations for everyone to eat when hunting was slim. But "sufficient" was not always enough in life. Zadilis knew that all too well herself.

"You're not wrong," Zadilis said. "But what if something happens and we have to move on? What if you don't any of the plants around the new area?" Zadilis looked up at the three girls as she scolded them. They nodded their heads in understanding.

The plants of the demon barrens, especially in the jungle and forest regions, could often be completely different even just a short distance apart. Anyone without the proper training wouldn't even be able to tell the difference, but a specialist could spot the differences between mosses or ferns a mere kilometer apart, or between different plants that looked almost identical. Then there were trees that were the same species even though they had completely different-colored leaves. Despite the different colors, their leaves and sap could be used to make the exact same medicines. Zadilis knew many of those sorts of plants too.

"Even I don't know them all, and you might discover new things for yourselves as part of your own research. But if you can learn everything I know, that will give you a leg up that I never had. That's what I can give you. Do you understand what that's worth?" Zadilis asked.

"Yes, Elder!" all three replied together.

Zadilis gave a satisfied nod. Bildy and the others saw her smiling and smiled back.

"You're so cute, Elder Zadilis. I just want to ruffle your hair!" Bildy said.

"That way you look up at me, it makes my heart skip! I can't say no to you!"

"You're like a little sister now. Although you were an older sister when I was a kid."

The three girls started to chatter about how cute Zadilis was. She wanted to maintain some semblance of authority as an elder while also passing on her accumulated knowledge to the next generation. But she couldn't help having to physically look up at the girls because they were all taller than her now.

Unfortunately, they had started to treat her as a mascot. Her magic had been fading because of her age over the last ten years or so, which was only making her lose her authority faster.

"Hey! No chatter!"

Her age had affected her hearing as well, so it took her a while to catch on to Bildy and the others talking among themselves.

After leaving the settlement, Zadilis and the girls defeated the weak monsters—goblins and such—that they encountered along the way, heading to the outer part of the demon barrens. In principle, the monsters appearing in the demon barrens were weaker the closer to the edge. That meant they wouldn't bump into any powerful enemies, like rank 4 Mad Boars or Crimson Bears, even if they went toward the barrens from the settlement. It allowed them to safely gather plants in the outer regions.

That said, monsters like orcs that targeted the female adventurers who came to the demon barrens also made their own settlements around the edges, so they had to be careful of them.

Well, there haven't been orcs here for a decade, thought Zadilis. *No problem.*

Orcs didn't just target human women, but also women from other races like Zadilis and Bildy, so they needed to be cautious. Luckily, orcs didn't appear half as frequently as goblins and other weaker monsters.

"Elder, we should have brought Basdia with us. I'd feel safer with her along," Bildy said.

"She's stronger than most menfolk," one of the others added.

"Girls, you know Basdia is out hunting with the other warriors. I'm pleased you rely on my daughter, but she won't be back until tomorrow at the earliest."

Basdia was the youngest of Zadilis's three children, even younger than Bildy and the other girls here. She couldn't use magic, but had been blessed with physical abilities better than any man. She was already a fine and proud warrior, swinging her axe to hunt alongside the others. Zadilis was proud of her, of course, but also a little concerned for her future. She could say the same thing about Bildy and the other girls, of course.

"You should stop pining for someone who isn't here and train to become strong enough to at least defeat weak monsters without using magic. Magical power has its limits. We don't have the luxury of quality staves or magic crystals like adventurers do," Zadilis reminded them.

Young people had a tendency to improve what they could do well rather than work on their weaknesses. That wasn't necessarily a mistake, but there were limits to such an approach. Zadilis knew that all too well herself.

"If all you do is hone your magic, as I did, you won't even be able to hunt in the future," she said. "You can't become like me."

"We won't, Elder!"

She had been trying as seriously as she could to impart this knowledge, but their replies were as formulaic as always.

That was youth, though. Nothing to get angry about at this point in her life.

I'll get Vigaro to give the women some training as well. She thought for a moment about the person who was, for all intents and purposes, the real leader of their settlement. Then she started to do what she had come out here for: teaching the girls about plants. She showed them grasses that could be pulped for a salve for festering, roots that could be boiled for a broth to break a fever, and tree bark that could be dried to ward off insects.

"You can't call any of this Alchemy, of course, and the effects won't match actual magic or magic items. But anyone can prepare these medicines, with the correct ingredients and knowledge. That makes them worth learning."

"Yes, Elder!"

Zadilis looked around, satisfied with the answer from the girls. A human alchemist or potion maker wouldn't give these plants a second glance. But Zadilis and her people couldn't go to a human town and collect the more potent alternatives for themselves. Using what one had on hand and learning to make do was an important part of life. An important part of survival. Of course, she wasn't going to deny any efforts to extend the range their hands might extend….

But I'm too old for that now. I can leave that for the youngsters. Now, to find some of those mushrooms with the spores that Huge Boars hate so much—?!

Somehow, the sound of a breaking twig reached her semi-deaf ears, a twist of fate either a good fortune for her and the girls, or misfortune for someone else.

"Ghruuu!" roared Zadilis, not even looking in the direction of the sound. It was a language used by their race during battle. It wasn't suited to everyday discourse, but proved useful for rapid conversations during battle. She said only one thing— "enemy attack." Bildy and the others looked up, raising their staves and starting to cast magic.

"They've spotted us!" said one of the incoming attackers.

"Because you screwed up!"

They heard the voices of multiple men beyond the thicket, and then arrows and rocks started to fly. The attackers were panicking, so their aim was off, but Zadilis and the girls were taken aback when the men finally showed themselves.

Adventurers! Five of them!

It wasn't goblins or kobolts, but five human adventurers. They were all men, with three Warriors in golden armor, a man who looked like a Scout with a short bow, and a man who looked like a Magician with a staff.

"If you've got time to complain, surround them!" one of them barked. "Don't let them escape!"

Still bickering among themselves, the adventurers moved to cut off lines of escape for Zadilis. Based on the way they moved, they didn't seem all that competent. Their armor and weapons showed obvious signs of wear and repair, suggesting they were cheap or old. They might have failed a request, or lost themselves to gambling or drink; they had a desperate look in their eyes—all of them did. One of them was throwing rocks by hand, not even using a sling. These men were adventurers from the very bottom of the barrel.

Adventurers rarely show up at this time of year, and now there are five of them?!

But for Zadilis and the others, these were dangerous foes. They had the advantage of numbers, with three frontline fighters compared to none. The adventurers only had one Magician, true, but their Warriors would end the fight before it came down to a battle of magic.

To make matters worse, it seemed these adventurers were actually here for them. *I don't think the materials they can get from us are of particular worth*, thought Zadilis. That assumption was backed up by the way the adventurers were looking at the bodies of Bildy and the others, with eyes like hungry beasts. They were here for something else, and they weren't going to let their prizes get away.

"Ghru-ul-uk, gaah!"

Zadilis gave more orders in the battle language, and then started to incant some magic herself.

"Hey, hurry it up! Those grunts are a special language only they can understand! They can cast magic with that too!" The Magician seemed to have some knowledge of what they were facing.

"You could have warned us about this before this started!" one of the men shouted. "Use the nets!"

Two of the Warriors took out concealed nets and threw them wildly. The Scout and remaining Warrior fired off an arrow and a knife, respectively. The girls' magic swelled up into a powerful gale, blasting the nets back onto the adventurers and knocking the arrow and knife completely off course. In the same moment, Zadilis unleashed a magical flash, blinding the adventurers, making them cry out.

"My eyes!"

"I-I can't see!"

"Gharl!"

Zadilis gave more orders between the screams, and the girls started to run for their settlement. Vigaro was still there, their young leader. If they could reach the settlement, they would be safe.

We have to run!

But first, Zadilis moved in the opposite direction from the girls, charging toward the adventurers. She passed the Warriors entangled in their own nets and kicked out the legs from under the blinded Magician, then turned and headed back toward the settlement herself.

"Ghaah!" She shouted again in the battle language, telling the others to keep running, while also shifting the attention of the adventurers onto herself.

"Damn it! After them! They're getting away!"

"Forget those three! Chase the other one!"

Just as Zadilis planned, the adventurers turned their attentions to her.

"Why? One runt can't be worth those other three!"

"They ran deeper into the demon barrens! We can't risk other monsters getting in the way!"

Other monsters weren't Bildy and the other girls' allies, but they were still the enemies of adventurers. The deeper into the barrens one went, the stronger the monsters got. Staying alert for other monsters while chasing the girls would be too much for them.

"But what about our money?!"

The men gave chase as ordered, but one of the Warriors didn't sound happy about it.

"No problem! That small one is a Mage! We can sell her for more than the other three combined!"

"What? Really?"

"I'm sure!"

The Magician had realized that Zadilis was a Mage. That worked for her plan, but it also meant they started to chase her even harder.

"That way!"

"Dammit, she's a quick one! Don't let her get away!"

"Watch out, she's a Mage! A higher class! Keep your wits up!"

"They couldn't be higher! We won't make it through winter if we don't catch her!"

Zadilis intended for all the adventurers to chase her, so that was working, but they were also more fixated on her than expected.

Hmmm. They saw through my illusions and won't give up the attack. I underestimated them.

They took out her light magic illusions with stones, and she tried to use wind attribute attack magic to slow them down, but the shield-wielding Warrior in front and the Magician blocked them too.

But I can't turn back and win by fighting now, either. She would have had trouble winning against five, even at her peak, but she could have done it. That wasn't possible for her now.

Her breathing was hard, panting like a dog. Her heart thumped, pain lancing through her.

I can't believe I'm so worn out already! My magical power is pretty much gone too. You really can't beat old age.

An arrow zipped to the left of Zadilis. She turned to the right reflexively, and then gave a yelp a second later when her feet kicked up in the air.

It was a cliff. A small cliff marking the border of the forest. The fall wouldn't kill her, and normally she could jump easily down from here into the forest.

But this time, it proved fatal.

Zadilis lost her balance and rolled down the surface of

the cliff, grunting and moaning, before ending up lying on her front.

She tried to get up, but her arms and legs felt like lead. Her life was in immediate danger, and yet all she wanted to do was take a nap. She was breathing hard and feeling the effects of leaving the demon barrens too. She really did hate getting old.

No matter. My death won't spell the end of our tribe.

Vigaro was positioned as the next chief. There were men the settlement could rely on too. She had helped the next generation escape. She had ten years left, if that—so this was for the best. She actually welcomed death, as opposed to becoming any more decrepit.

Laughing voices and footsteps closed in with her. The adventurers. They were going to finish off Zadilis and take her magic stones and materials.

She didn't care about that. She'd done the same thing countless times in her own life. She never went looking for them, but she'd killed adventurers. She didn't hold it against them. She just wanted them to finish her quickly.

Zadilis quietly closed her eyes, but then the adventurers rolled her over. If they were going to kill her, they could have just stabbed her in the back. She opened her eyes and saw the leering faces of the adventurers.

"Heh, I thought as much when she was giving us the run around. She's quite the catch."

"Really? I like them a little more mature."

"I don't care what you like. The most important thing is the price we can get."

When they started talking about prices, Zadilis worked out what was really going on.

"These females sell for a lot on the black market. We're all set for winter now."

The adventurers hadn't been chasing Zadilis to kill her for magic stones and materials. They were going to take her alive and sell her into slavery.

Zadilis opened her eyes again. That wasn't going to happen. She could accept her own death in defeat, so she decided to fight to make that happen rather than go into slavery.

"Never!" she shouted.

"See, she does understand us. A Mage! She'll sell for a high price."

The adventurers only grinned wider as Zadilis bared her teeth and glared at them. She gathered her remaining strength and prepared to take at least one, but then one of the adventurers stabbed her with a knife. She screamed out, pain coursing across her entire body. She saw white and broke down into wails like a little girl.

"You bet that hurts. You might be tough, but this knife is a magic item with Pain-Boost magic on it. Every wound caused by it does triple the pain."

"We used it on a bandit the other day and a little cut had him whining and selling out his allies."

Zadilis moaned, gasping for air. Any energy she might have had flew out of her along with her tears.

"Hehe, these monsters breed every chance they get. Let me get a taste before we sell her off, eh?"

"Hey, if you don't be careful, you'll be falling for monsters."

"Go ahead, but be careful. And quick. We don't need other monsters showing up."

One of the adventurers straddled Zadilis, and tore at her clothing. Her charcoal breasts were exposed, and the man grabbed at them hard, but didn't get the reaction he was looking for.

"Bah."

Upset that she wasn't playing along, the man reached for

the knife that was still sticking into her. Zadilis prepared to scream, tightening up at the thought of that pain...

"Wurgh!"

The other adventurers were watching for monsters coming out of the forest when the Scout suddenly made a gurgling sound. An arrow jutted out of his back.

For a moment, Zadilis thought her people had come from the settlement to save her. The adventurers were clearly thinking the same thing.

"Someone coming to save her?!"

All of the adventurers, including the one on top of her, grabbed their weapons and looked toward the forest. The Magician in the robes, however, shouted a warning as he pulled the arrow from their friend.

"You morons! It's not from the forest! Behind us!"

The Magician was looking at a wagon and a throng of bone-only beasts, racing toward the group at high speed and yet hardly making a sound.

"Undead monsters?" howled one of the Warriors. "Why are they coming from the plains and not the demon barrens?!"

"No idea! They have an archer so get in front of me!" gasped the Scout, who had been saved from death by his leather armor. He chugged a potion.

With his wound healed, the adventurers gathered themselves to try and face this new threat, but in that moment the undead were upon them.

Vandal had arrived. Skeleton fired a second arrow but the target dodged it this time. That couldn't be helped, as the Skeleton's skill was still at level 1. Vandal's party generally lacked in long-distance attacks. He needed Saria and Rita to learn to use bows.

Even as he considered that for the future, Vandal—his baby body hidden in the bed of the wagon—unleashed his own magic toward the adventurer Magician.

"Magic Absorption Barrier."

A glob of black magical power flew toward the Magician. He tried to block it with some kind of defensive magic, but the black glob simply absorbed that magic and rendered it useless.

He gave a frustrated cry. "That Ghost Carriage is using some kind of crazy magic! What's going on?"

The Magician was surrounded in a dome of the black magical power, but didn't seem to have taken any damage yet.

"Hurry up and cast something!" his friend shouted.

The frontline warriors stepped up with swords, spears, axes and shields ready, but in the next moment their defensive line was shattered.

Hyaah! Move aside or get run over! shouted Sam, clutching the reins of the Ghost Carriage, accelerating all the more. The pale haze-horse pulling the wagon rushed toward the men. *Charge!*

"Run for it, lads!" At the shout from the man with the shield, the adventurers all dived out of the way of the oncoming Sam.

It didn't matter what their defense stats were, or if they had Shield Proficiency or armor techniques like Stone Shield or Stone Wall—they wouldn't be able to withstand the Speed Driving and Charge combination from the bulky undead carriage. The adventurers' quick thinking got them all out of the way, leaving Sam to perform an incredible drift turn a few meters away from Zadilis's collapsed body. This turn was only possible because the spirit body horse was actually part of Sam. It would've ordinarily torn the wagon apart, but the Resist Impact skill kept everyone other than Vandal in place.

The undead bellowed and roared. Bone Wolf, Bone Bear, and Bone Monkey attacked the adventurers' crumbled frontline. The humans had some skills, it seemed, as they managed to get their weapons back into play and avoid the initial onslaught.

Screeeeeech!

Brrroooooagh!

With Bone Bird slashing down the from the sky and Skeleton climbing down from the wagon, the adventurers weren't just losing steam—they looked likely to get mopped up in a few more seconds.

"Why are there rank 3 monsters outside the demon barrens?"

"Like I know! Flicker Slash!"

"Hey! You got that defense magic ready yet?" The man with the shield somehow managed to hold off the crushing front paws of Bone Bear, while another used the basic sword skill Flicker Slash to avoid Bone Monkey's attack, and the third shouted at the Magician to hurry up and get them protected.

"Fire, gather in my hand . . . nope, it's no good! My magical power is being absorbed! I can't do anything!"

Each time the magician tried to cast a spell, his power was quickly syphoned off. That was the effect of Vandal's Magic Absorption Barrier. Every time he tried to use magic within the barrier, it got sucked away. The only ways to break it would be to expel more magical power than the barrier could absorb, use barrier-breaking magic, or run away at a speed the barrier couldn't keep up with.

Breaking the magical barrier created by Vandal's insane magical power was far beyond this particular Magician, however.

He couldn't use any magic from inside, either. If he ran at full speed he might be able to shake the barrier off, but he wasn't smart enough to think of that.

"Dammit! What is this thing? How should I even attack it?"

The Scout, meanwhile, was fighting Saria and Rita. They had superior strength, and he was outnumbered, putting him in a tight spot. That said, Saria and Rita were just flailing their weapons around, so the nimble Scout didn't have much trouble avoiding their attacks.

But the Scout was also having issues fighting them with just a dagger. Normally, it wasn't difficult to defeat living armor. He could use a blade to separate the pieces and split them apart. But in the case of Saria and Rita, they were pretty separated already. Rita was literally a two-piece, and neither of them had helmets at all. They couldn't get more split apart than they already were, being such risqué armor.

"They don't have a head! No weak spots! What should I do?!"

He was trying to keep it together, but his allies on the frontline were losing ground, and their Magician had been neutralized. Then, Sam ran over the panicked Scout, sending him bouncing like a rubber ball and making him howl like a dog.

Overwhelming the enemy's every chance to come back into the fight, Vandal's party quickly reduced the adventurers to corpses on the ground.

On Vandal's side, Bone Wolf and Bone Bear broke some bones, and Vandal suffered a few bumps from the wagon's drift turn.

My apologies for that, Young Master.

"No worries. I'll heal up quickly."

Vandal's head was cut and bleeding, but he had the Rapid Healing skill, which would fix him up in a few days. He recently learned that he could use death magic to directly heal the injuries of his undead, so he could cure them in a jiffy.

All in all, they hadn't taken much damage.

"Still, I'm going to have to reflect on this," said Vandal. Attacking a party of adventurers with so little thought had been a big risk. They had won so easily only because their charge paid off, because their enemies hadn't seen death attribute magic before, and because they weren't that skilled to begin with. Vandal checked their guild cards, a form of identification issued by the adventurers' guild, and saw they were grade D. If they had been C or higher, things wouldn't have worked out like this. It wasn't possible to tell at a glance how strong adventurers were going to be, so rushing into battle with them proved dangerous. That said, Vandal hadn't been able to overlook them attacking a woman.

"I'll use the advantage of surprise better next time," he said. And that was all the reflection he needed.

He put off picking over the rest of their possessions, dealing with the bodies, and gathering intel from the spirits of the adventurers who were already gathering around him until later. First, he needed to finish helping the woman.

He already used Detect Life to confirm she wasn't close to death, but she was still in rough shape. If need be, he could always break out the potion from the dungeon.

Meanwhile, Zadilis was sure she was about to die. It hadn't been her people who killed the adventurers, but some undead, meaning they were surely going to kill her too. But the attack didn't come, no matter how long she waited.

"Are you okay?"

Instead, a baby standing nearby—and bleeding from his forehead—asked how she was doing.

She was surprised, confused, and scared that this baby was some kind of spirit. But more than that, pain from the knife still stuck in her prevented her from replying.

Vandal looked down at her. She had oddly colored skin, but was quite cute. She looked in her late teens, or maybe a little younger. Her beautiful face and moist eyes prompted Vandal's desire to protect her. She could have been a teen sensation in the pop world back on Earth. Her grayish-brown skin was an oddity, but stuff like that probably wasn't all that rare here in another world. And her exposed chest....

Better not look at that.

Vandal quickly turned his gaze from the chest of the attractive girl. He was mentally and physically still an infant, so perhaps it was a relief that he hadn't yet awakened to sexual desire. He hoped she hadn't felt violated a second time.

Of course, his eyes were as lifeless as an undead, so she probably felt more fear from his staring than shame or embarrassment.

Vandal carefully reached toward the hilt of the knife still sticking into the girl, seeking to heal her wounds.

"Wait...stop...!"

The knife was a magic item that increased the pain it caused. Pulling it out would cause that pain again, and she tried to stop him from touching it.

"Nullify Pain."

Vandal saw the pain she was in and used death magic to negate it. The girl was surprised at the sudden change, and then

Vandal pulled the knife out in one smooth movement. Then he applied some drops of the grade 3 potion to the wound.

It closed up almost instantly. The wound in her flesh sealed itself back up, covered with smooth new skin. There was no sign of a scar at all. On Earth, this would have required time and effort—surgical treatment and plastic surgery to remove the scar—but on Ramda you just applied some potion. Ramda had some things better than Earth did, that was for sure, although Vandal might change his mind when he found out exactly how much a potion like that one cost.

"I'm Vandal," he said. "Shall I get you some water and a cloth to clean yourself up?"

He spoke quite naturally to the girl as she looked up at him in mute shock. It made sense for her to still be in something of a panic, considering she had just been stabbed and almost raped.

A female officer would handle this case back on Earth, Vandal thought. But the only women he had along were Dalshia (who only Vandal and the undead could see) and Saria and Rita (who were just moving armor and so hardly even counted as female). Vandal was the only one in any position to actually help her. *I'm really not suited to this.* On both Earth and Origin, he had little interaction with the opposite sex, rendering him completely unable to deal with such a delicate situation as the victim of a sexual assault.

The tears brimming in the girl's eyes seemed proof enough of that. She had been crying and sweaty before he healed her, but now she started to loudly cry again.

And then she threw herself onto him.

She hugged him so hard that the undead almost reflexively

moved to grab him back. He waved them off, letting the girl hug it out, but he couldn't exactly enjoy it.

She was much stronger than she looked. He wasn't at risk of broken bones, but it was hard to breathe. Her nails dug into him too.

This is pretty rough on a baby! Although I went through worse on Origin, with all the modifications and experiments. He put a brave face on, but he also was in no position to enjoy this hug from a cute girl.

"You saved me, you saved me. I owe you my life," Zadilis wept. "You not only defeated those adventurers but also used such a precious potion on me. How can I thank you?"

"Okay, okay…."

After waiting for Zadilis to calm down, they stripped the adventurers' bodies for items, and then headed into the demon barrens. Before long, the party was rumbling along in Sam's carriage, making quick progress toward Zadilis's home.

"Just a little farther to the settlement. Thanks again."

Her home was located inside the demon barrens because she hailed from a race that was generally considered to be monsters.

"We ghouls have a high tolerance for pain, but that magic item was hell itself. And then they were going to sell me into slavery! Humans are quite terrifying."

As it turned out, Zadilis was a ghoul. Vandal guessed she might not be human, mainly from the color of her skin, but he hadn't expected her to be a ghoul. She was sitting in the wagon and he was sitting in her lap, and she was so far from his image of a ghoul that it made him a bit nervous.

"I thought ghouls were undead?" he asked. In his mind, ghouls were like a kind of more powerful zombie, a monster that mainly ate dead flesh, sometimes with poison in their nails and teeth. But he felt a kind of warmth from Zadilis that he had hadn't experienced since Dalshia's death, and his use of the Detect Life told him she had life force. She might not have been human, but she was definitely alive.

Young Master, the general perception is that ghouls are a higher class of zombie, something more like vampires, Sam added. *In Ramda, ghouls live and leave descendants behind. On the other hand, they're violent monsters who attack people. They're physically strong and resilient to pain, and have poisonous talons on their hands and feet. They also use some kind of terrible rite in order to turn fresh corpses into more of their kind.*

"So they aren't exactly a higher class of zombie, but something like that," Vandal mused.

But then Zadilis corrected Sam. She explained that ghouls were like a variant of vampires, an inferior relative. They were also living beings completely unrelated to zombies.

"To put it simply," she said, "we ghouls are the descendant of the twin brother—or maybe twin sister—of the original vampire. That means ghouls are also the children of Vida."

"There was nothing about ghouls in my mother's stories," Vandal said.

"I don't know the details myself. This wisdom comes from the elders before me."

The myths Dalshia had shared with Vandal said that Vida created the lamia, scylla, harpies, arachne, centaurs, and others, but he hadn't heard anything about ghouls. Dalshia probably didn't know everything, of course, and mythology could always change between regions. He could always ask her about it when she was awake.

Regardless, the ghouls from the settlement Zadilis belonged to believed this story.

They didn't seem that friendly toward humans. After all, humans considered them monsters and wanted to kill them, or worse. Zadilis had killed numerous adventurers when she was younger, and lost friends to adventurers too.

"I can't believe they wanted to sell me into slavery. They got the better of me, so I was ready to accept death, but not that."

Zadilis seemed to have been shaken by the experience of getting targeted for human sexual pleasure. She didn't know that, in reality, it was far from an uncommon occurrence. There were numerous monsters that looked exactly like humans except for different-colored skin or certain abnormalities. It made all too much sense that humans would think of selling women from such races as slaves.

"I mean, they're not orcs who will just go after anything that moves. Am I wrong?" she asked.

Vandal looked up at her. "I think you're quite attractive."

Even after learning she was a ghoul, Zadilis still looked like a cute girl to him. Her yellow eyes and charcoal skin were unusual, and her fangs looked like cute double teeth. Youth still lingered on her cheeks, but her lips were full and luscious. If Vandal had been an older, normal boy, he might have fallen in love. He felt like maybe he was missing out on something there, but Vandal put that aside and rationally considered that—regrettably—he could see the value of Zadilis as a slave.

"I don't think they were looking for just any woman. They might have been targeting you from the start. You need to be careful—I'm sorry, is something wrong?"

"No, ah, it's nothing."

Zadilis was moved more than expected by Vandal telling her she was appealing. *Hold on, hold on, he might have saved my life, but he's still just a baby!* That thought didn't stop the fluttering of her heart. *He's certainly a strange baby. He's got undead serving him and uses strange magic. I feel strange when he's looking at me—hang on, is this the alluring gaze of a vampire?!*

She had some knowledge of dhampir, and it was confusing her feelings toward him.

"You're quite right. We'll have to be careful. I'll make sure the other women know. If they'll come after an old ghoul like me, the youngsters will need to be careful."

It also turned out that Zadilis was the elder of the ghoul community. She turned 290 this year. Ghouls had a life expectancy of around 300. She wasn't lying when she called herself "old." When Vandal used Detect Life, she hadn't seemed weakened because of the knife wound, but rather because of her age.

"I doubt many adventurers know much about the age of ghouls," Vandal commented wryly.

Zadilis smiled, her smooth skin gleaming with youth.

"Indeed, you tend to forget about that stuff, just living with other ghouls. Ghoul women stop aging around the time they have their first child, so most of those in the settlement don't know the ages of our women. Huh? What is it, boy? Are you sleepy?"

"No, nothing…." Something Zadilis said had made Vandal give a sigh, but he wasn't sure why himself.

"If you say so. Can you make me a promise, while we are here?" Zadilis asked. "You too, Master Sam, if you would.

Please keep it a secret that I wept like a babe."

"No problem."

I do as the young master commands.

"Thank you, thank you. Ah, as we've been talking, it looks like something has found us," Zadilis said.

They had been sharing a pleasant chat, but this whole time they were moving through the demon barrens. Monsters gathered here in densities far beyond those of normal forests and plains. Skeleton and Bone Wolf protected Sam, and so far only one crazy goblin had tried anything on, with predictable results.

At Zadilis's comment, Vandal used Detect Life and located a few dozen lifeforms maybe fifty meters up ahead, roughly man-sized if not a little larger. However, his permanently active Detect Danger: Death didn't react, and so it didn't feel like an ambush by bloodthirsty monsters.

Young Master? Sam asked.

"Just keep going for now," Vandal replied. Sending Bone Bird scouting wouldn't do much good here in the forest. They waited and watched the monsters start to emerge from the trees.

The monsters had a roughly human form, with four limbs, but their heads looked closer to those of lions. Distorted lion heads, with bared teeth and wild whiskers—more the king of the crazies than the king of the beasts. They had charcoal skin from the neck down, and arms so long their knuckles dragged on the ground even when standing upright. It would be easy for these features, Vandal noted, to distract from the hard-yet-flexible carnivore muscles they also sported. They were humanoid monsters, just like the goblins Vandal and his undead had been dealing with since he was born, but also clearly set apart from those. He wondered why they hadn't attacked yet.

Zadilis stood up, with Vandal still in her arms.

"Ah, menfolk. Thank you for coming."

"Elder, Bildy told us come help… Why you coming back with undead?"

"Glad you safe…but who all this?"

The ghouls had a growly tone, but did well forming words at all with their lion-lips.

Sam murmured to Vandal, who was also pretty perplexed by the situation. *Young Master, I have heard that ghoul males and females—that is, men and women—are very different in appearance, but this is my first time actually seeing them.*

They were the same race, and yet Zadilis looked human apart from her skin and teeth, while the men looked anything but. These ghouls seemed to have a unique genealogy.

"I was being attacked by some adventurers, and this boy appeared and saved me. The undead follow him," Zadilis explained.

"Small child defeated adventurers?!"

"He has undead following?"

The men looked at each other, unable to quite believe what Zadilis was telling them. Vandal didn't expect them to just get onboard right away.

Then, a ghoul even bigger than the others pushed out from deeper in the forest. He was over two meters tall, a real big one. He wore leather armor made from monster hides and his whiskers were decorated with vibrant bird feathers. He had a battle axe over his shoulder that could have chopped a bear in two. He looked like the leader of the male contingent.

"Vigaro, no need for you to come out here as well. I keep telling you that a chief must not leave the settlement for every little thing!" Zadilis said.

"You in charge, Zadilis. If you in danger, I lead warriors to aid," the big guy said.

"But *you* are our future!" Zadilis countered. "The settlement keeps running as long as you're there."

"Why is settlement running?" he replied. "You make little sense old woman. Did adventurers hit you on head?"

"I take it back. You need to work on your head, not just your body."

"I work on head plenty. I been nutting orcs for good ten years," Vigaro said proudly.

Zadilis gave a sigh, her breath tickling the back of Vandal's head. He couldn't take his eyes off the arms on that Vigaro ghoul. They were like logs. He wondered what his secret was—and if he was willing to share it.

"What plan for child?" the big ghoul continued.

"We will welcome him to the grotto, of course. He has promised to provide meat so we may feast with him. Do you have a problem with that?"

"Ghuu . . ." Vigaro tilted his head at Zadilis's words. Even though this child had saved her life, she wouldn't normally invite other races into their settlement. The ghouls lived in the demon barrens, after all, with everyone other than their own kind nothing less than their mortal enemies. In fact, conflicts with other groups of ghouls often happened as well. That was why Zadilis and Vigaro opposed mingling with other races. It was necessary for their survival.

Vigaro noticed that Vandal was a dhampir. He was interested in the meat the child might offer. But he was more concerned about the idea of letting anyone else know the location of their settlement. Vandal was looking up at Zadilis with an expression as dead as eyeballs floating in orc soup. The child certainly didn't seem dangerous or aggressive, but…there was something strange.

Vigaro started to realize that he wanted to see himself reflected in those dead eyes. He wanted to do something for this baby.

"If it's a problem, we'll just carry on our way…."

That comment from Vandal made Vigaro and the other male ghouls all give a little whimper. They felt guilty, and worried that they might chase Vandal away.

"No problem! Welcome you to grotto, welcome!" Vigaro immediately shouted.

The men all roared their agreement. "Vandal, you our guest! Welcome! Ghouuuuul!"

Vigaro threw back his head and howled like a beast. Vandal gave a start at the humming vibrations in the air, but Zadilis soothed him.

"He's letting the others know that I'm safe, that we have guests, and to prepare a feast."

And so, for the first time in his life, Vandal was welcomed by a community that was actually friendly toward him.

Name: Zadilis
Rank: 5
Race: Ghoul Mage
Level: 100
Job: None
Job Level: 100
Job History: None
Age: 290

—Passive Skills

[Dim Vision] [Resist Pain: Level 3] [Brute Strength: Level 1]

[Paralytic Venom (Claws): Level 2] [MP Recovery Speed Boost: Level 4]

—Active Skills

[Light Attribute Magic: Level 4] [Wind Attribute Magic: Level 2]

[Non-Attribute Magic: Level 2] [Magic Control: Level 5] [Alchemy: Level 2]

—Maladies

[Old Age]

The kobolt Gyahn, with ambition burning in his chest, just wanted to throw his oversized axe aside—along with all the other baggage. He was heading with his fellow kobolts toward their nest.

Kobolts were another common monster, just like goblins. They were generally rank 2 and didn't have any particular abilities. They looked a lot like dogs and would only reach the chest on a human even when fully grown. But they formed packs like dogs and wolves, making them more dangerous to fight than goblins. Still, so long as there weren't any ranked-up kobolts in the pack, they were good monsters for rookie adventurers to train against.

In this pack, though, there were multiple such promoted species—including Gyahn, who was a rank 4 Kobolt General.

The pack alpha was an experienced Kobolt Mage, and pack beta was a General with more experience than Gyahn.

The Kobolt Mage dreamed of taking control of the jungle demon barrens where Gyahn and the kobolts lived. Their pack had increased in number, with younger members like Gyahn ranking up into promoted species. In order to achieve that, they needed to head toward the center of the demon barrens. That was because their own settlement was surrounded by multiple groups of ghouls.

The biggest problem among these was a group of around 100 ghouls, led by a Ghoul Mage. Gyahn's pack had tried an attack, but failed completely. The ghouls were violent and dangerous, attacking and eating anything that came their way, even kobolts or goblins.

In order to beat out the ghouls and take control of the demon barrens, they needed to get away from them for the time being, find some new territory, and increase their numbers and strength. Thirty of them had struck out for just that purpose. The Kobolt Mage led the expedition, with Gyahn and another Kobolt General, and then a Kobolt Archer and Knight. Even just the regular kobolts on the expedition were the higher-level ones.

And now, only ten remained.

Whining like dogs, covered in blood and mud, ears and tails sagging, ten bedraggled kobolts. The Kobolt Mage and other General were missing. The Archer had been stationed at the rear, and the Knight had just gotten lucky, but after that they only had regular kobolts.

Their plan had been to do some scouting with enough strength to at least drive off any threats they might encounter.

But in the center of the demon barrens, Gyahn and his pack had encountered an unexpectedly powerful enemy.

Orcs.

Rank 3 monsters with top-class brute strength, full-throttle charges, and vitality. However, they were pretty dumb, unable to use much gear apart from sticks and clubs. If the kobolts had only encountered a few of them, the pack would have been able to prevail, meaning experience and food for them all.

This time, there had been close to ten orcs led by an Orc General and Mage, and all of them were equipped with reasonable armor and weapons. It was a proper military unit. They had even had goblin and kobolt slaves with them.

The pack had managed to defeat some of the orcs and their slaves, but their own alpha and beta had also been killed, forcing them to flee. Any of them who weren't here now were either dead or slaves to the orcs themselves.

And in the end, maybe the slaves were better off.

Gyahn gave a dejected howl, tugging at his ripped ear and wondering what came next. They could return to their nest, but there were only the untrained kobolts, pregnant females, and children there. One student each of the Knight and Mage had remained to stand watch, but they would hardly make up for the fallen numbers.

Kobolts matured in a matter of months. They could at least still hunt. But that wouldn't be enough to defeat the orcs in the center or the groups of ghouls surrounding them. They would have to eke out an existence, pinned between two superior enemies.

That was difficult for Gyahn to accept, after the lure of ambition had fired him once. But it was suicide to attempt a battle when the results were already so plain.

Suddenly, the remaining members of the pack started to bark and shout.

Gyahn looked up in surprise and saw a massive orc, no, a Mad Boar, charging right toward him and shrieking as it came.

This was the result of a ten-foot Huge Boar consuming enough prey to become a blood-starved wild beast. It was rank 4, just like Gyahn, and so in his exhausted state he couldn't hope to fight it equally today. Just looking at its orc-like face gave him flashbacks to a defeat he was yet to process.

Gyahn wanted to shout at his dazed comrades to get away. A Mad Boar was still a boar, in essence. It might get up some speed, but it couldn't turn for love or truffles. If they scattered, they could surely get away from it. Escape this threat, at least—but then what about the next one?

Before he realized what was happening, Gyahn had dashed past his comrades, howling as he rushed head-on for a collision with the oncoming Mad Boar.

"Awooooooooo!'

The strong led the pack. That was the rule, and that made him the alpha. This wasn't the time to be worrying about what to do—it was time to act. He would lead the pack and make the hard decisions that came with it.

"Awoooooo!"

"Roaaaaagh!"

The Mad Boar and Gyahn crashed into each other head on. The massive boar sought to just run this inconvenience over. Gyahn leapt up onto its head, then swung his broken axe down with all of his might. With a crash, both the Mad Boar's skull and Gyahn's axe shattered into pieces.

In that moment, Gyahn had pulled off something he had never done before—the Axe Proficiency technique Slice Steel. The light in the Mad Boar's eyes flickered out, and it collapsed to the ground with a hideous bellow.

Gyahn's allies were watching from the sidelines, but now they started to howl and bark for him. He stood atop the fallen boar, accepting their adulation with some howling of his own.

He had provided food for the pack. Food to make them strong again, and restore the warriors who would realize his ambitions!

At Gyahn's bold howling, the defeated kobolts started to recover their strength. A new leader—no, a new king had just been born for their pack.

✳

"Cheers! To Elder and Elder-saving baby!"

"Wow! This meat baby gives us taste good!"

The ghoul grotto was located deep in the demon barrens. They welcomed Vandal, after he saved their elder Zadilis and won the approval of their warrior and next chief, Vigaro. The settlement was much larger than Vandal had been expecting, and more civilized too.

The demon barrens were more like a jungle than a forest out here. The ghouls had chopped down trees to make a clearing, and lived in pit-dwellings with roofs of woven leaves. The construction had Vandal worried about moisture accumulation for a moment, but this wasn't an Amazon-like rainforest, so it probably worked out okay for them.

They had dug a well for water, and made fields for crops,

although they were primitive and limited in scale. They also fermented plants obtained from the surrounding jungle to make alcohol, and had stocks of preserved game meat from their hunting. They lived like forest-dwelling tribes Vandal had seen on TV on Earth. It was a far more intellectual and cultured community than, say, the goblins and kobolts that relied entirely on hunting and gathering.

A much more human lifestyle than the one I've led until now, that's for sure. Vandal had made ends meet by hunting and gathering himself—including hunting bandits—and seeing the ghoul settlement, he again felt the need for a stable foundation to work from. Clothing, food, and shelter, the basics required for life.

The ghouls threw a party with the meat Vandal had brought in and the bandits' wine, which Vandal he hadn't used as much of as he thought. There were almost 100 ghouls. There were around ten more warriors off on a goblin-hunting trip, meaning more would return at a later day. Vandal didn't know much about the ecology of monsters, but it wasn't hard to imagine this being the largest-scale monster settlement in the entire demon barrens.

Apparently, the leader of the warriors who were off goblin-hunting was Zadilis's youngest child. She had apparently been born more a fighter than a magic user.

The male ghouls, with their lion heads and elongated arms, and the female ghouls who looked just like human women apart from their skin color, were eating the meat and wine provided by Vandal, the savior of Zadilis, and singing his praises. Vandal watched them and felt warm inside. He'd done a good thing.

He felt that way, even knowing the source of the meat.

A meal is better shared, for sure.

"Vandal! Eat too, baby!" Vigaro offered him a skewer of well-roasted meat, but Vandal shook his head from side to side.

"I still have some hesitation about eating human flesh," he admitted.

It was true. The meat Vigaro offered had been spiced and cooked nicely, but it was sourced from the five adventurers that Vandal had killed to save Zadilis. In other words, it was human flesh. These ghouls were different from the image Vandal had held of them, but they did eat human flesh.

"You sure? This better than poison toad!" Vigaro gestured at the toad legs that Vandal was chewing on.

Zadilis, sitting next to him, stepped in. "Don't get too pushy. Vandal is a dhampir. He drinks blood, but doesn't eat human meat," she said.

"Okay. Drink, then! Drink, baby!"

"Vandal is still only 1 year old! Alcohol will be poison to him, nothing else. This isn't the place to start trying to build up his tolerances!"

"He 1 year old? Really? I thought he just small but old!" Vigaro opened his eyes wide in surprise. Based on the way Vandal acted, it was hard to imagine him not being much older. Indeed, that would be the normal reaction.

"He can use magic, has tamed multiple undead, and defeated five adventurers. I can see why you'd think he's a small adult," Zadilis offered.

"Really? I'm still just a 1-year-old baby," Vandal said.

"Doesn't look that way," Zadilis and Vigoro said at once, shaking their heads. Vandal understood why, but wasn't going to spend too long dwelling on it. Even with removing the magic and undead from the equation, there were few people who would look at Vandal right now and consider him a babbling baby. He was expressionless, with dead eyes, and it barely felt

The Death Mage
241

like he was there even when he was staring you down. His hair had grown out wildly in the six months since Dalshia died, and his clothing was basically just scraps of cloth. He was a ghost, a wraith, surely.

"Elder, can we thank your savior too?"

"Yes, please! Let us talk to him!"

But the ghoul women didn't seem to have that impression of him at all. A number of them were looking over, their yellow eyes glittering. Vandal blinked under the attention. He had never been popular like this at any other point in his life, apart from maybe with some ghosts. His surprise was palpable.

"Ah, boy. These are some of the youngest in the settlement. I'm in the process of teaching them all sorts of useful things at the moment," Zadilis explained.

The girls she introduced did indeed look very young. Maybe late teens or early 20s. It was strange how their elder, Zadilis, looked younger than they did.

"Thank you for saving Elder Zadilis!"

"You're so cute! Can I comb your hair?"

"Your eyes are lovely. You've got two different colors!"

Mentally, they were clearly much younger. As soon as he was introduced, they started squabbling to be the first to give him a cuddle.

"H-hey, be gentle with me!"

They lifted him up by grabbing one leg and lifted him up while upside down, treating him a lot more roughly than one should handle a baby. Being a dhampir meant he was hardier than a grown man, but still. He didn't appreciate being manhandled, but he also didn't get angry with them. *Hold on. Could I be...popular?*

He'd never had someone of the opposite sex treat him like this before. His third life, and finally spring had come for him? Vandal's mind was full of such thoughts, preventing him from feeling anything like anger. The ghoul women all looked young and attractive, and living in the demon barren jungles meant that their clothes revealed a lot. A human man would be drooling all over them. You just had to get past the flesh eating.

"I'm Vandal. Nice to meet you." Vandal certainly wasn't bothered by it. Thinking back, the adventurers hadn't been attacking a human girl, trying to rape and sell her into slavery. They had been attacking a ghoul, Zadilis, who was considered a monster by society. Selling her as a slave was illegal, strictly speaking, but that broke the law against bringing an untamed monster into a residential area, far from the level of trying to sell a human girl into slavery.

At the point they attacked Zadilis, they had been trying to rape a female monster. That wasn't a crime, or anything at all. No country would create laws prohibition fornicating with female monsters, with or without consent. Such laws might have stopped some strange monster STD, but that was about it. Female adventurers and guild staff looked down on it and disliked such behavior, but it wasn't against the rules.

Adventurers were the people who fought off monsters and protected the people. Ghouls had roots in the goddess Vida, but they were designated monsters in the Amidd Empire and its affiliate nations. Raping them before killing them was not considered a problem.

So, while Vandal attacking the adventurers and taking their belongings made him a bandit, the ghouls didn't care. Vandal was a dhampir, another race designated as a monster in the

Amidd Empire and its affiliate nations. Just like ghouls. Something that attacked and hurt humans. So, if he attacked a bunch of adventurers, killed them, took their stuff, and then shared their meat with his friends, there was nothing wrong with that. Those adventurers were like goblins and poison toads to Vandal, nothing more. There was no need to worry about them.

Vandal might have been more concerned if he had been planning on securing some kind of human rights for dhampir here in the Amidd Empire, but he wasn't planning that at all. He wouldn't attempt something as difficult as that even if someone asked him to.

The way the ghouls welcomed him made him feel closer to ghouls than he had ever been to humans. They loved the meat so much that he wished he had been preserving the bandits all along. He could start doing that now.

"I wish my boy was like you, Vandal," one of the ghoul girls said. "He's almost 30 but he's still not flown the nest."

"Hey, will you rub my belly? I want my baby to be born as strong as you."

"I'm Bildy. If my baby is a boy, can I give him your name?"

That brought Vandal back down to earth with a bump. They were all mothers—or soon to be. Their bellies were flat, so he hadn't noticed. Vandal hadn't been thinking such a relationship was possible, or even wanted such a development. His baby body was still 1 year old, so it wasn't possible. But it was still a downer—and at the same time, he had to wonder why something like this would upset him. It was the same gnawing self-disappointment that ate at him when he killed the adventurers.

"Enough! He's so exhausted he's gone limp! Let the poor boy be!"

From their perspective, his reaction looked like one of exhaustion.

Later that night, Dalshia told Vandal everything she knew about ghouls.

They were rank 3 undead monsters at lowest. They had higher intelligence and social skills than other similar demi-human-type monsters, like goblins, orcs, and kobolts, and their appearance differed greatly depending on gender. They shared yellow eyes and charcoal skin, strength, poisonous talons, and enjoyed eating meat. They were resilient to poison and pain, and had lots of vitality. The males had lion heads and made excellent warriors, physically stronger than the women and with more powerful poison. The women were all attractive, and while they were physically weaker than the males, many of them were blessed with magical abilities, allowing them to at least use simple magic. But that didn't mean there weren't some powerful female warriors, and skilled male magicians. Ghouls could also perform a special rite that turned human bodies into ghouls. Promoted species included Ghoul Warriors, Ghoul Berserkers, and Ghoul Mages. In the past there had been even higher classes, such Ghoul Tyrant and Ghoul Elder Mage.

That's everything I know about ghouls, Dalshia concluded. *And you plan to wait out the winter here in Ghoul Grotto?*

"Yes. But Mom, ghouls aren't undead. They are like vampires, a race with their roots in the goddess Vida." Vandal replied to his mother's concern with his normal expressionless face.

That just makes me worry more, Dalshia replied. *Your skills make undead like you, Vandal, but that won't work here. If they get hungry, they might try to eat you.* Dalshia had only just woken up, and being immediately confronted with Zadilis and the others had alarmed her.

"I'll be fine," Vandal said. "I think. I don't have that sense of death I felt when I crept into Evbejia."

They were so nice that he had started to drop down his guard a bit. Of course, while Dalshia and Vandal himself hadn't realized it yet, his Death Attribute Allure skill worked on the ghouls.

"It also doesn't change the fact we need to find a suitable place to wait until spring. They say we can stay as long as we like."

The top members of the community had already given their approval for Vandal to stay until spring, if he wished it. His allure skill and gifts of meat were really greasing the wheels.

"I also want to learn more about the world from Zadilis."

Can't we do that after reaching the Olbaum Electorate Kingdom? No?

"Not really. Not now that I know about the guild card problem."

Vandal looked over at the wagon—which was a lot lighter now the wine had been removed—and the five guild cards placed there. They belonged to the main course of the feast, the adventurers, and displayed their names and grade D status. He had been planning to dispose of them, but had also heard some important info from the adventurers' spirits, and so decided to check them out a little first.

Guild cards had a function that displayed the owner's status to other people. Seeing someone else's status normally required special magic or magic items. However, the owner of the card could make adjustments to decide how much they wanted to show other people. They could show just their names and current jobs, or their job histories, or all the way down to their status and skills. The owner was free to make that decision.

However, when you first created a guild card, you had to present all relevant information to the guild staff.

"Which means the moment I become an adventurer, my skills and curses will all be exposed," Vandal sighed.

Yes, that's a problem. A shame, too, because you normally get paid for those. The adventurers' guild paid money when previously unknown jobs and skills were discovered. Vandal had plenty of those already, with his death attribute magic and skills like Death Attribute Allure. Vandal had explained all of those to Dalshia when he told her about his past lives. When she heard the full breakdown of her son's skills, she had realized that he had some new and special ones.

You'll become famous the moment you register with any guild. The magician's guild will definitely want a piece of you. And those curses will definitely get everyone excited.

"I can't start forgetting skills or resolving my curses ahead of time, so I need to acquire a certain level of knowledge, techniques, and strength before I register with the guild."

Vandal had no parents in this world, so he needed something that could vouch for him in human society. That meant registering with a guild somewhere. But all guilds had guild cards, meaning his skills and curses would be exposed wherever he went.

However, guilds also existed to protect their members, so they weren't going to capture or detain him just because of some unknown skills or curses. The other members, and even people outside the guild, wouldn't be able to do anything to him simply because he had unknown skills or curses.

Not openly, anyway.

Vandal knew well that the world wasn't comprised solely of people who kept to the rules and abided by morality.

It looks like we don't have much choice, Dalshia said. *This Zadilis can use magic, so have her teach you whatever she can. Even if you can't learn the same spells she uses, you might be able to apply them to death attribute magic.*

"Okay, Mom."

And so, for the time being, Vandal became part of the ghoul community.

[Death Attribute Allures skill increased to level 3!]
[Enhance Brethren skill acquired!]

The next day, his cohabitation with the ghouls started in earnest.

They handed something strange to him. One of the ghouls told him to eat it. It looked like a purple fin of something or other. It was slimy and spongy to the touch. It really didn't look like something one could eat. He wondered if he was being punked, but timidly took a bite.

It had a strange texture too, and a slightly bitter, spicy flavor. But it didn't smell bad, or of much of anything at all. Without asking more about it, he couldn't even tell if it was meat or fish or vegetable.

"How is it, Van? The gobgob?" The tall female ghoul who handed it to him called him by a shortened version of his name.

"It's delicious." Vandal replied without really thinking about it. His issues with communication continued to show themselves in some areas.

"Van, what have you been eating until now? There aren't many ghouls who would call that delicious."

The fact his expression never changed didn't help with expressing his emotions. He wanted to come up with a good response to this golden-eyed ghoul, but there wasn't much from his diet that he could counter with.

"The legs of giant frogs." Those had been the best, apart from blood and his mother's milk and blood.

"Well, there are plenty of delicious monsters and fruit in the demon barrens. You're only 1 year old, don't worry."

The ghoul—who was called Basdia—reached down and patted him on the head. She was Zadilis's youngest daughter and leader of the warriors. She had come back that morning from hunting goblins. She was six feet tall, a beautiful woman who looked in her late 20s with a muscular body but gentle curves. On Earth, she would have been a female athlete or fighter known for a face too pretty to hit.

She also looked a lot like Zadilis. A sister with some years between them, surely—and Zadilis as the younger sister.

"So, humans don't make gobgob," Basdia pondered. "Is everything else in human settlements so nice? That might explain why the adventurers tasted so good."

"No, I think they just don't know how to make it," Vandal replied.

"They don't? Why not? They must have plenty of materials, they hunt them all the time." Basdia said the ingredients could be found everywhere, and were often hunted by adventurers.

Those ingredients were goblins and juice from gobgrass.

Gobgrass was a common weed known as the "goblin of plants." It could spread rapidly anywhere and crushing it produced a purple juice. It wasn't strictly edible, but it also didn't do any direct harm. It was the natural enemy of farmers everywhere, spreading across fields in the blink of an eye and sucking up all the nutrition from the soil. It also tasted horrible, wasn't suited to eating, and couldn't be made into any useful potions. It was simply a weed, multiplying quickly and providing no benefits—hence the connection to goblins and the name "gobgrass."

As for goblins themselves, everyone knew their flesh smelt awful and couldn't be eaten. Same for their blood and internal organs. If Vandal was faced with the choice of goblin blood or crushed bug juice, he would take the latter, no questions asked.

Gobgob was created by cutting goblin flesh into chunks, and then pickling it for a full day in the juice extracted from the gobgrass. That removed the odor from the meat, and while it didn't make it taste good, it at least made it possible to eat. It also preserved it nicely, as gobgob would last for at least a year.

"We survive on gobgob when we have nothing else to eat," Basdia explained.

"It's easier and faster to make than dried meat. I can see it being a useful emergency ration," Vandal said. "But humans simply wouldn't go so far to try to eat goblin." Rather than find ways to make disgusting goblin palatable, humans would just find things other than goblin to eat, and then spend their energy cultivating or rearing those.

"If you say so."

Maybe she understood, and maybe she had given up on understanding. Basdia went back to chopping up and draining the blood from the goblin flesh. She still had ingredients for gobgob from what looked like plenty more goblins.

Basdia was the strongest among the young ghouls, even including the men, but she was still low ranking in the community. In ghoul society, male status was derived from strength, and female status from magical abilities and the number of children they have had. Basdia wasn't good with magic and hadn't had any children yet, so it didn't matter how well she could fight. She wasn't rising up the ranks any time soon.

As he chewed the remaining gobgob, Vandal pondered that certain passionate groups on Earth would be quick to shout "Discrimination!" about this. But since ghouls were treated as monsters in Ramda, he supposed they had less leeway to complain about the basic structure of society.

"I want to have a kid and make something of myself," Basdia said. "Then I won't have to hunt goblins or make gobgob. I'll be able to hunt things that taste better and spend my time on getting stronger rather than on chores."

The low-ranked ghouls did things like keeping the grotto tidy, making everyday goods, and fixing the homes and fence surrounding them. The work of collecting goblin and gobgrass to make gobgob also fell into that category. The exception was making weapons and armor. Ghouls capable of that were respected even if they were weak or hadn't had children.

"So you want to advance in the world and become stronger?" Vandal asked.

"Yes. I like strong people, and I want to be stronger myself," Basdia replied. She looked like a female warrior and had the personality to match. "I have to think of my age as well." Basdia had recently turned 25. The appearance of ghoul women stopped aging at the point they got pregnant, so she was worried about pulling too far ahead of her mother. From Vandal's point of view—looking up at her—Vandal didn't think she had anything to worry about.

"If you were a little older Van, I would have taken your seed," she said.

Vandal gasped.

"What's wrong? You got gobgob stuck in your throat?"

Basdia put down her chopping knife (which looked big enough to chop a cow's head off) and picked Vandal up. She didn't seem particularly embarrassed by anything she had said.

"No, I just don't want you…saying things so provocative in such a cheery tone. You surprised me, that's all." The phrase "taken your seed" would surprise pretty much anyone. But Basdia just tilted her head, unsure of the problem.

"My mother told me that, in the past, when there was a ghoul woman having trouble getting pregnant, they would capture human men alive and then take their seed in exchange for sparing their lives. The seed from other races, such as humans, seems to have a higher probability of causing ghoul pregnancy. The human men were often quite happy to play their part, so I'm told," Basdia explained.

"I bet they were. Especially if the alternative was death."

If a man had to choose between dying or making babies, there was only one choice. Ghouls looked pretty much exactly like human women, apart from the skin color and the eyes. Furthermore . . . .

"Ghoul women are all so attractive." All the ghoul women Vandal had seen since yesterday were beautiful. Any man asked to have sex with them, to save his life or otherwise, would probably shout "Yes!" without any hesitation, unless he were some super-devout follower of Alda. Vandal definitely would, if he had the right equipment.

"Humans think that too? It's nice to hear, but it's too late for me," Basdia said.

"Why?"

"I'm 25. Most adventurers are mankind, and they make fun of women over that age, calling them over-the-hill."

Here in Ramda, medicine was far behind Earth and Origin, meaning average lifespans were shorter. Magic was an alternative, but only those with certain resources had access to medicinal magic. There also weren't many Magicians who used obstetrics- and gynecology-related magic.

Making children was an important issue in this world. Because mechanical technology hadn't yet developed, human labor drove production. People tilled the fields, people made the clothing, people procured the stone to make the houses, and people made the magic items.

That was why humankind tended to get married before 25. It wasn't rare for female adventurers to get married past that, but that was because female adventurers had assets and connections. Many of them also had spouses, for all intents and purposes, even with nothing on paper. Of course, the pregnancy rate on this planet was no lower than on Earth, and women could still get pregnant even into their 40s. But "over the hill" applying to women in their late 20s was a product of that society, pushing women to keep society ticking.

Basdia didn't know these things about human society, and was probably just getting this second hand—or third hand—from another ghoul who overheard some adventurers talking.

"No need to worry. You're very young, Basdia."

Vandal wasn't knowledgeable about human society and customs in this world, and so he did think she was a little overly concerned with age. On Earth he had only lived to high school, and on Origin until 20, so he wouldn't understand the importance of having children or the difficulties caused by differing medical technologies.

"Thank you. That's nice to hear." She smiled, and glowed with beauty. Her skin looked even more lovely as she lifted him up, and if he had been going through puberty then he wouldn't have been able to keep his eyes off her impressive cleavage. Being able to look so beautiful while mainly eating meat had to come from some difference in the physiology of humans and ghouls.

"My mother mentioned that you have some rare magical abilities, Vandal. Maybe you could use those to allow yourself to give me your seed? Use life attribute to make some parts of you grow faster?"

"I don't think that's going to happen."

It sounded like Basdia was more hung up on this than Vandal had expected. He wondered if he should keep a few men alive from among the next batch of bandits or adventurers, but ultimately that question was no less tricky to answer.

"I see. I'm sorry my daughter put you on the spot like that." Zadilis gave Vandal a small bow in apology.

They were in her house and Vandal was explaining the earlier discussion. Zadilis was also very interested in her daughter becoming pregnant.

"It's going to be at least ten years before you can perform any such duties," Zadilis said. "She isn't going to wait that long. I might be rushing her myself because I want to see my first grandchild! I'm surprised you understood the meaning of her 'seed' talk, anyway."

"I'm full of surprises," Vandal quipped. A normal 1 year old wouldn't have a clue what they were talking about. Vandal tried to play down that slip on his part. Zadilis, Vigaro, and Basdia were all very nice to him, but that didn't mean he was ready to tell them about his freaky past lives.

"When you say 'first grandchild,' does that mean…no, I get it." Vandal gave a shrug at the sounds of lovemaking coming from some of the other holes. Those "houses" only had leaves and sticks for a roof.

The sounds came from the ghouls living in the settlement. It seemed that the ghouls had no concept of marriage, and generally slept around. This was because the ghouls lived in the dangerous demon barrens and because they would keep on aging if they didn't get pregnant. Because of their long lifespans it was a lot harder for them to get pregnant than other races. They wouldn't be able to keep the settlement going if they restricted themselves to a single partner. Vandal presumed those were also the reasons why Basdia's child would be Zadilis's "first" grandchild. Zadilis also had two sons, but there was no DNA testing in this world to work out if they had fathered any children of their own. During the celebrations, he hadn't been introduced to anyone's husband, wife, grandchildren, or grandparents.

"It looks like you get it," Zadilis said. "But I do know who Basdia's father is."

"You do? Who?"

"Vigaro."

Basdia was 25, meaning Zadilis had given birth to her at the age of 265. That put her into old age for a ghoul, normally without the strength or inclination for childbearing. However, the ghouls had been celebrating a victory over some kobolts, and cracked out some wine they had stolen from humans.

"That wine was far stronger that the stuff we brew ourselves. I got sloshed and woke up in his bed the next morning."

"I see."

Hardly the most romantic of tales.

"You need to watch out for the drink, boy. Swallow it down, but don't let it swallow you, hah! Now, shall we look at some magic?"

Zadilis was old, but she was still a Ghoul Mage. She couldn't use death attribute magic, of course, but her knowledge would be very useful for Vandal. While Zadilis trained Vandal, the ghoul warriors were training Skeleton, Saria, and Rita. Sam and the other undead did what they could to help out around the settlement. Aiding with hunting demon barren monsters would provide them with experience and promote further growth.

This was Vandal's first time learning from someone else since his fateful school trip.

Name: Vigaro
Rank: 5
Race: Ghoul Barbarian
Level: 78
Job: None
Job Level: 100
Job History: None
Age: 167
—Passive Skills
[Night Vision] [Brute Strength: Level 4]
[Resist Pain: Level 4] [Paralytic Venom (Claws): Level 1]
—Active Skills
[Axe Proficiency: Level 4] [Brawling Proficiency: Level 2]
[Command: Level 3] [Cooperation: Level 2]

Name: Basdia
Rank: 4
Race: Ghoul Warrior
Level: 17
Job: None
Job Level: 100
Job History: None
Age: 25
—Passive Skills

[Night Vision] [Brute Strength: Level 2]

[Resist Pain: Level 2] [Paralytic Venom (Claws): Level 3]

—Active Skills

[Axe Proficiency: Level 2] [Shield Proficiency: Level 1] [Bow Proficiency: Level 2]

[Thrown Projectile Proficiency: Level 1] [Sneaking Steps: Level 1] [Cooperation: Level 1]

—Maladies

[Infertile]

"Can you start by telling me about the magic and skills that you know, boy? If you don't want to share everything, no need," Zadilis said.

"No, I trust you. And I can think of at least 100 people who are going to know all this at some point."

Having accepted her offer to teach him, Vandal needed to share with her all of the magic and skills that he had. That would enable him to get instruction and aid from her based on her knowledge and experience.

However, that would also mean that Zadilis would receive information about death attribute magic. Even if she didn't, though, it wasn't normal for adventurers or even monsters to casually share information on their own skills. It was equivalent to sharing your weaknesses. But for that reason, sharing them with someone more trusted wasn't uncommon. Adventurers couldn't form an effective party or work together well if they didn't know what each other could do. Vandal wasn't sure about monsters, but presumed the same practice applied.

And while it wouldn't probably happen until decades later, everyone to be reborn here from Origin were going to come in with the knowledge of Vandal's death attribute magic. Even if Rodocolte didn't warn them in advance, by some miracle, there had to have been documents left in the lab, and magic items created using Vandal's death attribute magic had already dispersed into multiple nations in Origin. At the time, they had been falsely distributed not as death magic, but as a proprietary offshoot of life attribute magic, but the ship would have sailed on that lie by now. After Vandal's death on Origin, Hiroto Amemiya and the others would have easily found out about death magic. Them somehow not discovering it was more unlikely.

So Vandal couldn't think of a reason to keep it from someone like Zadilis, someone he trusted.

"One hundred people? Well, let's stick to your magic for now, boy."

At that point, Zadilis also thought Vandal's magic was some kind of unique life attribute magic. Life magic and undead might seem completely opposed, but in Ramda, life Magicians created undead. They forced vitality back into a corpse, turning it into an artificial lifeform. The process had a lot of issues, and the resulting undead were nothing compared to the undead that appeared in the demon barrens or dungeons. Zadilis had thought he had simply overcome these issues with some new technique, and so she was stunned when he explained about death magic.

"Death? Death attribute? A new…a ninth attribute? Is that even a thing? No, of course it is. You have the undead following you, and you've used magic I've never seen before."

On Origin, death attribute magic was the eighth type of magic, but Ramda also has the time attribute, making death the ninth here.

"Kinda surprising, huh?" Vandal ventured.

"Of course I'm surprised! Any monster aware of the value of a new attribute would be!"

Magic enabled monsters to survive. It was a means for them to force their way to the top of this survival-of-the-fittest society. Unknown magic meant no one knew how to deal with it, providing all sorts of potential to wipe out adversaries with the element of surprise.

Ramda was the same as Origin in that you could only learn attribute magic for which you had an affinity. That applied to monsters too, so every single monster wasn't going to jump at the chance of a new attribute, but those with "mage" in their name were definitely going to try to steal it.

"Interesting. So that adventurer Magician couldn't get his own magic off because of death attribute magic."

Zadilis recalled the deaths of the adventurers who had attacked her—especially how the Magician had died—and gave a shudder. As a Ghoul Mage, she could imagine the terror of having her magic taken away. It was like a swordsman losing both arms and being told to fight. Putting it that way, Vandal almost felt (retroactively) bad for them.

"My affinity is with light and wind attributes," she said, "so I won't be able to use death attribute magic directly for myself, but I might be able to apply it. That's how magic works."

Fire attribute and water attribute might appear complete opposites. But the essence of fire is the control of heat, and the essence of water is the control of liquids and cold. That meant a master fire attribute Magician could use heat to burn things, but also draw heat away to freeze them, and a water master had complete control of molten magma. Other attribute users could control mercury or magma as well, and wind attribute users could even extract flammable elements from the air to cause massive explosions.

"I read that in a book the elder showed me when I was a child." Zadilis had obtained this information from prizes taken from adventurers. The only way for monsters to get books was to steal then from humans or other monsters. "The point is that the number of attributes you have affinity with isn't important. It's how well you can master the ones you have. Of course, being able to use multiple attributes is more convenient. But an adventurer who can use multiple attributes a little can be defeated by a Goblin Mage that only uses fire."

"I like the sound of that," Vandal said. On Origin, the researchers had slated him as having nothing but the death attribute magic and a massive pool of magical power, so the teachings of Zadilis were a fresh joy for Vandal. He was even moved to hear this.

His expression still didn't change, of course.

"This technique requires magical power. The more MP you have, the longer you can train for. How much magical power do you have, boy? I can make adjustments based on that."

"Okay. I have around 100 million."

"I see, 100 million…hold on?!"

Zadilis looked shocked all over again. It was a cute expression on her, more suited to the age she looked.

"One hundred million? Are you sure? I don't even have 10,000 myself! But I guess, with your unknown attribute magic too…it's not impossible."

Zadilis was definitely taken aback by the massive number Vandal had professed to possessing. Normally she might laugh it off as a crude lie, so easy to see through, but she knew that the child in front of her made a good argument for why that wasn't the case.

There was no reason for Vandal to lie so poorly anyway. Even if he wanted to brag and inflate his number a little, there was no reason to go so high. This was magic training, too, meaning any lies would quickly be exposed.

"Well, okay. We'll get to the bottom of that soon enough." Zadilis managed to swallow her surprise.

Vandal, for his part, received confirmation from her reaction that 100 million MP was considered out of the ordinary. He'd have to keep it to himself when he went into human society, at least until he registered with the guild.

"What about magic-related skills?" she asked.

"I have Skip Incantation," Vandal said. "I'm guessing Golem Creation counts as a magic-related skill too?"

"Boy, are you looking to surprise me into an early grave? How did you learn Skip Incantation? You should be teaching me that. And I've never even heard of Golem Creation!"

Dalshia had told Vandal how rare Skip Incantation was, but having the nearly 300-year-old Zadilis react with such surprise really brought the point home. In regard to Golem Creation, Zadilis had learned Alchemy, and so Vandal had expected her to know about that one. Knowledge from Earth led him to assume that golems were something created via Alchemy.

"I mean, for training with Skip Incantation, all you need to do is use a lot of magic in a situation where you can't incant it," Vandal said simply.

"Easy for you to say, MP-monster baby," Zadilis replied. Achieving the same effect as normal magic without incanting required tens if not hundreds of times the magical power. Maybe a Magician could try it once a day. Vandal had picked up the skill because he had the magic to burn. It was normally only certain geniuses, Magicians who had mastered magical jobs, and legendary monsters that obtained the Skip Incantation skill. "I'm not sure there's anything I can teach you. Your non-attribute magic and Magic Control must be perfect too."

Now it was Vandal's turn to react with surprise.

"Non-attribute magic? What's that?"

"You don't know? That's one of the basics of magic!"

In the end, Zadilis was surprised yet again. Non-attribute magic was magic that used magical power prior to changing into attribute magic. Anyone could use magical power that wasn't imbued with attributes, so Magicians started out by learning non-attribute magic in order to pick up the basics of magical control. Non-attribute magic was less effective than other kinds, and more simplistic, but it was also versatile.

"I live in the demon barrens and I know all about it!" Zadilis exclaimed.

"I taught myself everything, up until now."

More than that, non-element magic hadn't existed in Origin. Either that, or the lab staff kept it from him on purpose. The latter sounded far more likely, but there was no way to determine the truth now. Once Hiroto and the others showed up, he might have a chance to ask. The researchers, at least, had never said anything about non-attribute magic around Vandal. The spirits might have known about it, but they had rarely offered anything other than answers to Vandal's questions. Their personalities might have been maintained by supplying them with MP, like Vandal was doing for Dalshia. Regardless, he hadn't been able to use his power freely on Origin.

Dalshia, it turned out, had known about non-attribute magic. When Vandal asked her about it later, she had thought it was so fundamental that she didn't need to teach it to her.

You could already use magic without me teaching you anything, so I thought you knew about it, Dalshia said.

"Okay," said Zadilis. "I'll start by teaching you non-attribute magic. It took me three years to pick up the skill, but I bet it won't even take you a year. You can train all day long, after all."

The ghoul warrior Vigaro looked down at the grasses at his feet. Spring was coming.

The ghouls didn't have a calendar and didn't conduct sys-temized agriculture, so the seasons didn't mean so much to them. The damp and wet rainy season, the heat of summer, the cool and fruity fall, and then the cold and crisp winter. Once it got warm, more nameless plants started to bloom again.

"It been close half year since you show up," Vigaro com-mented to Vandal, who was clinging to his back like a baby monkey to its mother. The infant spent most of his time in training with Zadilis in the settlement or making walnut sauce with the women, so he didn't normally join in the hunting. But today he came along for a change of pace.

The half year since Vandal arrived didn't represent a mas-sive chunk of time, compared to how long Vigaro had been alive already. But that short span had brought many changes to the settlement, which had been relatively unchanged for 100 years.

"It's been that long already?" Vandal was clinging on with strength beyond what one would expect from his baby body.

The ghouls had done so much for him. The least he could do, for example, was to use death attribute magic to preserve their food. He used good old Maintain Freshness, and now the meat that even a sturdy ghoul stomach hadn't been able to handle after a few days, depending on the season, would last for months. In the past, the only preserved food they had access to was gobgob and sun-dried meat when the weather was nice, so this change had seriously enriched their lives. Now the ghouls didn't have to go hunting every single day, increasing their time for training, and reducing the number of hunting-related injuries.

Ghouls could be a lazy species, so this leeway had led some of them to start slacking off. But with Zadilis and her constant reminders about the importance of building strength daily, and Vigaro who understood what it took to win battles, the problem wasn't too severe.

"Yeah. Thanks you, we get delicious meat all days."

Vandal was also applying Mature magic to the meat right before it was cooked each day. That allowed the entire settlement of pit-dwelling ghouls to enjoy the kind of mature meat it would have taken weeks to prepare in a carefully curated space back on Earth. The ghouls just loved it, of course.

"I eat it too, so don't worry about it," Vandal replied.

"Delicious meat making stronger. I stronger than before! Big help, you big help us." Vigaro reached around with one long arm and rubbed Vandal on the head and back.

Vandal's expression didn't change, but he gave some small shudders. He wasn't angry—indeed, he was laughing at being tickled, in his own way. The two of them were close enough now for each to understand the other that well.

Vigaro wasn't the only one he had become friendly with, and many of the ghouls were hoping that Vandal would change his plans to leave once spring arrived. If he had been an adult, they might have tried to keep him with the offer of women, but that wasn't going to work for an infant who wasn't even 2 years old.

"What about Basdia? You like, right?"

"She does have an incredibly beautiful, muscular body, but your lats are nothing to sniff at either, Vigaro," Vandal replied.

Vigaro shook his head. Vigaro gave it a shot, but he was getting nothing from the under 2s.

Still, it was taking a while for Zadilis to impart all of her knowledge, and so hopefully he would stay until summer. Vigaro liked Vandal, so he wanted the training to go well, but at the same time he also wanted Vandal to stay in the village for as long as possible. It was a complicated feeling.

As he struggled with such feelings, his students were tackling the hunt of a powerful prey.

"Raaaaaaaah!" they bellowed.

"The one with bow—no, one with staff first!" he shouted from the sidelines, amid the snarling and howling. The young warriors under Vigaro's tutelage were fighting a pack of enemies, monsters, not adventurers. Adventurers attacked Vigaro and the ghouls much less than he had been expecting, and indeed, adventurers hardly came to the demon barrens at all.

When their Elder Zadilis had been younger, adventurers wiped out two thirds of the settlement, and so they had kept out of adventurers' way as much as possible since then. If they found some, they hid, and only fought back if they were attacked first. The ghouls knew how delicious adventurers were, and about the booty they carried with them, but they also understood who terrifying they could be. Vandal didn't know how other ghouls handled things, of course.

Vigaro and the ghouls didn't know this, but the reason not many adventurers came to this demon barren was related to its location. The size of the demon barrens and the monsters that appeared made them perfect for grade D and C adventurers, but the nearest human town was three days away, the town of Valcheburg. Furthermore, there was a demon barren of pretty much the same type only a few hours away from there, and multiple dungeons too. That meant adventurers naturally gravitated toward the demon barrens that were close to the town and had dungeons. Of course, allowing the demon barrens to overflow with monsters could cause problems down the line, but the adventurers' guild had determined there was little risk of that.

That was because there were many demi-human-type monsters living in this demon barren—races like goblins, kobolts, orcs, and ghouls that made their own settlements and the whittled each other's numbers down by fighting amongst themselves. No adventurers needed. So the guild decided they didn't need to bother with the place all that often. Leaving it completely unchecked would be a different problem, so they did send scouting parties out every now and then. Apart from that, the only adventurers coming over were those who thought they might be able to get a particularly big haul, and those with specific goals such as the group who targeted Zadilis. All of these factors meant the ghouls maybe encountered adventurers once a year.

So at the time, Vigaro's students weren't fighting humans, but kobolts.

"Raaaagh!"

"Awoooo!"

These snarling monsters were slightly smaller than humans, and looked like dogs standing upright. They were about as strong as humans, maybe a little weaker, but they had keen agility to compensate and were good at fighting in a pack, making them much smarter than goblins. Kobolts averaged rank 2, and had higher classes including Kobolt Chief, Kobolt Geronimo, Kobolt Mage, and Kobolt King.

The students were fighting thirty regular kobolts, armed with short swords and bows, five rank 3 Kobolt Chiefs, armed with larger swords and spears and wearing armor, and a rank 4 Kobolt Mage armed with a staff. Vigaro had thirteen students plus some boney undead in the battle. This put them at a distinct disadvantage in terms of numbers, but ghouls were rank 3 monsters. They could win on quality, not quantity.

That was the plan, anyway. The fact they were losing ground suggested they hadn't been ready for this.

"With you still around, it be nice to stock up on meat today," Vigaro ventured.

"How do kobolts taste? Any good?"

They had dog-like heads, so from Vandal's point of view they didn't look all that delicious. People apparently used to eat dog in Japan, but long before Vandal was born.

"The meat tough and bad. Not goblin bad, but bad. But cook it certain way and it taste good."

So it was bad, but just like gobgob the ghouls had invented a way to make it edible. That seemed necessary to survive here in the demon barrens, with so many demi-human monsters around.

"They giving more trouble than expected. Should be fine, but trouble."

Ghouls had low birthrates and so they couldn't afford to casually lose members of the tribe. Vigaro would join the fighting if needed, but he still believed his students would prevail through the hardship. They already had some helpers down there with them, after all.

Halberd Technique Flicker Flash!

The halberd blade slashed through the air, taking off the head of a kobolt directly in front and the head of one standing to its side.

Sis, I'll handle the right! Naginata Technique Two Tier Thrust!

Another kobolt tried to circle around from the right, and got a glaive rammed into its throat and then solar plexus, ending up with the blade jutting from its back.

There are a lot of them, and they're quick too. Stand firm, everyone! We'll handle the frontlines! Make sure they don't circle around!

It was the Living One-Piece Swimsuit Armor Saria and the Living Bikini Armor Rita. As a result of their training for six months with Vigaro and the other ghouls, they had learned some skills, although still level 1, as well as some battle techs. Battle techs allowed frontline fighters to imbue their weapons with magical power, making them a higher class of technique compared to normal attacks. Once mastered, they could allow a user to perform dozens of thrusts in an instant, or turn a lump of steel into scrap with a rusty old sword.

At level 1, battle techs were slightly less insane—the powerful horizontal slice called Flicker Flash and the double-striking Two Tier Thrust, for example. But the two of them were proving that even beginner battle techs could work wonders in combat.

Leveling up had also allowed them to start talking. This had pleased not only Sam and Vandal, but also Vigaro and the ghouls. The two armors didn't even have faces, and so communication with them had been difficult up until that point.

"Grooooooagh!"

"Awooooooo!"

Then there was Bone Monkey, Bone Wolf, and Bone Bear, who had ranked up from rank 3 Bone Beasts to rank 4 Rotten Beasts. The regular kobolts couldn't hope to match their level, and for this battle they were watching from students training from the rear. Sometimes they would fire off a poison breath attack, making the kobolts roar and growl but keeping them in their place.

I am lucky indeed to see the growth of my children even after my death. Sam was there too, watching the battle with them and Bone Bird. The bird had done some recon already, and Sam would go into action once the fighting was finished.

The tide was finally turning in the ghoul's favor.

In the bushes on the opposite side from Vigaro, Kobolt King Gyahn growled as he watched the battle alongside his underlings.

In the last six months, he had managed to grow his pack in strength to a point even beyond that of when the central orcs had defeated them. Kobolts bred quickly, even if not as quickly as goblins. Children could be ready to join the fight in just six months.

Gyahn had also used his ascension to Kobolt King to absorb the other kobolt packs in the vicinity. Monsters with the "King" title possessed powerful charisma among other monsters of the same race, and he had the Enhance Brethren skill that provided boons for every other monster in his pack. All Gyahn had to do was show up, show himself off, and other kobolts would fall in line to join with him.

But he wasn't done yet. The pack still wasn't strong enough for kobolts to take over the jungle demon barren for themselves. The orcs holding the center were also a race that could propagate quickly. They only had one child at a time, but Gyahn still knew they were behind them in terms of power.

Gyahn vowed to wipe away the stale taste of defeat and drag them down from the throne they sat on. In order to do that, Gyahn needed ghoul females. He was going to attack the Ghoul Grotto, home of their fated foes for generations, and get his doggy paws on as many ghoul females as he could. Then he would have them give birth to kobolt children.

Ghoul females, like other humanoid races, were fertile when it came to being impregnated by demi-humans, including kobolts, while also being far tougher than most other races. They were strong, and many could use magic, meaning it would be hard to keep them alive and subdued, but the rewards would most definitely be worth it.

That was why, when Gyahn found these young ghouls out

here training, he had put together a party of his own young kobolts and sent them in to attack.

But they were a decoy.

When they got these unexperienced ghoul warriors on the ropes, the more powerful ghouls watching in the back would have to intervene. That was when Gyahn and his elites would enter the fray. Once the ghoul warriors had been wiped out, the kobolts would attack the Ghoul Grotto. The females might be able to use magic, but they wouldn't even have the time without the males to stand in front of them.

That was the plan.

But at this rate, the decoy party was going to get wiped out before the ghoul elites made a move. That's the way it was starting to look to Gyahn.

A Kobolt Mage, formerly the leader of a different pack, let out some yips and barks, stating they should have started with a smaller group of ghouls after all. Gyahn gave him a glare and a snarl in reply, shutting him up.

Unlike kobolts and goblins, ghoul settlements would band together in the face of adversity. If they had attacked with a smaller group, they would have faced a counterattack from a large and powerful force of united ghouls. By then, Gyahn's pack would also be busy having to feed the babies born from the ghoul women that they did manage to capture. They wouldn't be having any more children if they were dead, and the children wouldn't become warriors either. That wasn't the kind of situation in which they could drive off a bunch of ghouls. Even if they won, they would probably lose half of their newfound strength.

So they needed to attack the largest settlement first. That would allow them to secure the number of females they needed, while also significantly reducing the number of ghouls who could organize against them. Even as Gyahn was annoyed with this underling for not seeing all of this, not seeing the big picture, the decoy kobolts were getting ripped apart.

It wasn't that the young kobolts he had sent on this mission were completely worthless. Rather, there were some strange non-ghouls mixed in among the normal ones. The Kobolt Generals were tilting their heads and growing in puzzlement, and Gyahn started to feel the same way.

First, he saw two sets of walking armor, one with a halberd and one with a glaive. From the shape, they looked like armor for a human or ghoul female, but no one was actually wearing them. Yet the armor was there, fighting on the frontlines.

Gyahn had no idea what to make of it. He had ranked up to Kobolt King, getting a boost to his stats and his intellect, but he hadn't learned anything that might prepare him for this. He could have had the Kobolt Mage use non-attribute Appraisal magic, but that could give away their position.

Then, there were the undead bringing up the rear, intermittently spitting venomous poison breath. The carriage back there might be something they had stolen from adventurers, but his kobolt brain couldn't work out why ghouls had undead working with them. Maybe the ghouls had a Tamer among their ranks, although he wasn't sure undead could be tamed. Gyahn had found undead—mainly skeletons—a couple of times, when defending the pack's nest, and he had found them to be very different from other monsters. They didn't care about their own fallen, and just continued to attack until they couldn't move any longer. He couldn't see any other monster managing to tame them.

Did that mean the ghouls had a Tamer who could do the impossible? A Tamer Gyahn couldn't conceive of? Or were the undead magical items, like the armor that fought on its own, similar to golems that just followed orders?

They were here, anyway. That was the problem. They provided unexpected and powerful resistance to Gyahn's forces. Maybe something was going on among the ghouls, something like Gyahn's own emergence as king. There might even be other, even more powerful enemies waiting among them.

He considered abandoning the decoys and withdrawing. He had comprised the force of the young ones because they could be replaced in six months. They were expendable, unlike the other elites he had with him.

It was the presence of those elites, however, that erased the weakness from Gyahn's brain. Elites. It was right there in the name. They weren't going to lose to these foolish ghouls.

Gyahn didn't have time to back down anyway. Even now, the orcs who had beaten them once were rebuilding their strength, capturing more slaves, having more children. There was no telling when they might attack. He couldn't back down now and lose this chance to expand. They didn't have six months to waste.

With a wolf's long, wild howl, Gyahn burst from the bushes with the other elites.

"Awoooooo!"

Sensing that their forces were starting to lose ground, the Kobolt Mage started to incant magic in the kobolt language. The spell created a flaming spear in front of the Kobolt Mage. Attacks across a wider area, like fireballs, would also hit his allies. Choosing a powerful spell that could attack single targets spoke to his intelligence as a mage.

The flaming lance launched, burning the very air. The target was one of the living armors swinging around that massive weapon. The fire lance weaved between the allied kobolts, closing in with one of the living armors. Rita swung her glaive down toward the fire lance.

Not today!

The fire lance blew apart, scattering clumps of fire outward. No normal weapon could cut down magic, no matter how big and heavy it was. But Rita's glaive was a magic item obtained from a treasure chest in a previously unexplored dungeon. It was more than capable of cutting apart and scattering magic on the level of a flaming lance.

It was better than taking the full force of the attack, but the tactic did still scatter fire everywhere. Luckily, the Bikini Armor that Rita had possessed was also resistant to fire. Furthermore, her body was nothing but the armor, meaning she really had nothing that could get burnt.

The kobolts that had been engaging her yelped as the fire hit them, while Rita herself was unharmed—completely the opposite of what the Kobolt Mage had intended.

"Hiyaaaah!"

Rita swung the glaive again, scattering the burnt kobolts in front of her and stamping down into enemy territory. Saria and the ghouls rushed in behind her to exploit this new opening.

Two of the Kobolt Chiefs growled, standing in Rita's way. They had weapons, armor, and shields made from insectoid monsters.

Rita swung her glaive downward toward one of them. The Kobolt Chief managed to catch the weapon on his shield. His doggy face twisted into a smile. Having blocked her blow, the plan had surely been for the other Kobolt Chief to then attack Rita.

"Flicker Flash!"

But the horizontal halberd slice unleashed by Saria, coming up close behind Rita, put an end to that by slicing the Kobolt Chief in half with a single stroke.

Of course, if Rita had been a normal living creature, then she would have paid the price for her sister's surprise attack. But Rita was Living Bikini Armor. The space all her squishy organs would normally have occupied was just a vacant, empty space.

Seeing his ally cut in half so brutally—a monster the same rank and type as him—the other Kobolt Chief understandably froze.

"Yah!"

"Die!"

The sisters didn't stop their attack, Rita swinging her glaive and Saria her halberd. The kobolt took the glaive on its shield while also managing to avoid the incoming tip of the weapon. He was a chief, after all.

But throw in the claws of the growling ghouls, and the Kobolt Chief was finally overwhelmed. It joined its friend with a howl.

"Gyaaaaaaaa!"

That accounted for half of the four Kobolt Chiefs. The Kobolt Mage gave a howl. The other kobolts still alive on the frontline also lowered their ears, eyes watering with fear.

It looked like they were just going to break and run. That's what Vigaro thought, watching the battle unfold.

"*Awoooooooo!*"

A new howl sounded. A howl that rang out with strength and authority on a completely different level from every other kobolt so far. The eyes of the remaining kobolts started to glow again when they heard it, and their ears perked back up.

What was that howl?

Not reinforcements?

Rita, Saria, and the ghouls, meanwhile, where shaken by this new development. They reflexively stopped attacking and looked around for new enemies. Vigaro thought things looked bad too, and prepared to give a shout to bring his students back toward him.

"Ah. They're coming this way," Vandal said.

The elite kobolts, led by Gyahn, came rushing toward Vigaro and the others, howling and roaring. The incoming charge of a Kobolt Rider, from atop an Imperial Bull with horns like deadly spears, charged straight at Vigaro.

"They come for us?" Vigaro shouted.

He grabbed the Imperial Bull by the horns and bit into the neck of the Kobolt Rider clinging to its back. The sharp fangs growing in that grey-black lion head tore half the kobolt's neck out.

"Warriors! They bring more meat to our table! Finish them!"

Vigaro then twisted his hands to break the Imperial Bull's neck, the smell of blood and rage turning the rest of the ghouls' hesitation into determination.

"Interesting. It can take a single word from a commander to instill terror or calm the troops down," Vandal analyzed.

"You calmest here," Vigaro replied.

Vandal was still clinging to his back, and chuckled wryly. Vigaro had only managed to defeat the Kobolt Rider and Imperial Bull so easily because Vandal had spotted the incoming threat.

"Oh, I still have a way to go." Vandal had noticed the incoming kobolts ahead of everyone else because of his Detect Danger: Death technique that he always had active, but normally it would have pinged even earlier. His location on the back of the mighty Vigaro really raised the bar for what could potentially kill him.

But now, danger surrounded him on all sides.

"Graaaaa!"

"Gyaaaa!"

About thirty kobolts rushed in as reinforcements, clearly stronger than the enemies Saria and the others had fought until now. There wasn't a single regular rank 2 kobolt. They were at least rank 3, including Kobolt Chiefs and Kobolt Warriors, and then Kobolt Riders atop things like massive wolves and bears. There was also a Kobolt Knight with a big shield, a Kobolt Mage with a staff, a Kobolt Berserker twice the size of a normal kobolt and swinging a club taller than it was, and a Kobolt Grappler who, at a glance, didn't look like a kobolt at all. Some of these elites were rare even among rank 4 kobolts.

Gyahn was on the very frontline, growling. He was almost man-sized, and had a head like a wolf's. Vigaro and Vandal couldn't use Appraisal magic, but they knew this was even more powerful than the other rank 4 kobolts.

"Strong foe. We get hurt! Someone, take Vandal..." Vigaro started.

"No, I'm fine. I'll support you with magic."

Vigaro was confused for a moment by Vandal's offer. He knew that the baby could already use magic, and had vast magical power over 100 million, a number Vigaro couldn't even conceive of. But he also knew that he couldn't use magic capable of directly attacking, like Zadilis. The only magic of Vandal's that Vigaro really knew about was his ability to preserve meat and make it taste better. That said, it might already have been too late to get him to anywhere safer than his current location.

"Hang on tight! Ghouuul!"

Vigaro charged at the boss kobolt with Vandal still on his back,

The dog howled and Vigaro roared back. "Whip Axe!"

Gyahn's axe and Vigaro's axe clashed together. Both of them used battle tech attacks, and both seemed about the same strength, meaning neither could get the upper hand over the other. Then Gyahn and Vigaro started fighting in earnest.

We need to defeat these fiends and aid the young master! Saria, who considered herself to be Vandal's maid, was looking over at Vandal clinging to Vigaro's back. If she had a face to look panicked, it would have, but instead she could only shout and swing her halberd around, the kobolts desperately avoiding her attacks.

I know, sis, but these are stronger than the others!

Rita was launching her own attack on a Kobolt Chief, but it wasn't working like before. The kobolts had been on the back foot before, but now they were fighting boldly. They were using all their might to hold the undead off until Gyahn and the other kobolts finished off Vigaro and the ghouls.

The Enhance Brethren skill of Kobolt King Gyahn boosted the abilities of the other kobolts, strengthening them. But with fewer than 1,000 kobolts under his command, Gyahn's Enhance Brethren was only level 1. Its effects as a boost were not especially powerful. Still, monsters also had absolute loyalty to their king. That gave them incredibly high morale, more than enough to put Saria and the others on the ropes, with their own lack of combat experience. But there were limits to even that loyalty—mortal limits.

"Groooooagh!"

Bone Wolf, Bone Monkey, and Bone Bear, who had been doing little up until that point, finally got fully involved. They rammed into the kobolts, sending them flying, and then unleashed their poisonous breath at close range. The kobolts didn't even have time to scream. They just started dying.

And it wasn't like all of their allies were out of the match, either.

Bone Bird squawked, soaring into the air as Sam started to spin his wheels and speed toward Gyahn. *This is hardy the time to be sitting on the sidelines!*

The enemy might have noticed Bone Bird, but Sam had looked like nothing more than a wagon, and one of the Kobolt Chiefs was quickly run down and killed, crushed into the ground with a whimpering scream.

Too dangerous to just charge in there, though! Sam might have skillful control of the carriage, but this was a jungle demon barren—he hardly had any room to maneuverer at all. He also had to be careful of hitting not just enemies but also allies.

Bone Bird screeched as it freely flew above the trees, attacking the Kobolt Mage at the back and the enemies isolated from the chaos with spirit feather missiles. It used the trees around it to block any attempts at counterattack, and was putting up a good fight.

If only I could fly too, Sam commented. It didn't look like he would be feeling powerless for too long, however.

Vigaro and the ghouls were on the receiving end of a surprise attack by a powerful foe, and yet the efforts of the kobolts were running off them like water off a duck's back. But regardless of skill, the kobolts had far superior numbers. Anyone considering this rationally would have thought the ghouls would be in trouble.

If they didn't take Vandal into account.

First, there was the Kobolt Berserker. Faced with the risks of injuring his own allies, he had moved apart from them and rushed in alone.

"Rise, rise, rise, rise!"

Vandal saw the Berserker charging from Vigaro's back and started turning the ground directly in front of him into earth golems and moving them away.

"Rooooooaaa!"

That naturally left massive potholes everywhere. The Berserker quickly lost his footing and took a serious tumble.

"Cover him! Rise, rise, rise!" Vandal had more golems pile down on top of the Berserker, before he could get up again.

The powerful kobolt still looked like it might escape for a moment, so Vandal created more earth golems and piled those on too, burying the kobolt alive under a mountain.

"One down."

"Cowardly. Nasty," Vigaro commented.

Even the other ghouls looked a bit shocked at these tactics, but that took care of one of their most dangerous enemies. The other kobolts were whimpering and howling, too. Seeing their Berserker laid low so easily and nastily had a big effect on them. All they knew was that the earth suddenly came alive and buried the guy. They couldn't concentrate on the ghouls in front of them, now the very earth might rise up to smother them.

Gyahn, their king, gave a fierce howl, ordering them to stand firm and kill the magician. That snapped them back to the battle, a little, but their movements were still more sluggish than before.

Vigaro laughed diabolically. "Doggies in trouble!"

Gyahn was still locked in combat with Vigaro, so the kobolt didn't have time to think his way out of this one. There was no way the ground could just start moving around, and the kobolts were the ones who launched this attack, so the ghouls couldn't have prepared those pits in advance. He understood that this had to be the work of a magician, but he had no idea where the magic was coming from.

If someone was spell casting, they should have been able to hear the incantations. Even with all the swords clashing off each other and shouting of the battlefield, someone standing still and incanting magic would stick out like a sore thumb. And there wasn't anyone who looked like a magician among the ghouls, anyway.

Vandal, meanwhile—the very magician Gyahn and his goons were looking for—was having trouble closer to home.

I'm getting shaken about more than I expected! I can barely hold on! His arms were nearing their limits, clinging to Vigaro's back while he bucked like a bronco. Vandal could only remain in place for maybe a few more minutes. His Limit Break skill was already in effect, and he couldn't possibly ram his nails into Vigaro's back. *We need to settle this quickly.* If he fell from Vigaro's back into this chaos, then his small body would get trampled. A growing urgency of the danger of the situation pressing into him, Vandal executed death magic spells one after another.

The kobolts yelped out and wailed as Vandal started by unleashing a Magic Absorption Barrier at the staff-wielding Kobolt Mages. That removed the threat of their magic, the black mist weaving between their allies to surround them, further confusing them when their spells stopped triggering despite their incantations. That took the two Kobolt Mages out of the battle.

Then, he applied Absorb Energy defense buff magic to every ghoul, meaning even if they got hit, the kobolts would only be able to do minor damage. The ghouls immediately started to comment that the attacks didn't hurt anymore.

There were many ghouls, so this took a while. Vandal had Skip Incantation, but that didn't mean he could activate multiple spells at the same time. After making sure everyone got Absorb Energy, he didn't have the leeway to also provide Lethality Enhancement, which would have made the ghouls' own weapons more effective.

"Protect Vandal! Push back!"

The kobolts yipped and cried out. Simply enhancing the ghouls' defenses made a massive change to the battle. The kobolts had come into this with the element of surprise, but now their Berserker had been buried alive without doing anything, and the magic of their Mages had been sealed away.

Bone Bird continued to rain down feathers from above. The Mages should have been the ones to deal with that problem, too, but they were indisposed. That left the Kobolt Archers to try and take down Bone Bird rather than pick off ground targets.

The king Gyahn was still alive, but Vigaro was fighting him to a standstill, completely pinning him down.

Meanwhile, the ghouls were recovering steadily from the surprise attack. They had been backpedaling for a few moments, but Vandal's magic allowed them to step forward again.

Young Master! One more push!

Saria and the rest of Vandal's undead had nearly wiped out the original decoy kobolts. The kobolts' morale was still high, but that didn't stop them from being taken out one by one. Once the undead rejoined the ghouls, they would be able to overwhelm the remaining elites. The issue was that Vandal's arms weren't going to last that long.

I need to speed this up!

In a strange twist, both Gyahn and Vandal were thinking the exact same thing. Maybe that moment of connection was why Gyahn happened to notice the odd-colored eyes peering at him from over Vigaro's shoulder.

The kobolt yelped in surprise. He had seen Vandal's white hair numerous times during the exchange so far, but what thought it was just Vigaro's own white locks—that this ghoul was older than he looked, and some of his hair had turned white.

This ghoul has some kind of creature leeching from it? A mutant? Some kind of strange variant? Gyahn was so stunned, his focus slipped for a moment.

Vigaro wasn't one to let such an opening get away.

"Rock Splitter!"

Vigaro triggered his own battle tech, swinging his mighty axe down with—aptly enough—the force to split a rock. Gyahn's shoulder plate cracked, with blood splashing onto Vigaro's face as the kobolt screamed in pain.

While he had left himself open for a moment, Gyahn was not so weak a foe that one such error would end the battle. He had started to drop back almost immediately after leaving the opening, and so while his shoulder and chest armor was destroyed, Vigaro's axe only scraped the flesh beneath.

Gyahn let out a howl of rage and pain. Vigaro didn't seem too concerned about failing to finish the kobolt off and licked at the blood on his own face with a smile.

"Blood tastes bad! Worry not! We cook you nice and tasty!" Vigaro shouted, a ball of carnivorous energy, and Gyahn's determination wavered for just a moment at the prospect of being cooked. While some of the decoys were still alive, he did wonder if a retreat would be a better idea.

But even if they did turn and run, there was no guarantee they would actually be able to escape. Even if some of them did get lucky, it would clearly take longer than six months to recover from these losses.

"Awoooooooooo!"

No matter the cost, winning this battle was now their only choice. He bolstered his strength again, activating a draining but powerful Limit Break skill. At his call, the other kobolts also prepared themselves for nothing less than victory or death.

"Ao-ao-awoooooo!"

The Limit Break bulked up Gyahn's muscles, swelling him in size. He swung his axe to cleave his foe in two. Vigaro responded with his own growl, thrashing his own axe. The weapons clashed together, but in terms of pure strength Gyahn now had the upper hand. Gyahn's axe was inching toward Vigaro.

That was the moment Vandal moved. He leaned forward from Vigaro's shoulders and pursed his lips.

Then, he spat.

His phlegm arched through the air and hit Gyahn on the shoulder. Gyahn's wolfish features contorted in surprise and rage. He growled and snarled, pushing the Limit Break skill even harder to bring all of his strength to bear in one decisive moment, but then—with no forewarning of any kind—one of the kobolt's hands simply left the haft of his axe.

"Gya—gyaa?!"

Shaken, Gyahn tried desperately to grab his weapon again, but his arm was hanging limp and useless. He whimpered, but before he could even work out what was happening with his body, Vigaro's axe was closing in on his neck.

"I cut off boss dog's head! This meat all ours now!"

Vigaro kicked over the headless corpse of Gyahn and raised his axe in the air.

The morale of the remaining kobolts bit the dust along with their king. The remaining elites gave whimpering cries, and all the kobolts started to run for their lives.

"Meat thinks it escape us!"

"Chase! Chase meat!"

The ghouls now saw the fleeing kobolts as nothing but meat and gave chase to fill their pantries.

We took too long after all!

Let's finish them off to make up for it!

The armor sisters and the Rotten Beasts finally wiped out the decoy kobolts, although not in time to help Vandal as they had hoped, and joined the ghouls in hunting down the remaining members of the pack. It certainly didn't look like it would take long to finish the rest of the kobolts off.

The remaining ghouls treated their wounded, while those with only light scratches started to butcher the kobolts. First they stripped off their weapons and armor. The kobolts mainly used weapons like daggers, which weren't much good for the brute-force ghouls, although they could be turned into spears with some sticks and a little ingenuity. The armor could be broken apart and refitted for ghoul use too.

The long swords and axes used by the Kobolt Chief and Knight were still a little small for the ghouls, but they could use them if they had to. Their armor could be adjusted using hard insect carapaces or split apart and completely refitted, allowing ghouls to use it as well. The staves used by the Kobolt Mages were trash sticks from the perspective of adventurers, but twigs of treasure for the ghoul women. Kobolt pelts weren't a hot commodity in human markets either, but in the unforgiving demon barrens they could make clothing for the winter that would inevitably return. The fangs from the Kobolt Chiefs, Knight, and Berserker could also make knives or spear heads, and the magical-power-infused eyes and organs of the Kobolt Mages could be used to make potions. The Kobolt King was brimming with magical power right to his bones, so he was a lump of potent ingredients.

Not to mention all the meat.

Adventurers would take the right ears, which were the bounty parts from kobolts, but the ghouls didn't care about those. They had no reason to.

"Vandal. What you do? With spitting," Vigaro asked, as Vandal turned the earth back into golems and uncovered the body of the Kobolt Berserker.

"I used a toxin."

"Toxin?"

"Yes. I used magic to turn my saliva into a paralytic, and then spat it into the kobolt's wound."

Gyahn had been leaning forward, pushing in with his axe, and so all Vandal had needed to do was lean forward a little himself and spit at the immobile target. The paralytic had been stronger than the one from the ghouls' claws, but made using the same composition, meaning it wouldn't have had any effect on Vigaro even if it hit him.

"It did leave my mouth a little numb, but I handled that quickly too." His only error—and a minor one, all things considered—was having creating a toxin so powerful even his Resist Maladies couldn't keep up.

"I see. Saved us good! We win and no one bad hurt!"

Vigaro was happy with the results. He didn't mind that Vandal had helped out since it wasn't like he was in an honorable duel with Gyahn, and the ghouls had such toxins in their own claws, so it wasn't an act of cowardice to win in such a way.

This was a battle between carnivores. The loser didn't get to cry foul.

"Felt good to fight. Make nice steamed kobolt once back home. Collect some kobol fruit and leaves first." Kobol fruit grew on kobol trees, which could be found only in the demon barrens, only in areas where kobolts lived. They were round with a bluish rind, about the size of a baby's head. They had a delicious texture and bitter-sweet flavor, making them popular in human society, too. The ghouls sometimes ate them whole, or squeezed them into juice, but they had another important purpose, so the ghouls always harvested them after hunting kobolts.

The massive task of carrying back the bodies and gear from dozens of kobolts, along with the kobol fruit and leaves, fell mainly to Sam.

Do your best, Father! Saria said.

I've got this! Sam replied. *But you did drain all the blood out of them, right?*

Of course, Rita responded. *We'll give you a good wash down afterward, don't worry.*

The Ghost Carriage considerably boosted the transportation capabilities of the ghouls. Sam was better than a normal carriage in that he could travel over far rougher terrain without any issues, and was also essentially self-powered and self-driving. That make him perfect for operating in the demon barrens. He could even run down a kobolt grunt or two if needed. It wasn't just the ghouls who appreciated him. Every adventurer who had ever hunted a demon barren would have wanted Sam along for the ride. Although most would balk at him being undead.

"Kobolt meat best steamed. Taste good! You like, I promise."

Vandal could tell Vigaro was hoping he would like it so much, he'd decide to stay with the ghouls. "It's taking long to finish my training than I expected. I'll be staying at least a little longer, don't worry," Vandal assured him.

"It only been one year. That normal," Vigaro replied. The ghoul had no magical ability himself—whatever affinity he might have would take him decades of hard work to turn into anything usable—and yet he was still the next chief. He knew how hard it was for the female ghouls to learn their magic. None of them had mastered the art in less than five years.

So it looked like Vandal would be with them for a while longer. That fact made Vigaro happier than anything else they had acquired today. With a grin on his lion face, he led Sam and the others back to the settlement.

Name: Bone Monkey, Bone Wolf, Bone Bear
Rank: 4
Race: Rotten Beast
Level: 7 - 10

—Passive Skills
[Night Vision] [Brute Strength: Level 2 (UP!)]
[Spirit Body: Level 2 (NEW!)]
—Active Skills
[Sneaking Steps: Level 2 (UP!)]
[Breath (Poison): Level 1 (NEW!)]

The kobolt meat tasted as bad as Vigaro had said. It wasn't quite on goblin levels, but it smelled much more pungent than meat from regular livestock and simply piling on the spices wasn't enough to cover the problem. Even if that hurdle could be climbed, the meat itself was stingy and tough, like chewing an old boot.

There were no humans who ate kobolt unless the alternative was to starve. But the ghouls, eking out a living in the demon barrens, didn't have that luxury. They had worked out a way to make goblin taste palatable, and so they had done the same with kobolt.

First, they cut the kobolt meat into large chunks, and then put slices of kobol fruit on top. Then they wrapped it all in kobol leaves and steamed the parcels. That made the kobol meat unbelievably soft, and removed the odor too, leaving a flavor that could still be called "unique" but not in an overpowering way. It wasn't going to blow anyone's taste buds off, but even humans would probably be able to make a meal of it. It might be possible to really go gourmet with the skill of a professional chef.

That wasn't to say this discovery would cause a kobolt sensation in human society, should the recipe ever make it out of the barrens. A single kobol fruit sold for 10 Amidd, which was around 1,000 yen. The kobol leaves had no market value, however, so maybe poor people would be able to at least make the meat semi-palatable just by using those.

"That sounds more like a welfare scheme than a business one," Vandal mused. He didn't even know if there were poor people like that anywhere in this world. He kept thinking, eating more kobolt.

The cooked meat tasted even better with some of his walnut sauce, a sentiment to which Zadilis and Vigaro heartily agreed when he recommended it to them. The ghouls had experimented with various approaches to cooking, but had never set foot into sauce territory. Culinary culture could be a strange beast.

As a result, Vandal's main task in the settlement at the moment was making his sauce. Luckily enough, there were walnuts to be found in the demon barrens all year round, providing all the raw materials he required. Some of the female ghouls helped him with the work, so it wasn't all that hard. In fact, he actually enjoyed it.

The main issue was that they were running out of salt. He needed to track down some more bandits and resupply. With more salt, Vandal could try making some walnut paste, too.

But before that, he was going to try making some cookies using the acorns that could also be found here all year round. There was a small river close to the settlement for washing the lye from the acorns. He didn't want the carbohydrates in addition to the protein, so it was definitely worth a try.

"I guess this means I'm making a contribution to society," Vandal commented. "I'm a member of this community. Every day feels fulfilling."

"An impressive sentiment, coming from a baby. You are a big help, I'll tell you that." Zadilis had a wry smile on her face, but she also wasn't trying to deny the difference Vandal was making to the grotto. It wasn't just walnut sauces. Boosting Vigaro's fighting strength with Saria, Rita, Sam, and the other undead was big too, even taking into account the need to train them.

In regard to the sisters, the spirits themselves had only been maids in life, but now that they possessed powerful magic items, they were actually stronger than your average ghoul. They were also originally human, and their diligence provided excellent stimulation for the younger ghouls prone to laziness. Because they served Vandal, in the eyes of the ghouls whatever contribution the sisters made was a contribution made by Vandal.

Zadilis liked Vandal on a personal level, too, and wanted him to stay with them. If that wasn't possible, then she wanted him to stay as long as possible. But she also wasn't holding back on training him in order to make that happen.

"Your non-attribute magic training is still taking a while. Not that I'm saying you're going slowly," Zadilis commented.

"It's harder than I expected," Vandal said. "I still can't form the magical power without bringing an attribute into it."

Seeing as he could already use death attribute magic, he would have been lying if he said that he thought the far more fundamental non-attribute magic was going to be difficult to pick up. That had been a mistake. Forming the raw magical power into the desired form and then activating it proved much harder than anticipated. He was so adept at using death attribute magic by now that having to stop that from happening became a stumbling block.

All Vandal really had was his massive MP and the imagination and ideas he had been exposed to through pop culture on Earth. When it came to actual magical ability, he still fell short. He had mastered death attribute magic on Origin in a very short period of time, but that had been due to the twisted will engendered by his living hell, and the enforced backup provided by top-class scientists who had also been cut free from any moral mooring.

Without that, Vandal was just a normal baby. Having all that MP gave him the singular advantage that he could train for longer than a normal person.

"If I had access to non-attribute magic, the battle today would have gone a lot more smoothly. I want to learn it as fast as I can," Vandal said.

"It took me three years to get my first non-attribute magic skill. Take it easy. It will come."

"As you say. That reminds me, one of the kobolt spirits told me that there's orc territory in the center of these demon barrens. I didn't get all the details, but apparently they were seeking to expand in order to fight those orcs," Vandal reported.

Zadilis gave a shrug. "Fine, so long as they don't come for us. We just need to keep training and we can handle anything that comes our way. No rush. No panic. You too. Here, have my meat."

She handed over her portion with a smile. For her, she probably felt like they were grandmother and grandson, but appearance-wise they looked more like slightly removed siblings.

"Thank you."

Even as he chowed down on Gyahn and the tasty kobolts, Vandal hadn't forgotten about all the issues he faced. Vandal wanted to revive Dalshia, have his revenge on High Priest Goldan and the Five Hue Blades who had killed her, and finally get to live a luxurious and happy life. But he still needed a lot more strength and technique before he could reach that point.

Gyahn, whom they had defeated today, had been rank 5, while his minions were rank 4 or below. Vandal needed to be able to defeat those kinds of enemies, but on his own, in order to fulfill his goals. That said, Zadilis wasn't wrong in her estimation of the situation.

"Good. Eat up, boy," she said.

There was no need to panic. All he needed to do was keep an eye on his goals and continue his daily training. His third life had only just begun, after all. "You're going to be big and strong before you know it."

"You think I could become like Vigaro?" Vandal pondered. He didn't just want strength and technique, but also muscles.

"I'm not sure about that," Zadilis replied.

"Vigaro would spend all day swinging his axe, even when he was a child," Basdia said, naturally joining the conversation. "If you do the same thing, you might reach the same point in …100 years?"

"You talk about me?" Vigaro appeared too, hearing his name. Sam came with him, along with his daughters who had finished cleaning him.

Young Master! Pay us some attention too, please! We've finished washing Dad and have nothing to do!

We don't have mouths or stomachs! Tell us what the food tastes like!

Meanwhile, the skeleton undead gnawed on kobolt bones, and the ghouls were celebrating their victory. The only one simply relaxing and taking it all in was Sam.

It was lively and fun, but the mountain of issues Vandal faced was certainly not a small one.

But here, in a place like this, I can put the work in to become strong enough, Vandal thought.

He just hoped it wasn't going to actually take 100 years.

Afterword

Thank you for picking up *The Death Mage*. My name is Densuke. I made my debut with this book. Nice to meet you.

I posted this book on the novel website *Shousetsuka ni Narou*. It won an award during the Fourth Internet Novel Awards, held by the same site, which then led to its publication.

I decided to write this book because I couldn't find the exact kind of story that I myself wanted to read. I'm overjoyed that so many enjoyed it online, that it went on to win an award, and then became published like this. I will work to ensure that even more people have a chance to pick up my work and enjoy it.

In regard to the published version, the main flow of the story is the same as the online version, but I've added new episodes along the way. Some characters appear more frequently or get more to do, there are some completely new characters, and other characters from the online version show up earlier than before, so there's a lot going on!

We also have numerous beautiful illustrations penned by Ban! These should help you to imagine key scenes and the characters in action, drawing you more deeply into the world. I think people who have already read the internet version can still enjoy it. They can, right?

Our main character has started his third life, acquiring a family, allies, and powers that he never had in his first or second lives. However, he and his allies are still very weak within the world of the series. They are at risk not only from gods, but also powerful adventurers, warrior priests keen to wipe out undead, and raging monsters. If they encounter these threats under the wrong circumstances, they will face certain death with no hope of escape.

I hope you will continue to watch over them as they seek to become strong enough to survive such threats, and eventually achieve their goals. There will be more heroines, skeletons, and muscle-heads turning up in the future too!

Phew. It's not easy to be the one writing the afterward. It's taken me close to an hour to write this much. Lastly, allow me to offer some thanks.

To the staff at Himifushobo, who noticed my work and selected it to win my award, to my editor who worked so hard to achieve this publication, to Ban! for all the wonderful illustrations; to everyone else involved in this publication; and to my readers, for all their support of *The Death Mage*—thank you all so much! I hope to see you again in the next volume.

—Densuke

Glossary

—Monsters
Ghost Carriage
Living Armor
Ghoul Mage
Ghoul Warrior
Ghoul Barbarian
Rotten Beast
Kobolt King

—Skills
Spirit Body
Spirit Pollution
Cooperation

Ghost Carriage
An undead created when a spirit with lingering attachments to the world inhabits a carriage and turns evil. A horse and driver comprised of white fog can sometimes be seen, but the carriage is the actual body, with these other elements nothing more than materializations of its expressions. Defeating a Ghost Carriage therefore requires the evil spirit to be purged or the carriage itself to be destroyed.

Its primary form of attack is to ram into enemies. In fact, that's more or less the only form of attack to which it has access. In some cases the original carriage may feature additional armaments, such as spikes. People rarely ride in such a carriage, but the Off-road Handling and Resist Impact skills it possesses make for a smooth ride for anyone "lucky" enough to give it a try.

Bounty parts are sections of the wagon with magic stones attached. Raw materials come from the carriage itself; there are various productive ways it can be repurposed, such as breaking it down for parts. However—ironically so—a horse or even a wagon will be required in order to transport the spoils.

A rare type of monster, Ghost Carriages are not generally seen in the demon barrens. However, after ruins have turned into demon barrens, there have been reports of all the carriages left there turning into Ghost Carriages.

In the case of Sam, he has access to Precision Driving and Sneaking Steps, skills a normal Ghost Carriage would not learn. The first comes from Sam's life as a professional carriage driver, and the second from all the sneaking around he has been forced to do since becoming undead. This combination allows him to drive with more skill than a normal Ghost Carriage, and to do so without making any undue noise.

Living Armor

Armor possessed by an evil spirit. Many of them are formed from the spirits of the one who wore the armor in life, such as soldiers, knights, or adventurers, but few retain memories or the personality from that life. The majority become mindless killers that simply attack anything alive.

Strength depends on the armor being possessed and the weapon it uses. Those in chain mail or half plate are rank 3. Those in full plate armor are rank 4. In very rare cases the armor that is possessed is a magic item. In those cases, the rank depends on the functions of the magic item in question.

The bounty parts are magic stones, which are obtained almost universally regardless of rank. Materials are the armor that was possessed, and the weapons, shields, and other gear the armor was carrying. As the armor has been exposed to magic, it can turn into a magic item after being defeated. Using it without taking any measures first can result in getting cursed, but the armor can be used safely after purification.

In the case of Saria and Rita, their spirits possessed magic item armor, but as they were maids in life with no knowledge of handling weapons, their rank was accordingly reduced. The functionality of the armor itself is not affected, so its defense and resistance skills remain intact.

Ghoul Mage

A ghoul that has learned a certain amount of magic. It is more powerful than a newbie adventurer, and has reasonable physical strength, as well as a paralytic toxin that allows it to fight well in close quarters.

Mages are smarter than other ghouls, often placing them in leadership or tactical positions. That means they are rarely found alone, and normally have multiple other ghouls around them. The adventurers' guild therefore recommends that any combat against them is performed in parties.

The bounty part is the right ear. Materials are the claws from their hands and feet, their magic-filled eyes and tongue, and their liver as materials for medicine. The spinal cord is a medium for alchemy. It is comparatively difficult to defeat a rank 5 monster, and many adventurers don't consider the reward and sale price of the materials worth the hassle.

However, many Ghoul Mages are female, meaning they sell for a high price as slaves on the black market. That means, however, that the ghoul must be captured alive, which is extremely dangerous and greatly increases the chances of being killed. Ghoul Mages sold on the black market are generally sourced by teaching a captive female ghoul enough magic to rank them up. Ranking up to a Ghoul Mage requires at least one attribute magic skill of level 3 or higher.

In the case of Zadilis, she possesses exemplarily magical control and is stronger than the average Ghoul Mage, but her advanced age has diminished her physical and magical powers, greatly reducing her capabilities in combat.

Ghoul Warrior

A ghoul with enhanced combat abilities. They act as commanders in packs of ghouls, and can be leaders when no more powerful ghouls are present. In addition to their toxin-laced claws, they are also skilled in martial arts and the use of weapons, and can use battle techs. Appearance-wise, they don't look that different from normal ghouls, meaning adventurers can mistake them for being weaker than they are and take a beating as a result.

The bounty part is the right ear. Materials are the fangs and claws from the hands and feet, and their livers are used as an ingredient in medicine.

A normal ghoul can become a Ghoul Warrior by learning multiple combat-based skills at level 2 or higher. This sets the bar comparatively low, with many ghouls fulfilling those conditions prior to even reaching level 100.

Basdia is blessed with physical abilities rather than magic, and her stats are a result of her training focused on extending such abilities. She suffers from the status ailment Infertile, but that has no adverse effect on her other abilities or skills.

Ghoul Barbarian

A ranked-up ghoul that has further honed its skills, greatly increasing its physical strength. It is about twice the size of a normal ghoul and will often rely simply on smashing enemies by swinging a massive weapon around. Many of them have low intelligence, however, with nothing in their heads besides fighting. That places them lower in the pack hierarchy, and they are generally put to use by Ghoul Mages. Barbarians are always male; a female barbarian has never been confirmed.

The bounty part is the right ear. Materials include fangs, claws from the hands and feet, tendons that can be used as bow strings, and their magical mane. Ghouls can become a Barbarian by achieving Brute Strength at level 3 or higher, and skills for handling two-handed weapons at level 4 or higher.

In the case of Vigaro, he is smarter than other Barbarians, and is positioned to become the next chief. He also has incredible command abilities: while normal Barbarians prefer to fight alone, Vigaro always fights alongside allies. That makes him significantly harder to defeat than other Barbarians.

Rotten Beast

Rank 4. A monster holding the grudge-filled power of a bone beast, reinforced by anger and regret from all the living creatures they have killed. The bones that comprise their bodies are blackened in places, maintaining their flexibility while reaching a strength almost equal to steel. Furthermore, they are capable of spitting poison breath, regardless of the monster they originated from.

For grade D adventurers, a single Rotten Beast is not too much of a threat so long as they have means to deal with that poison. However, Rotten Beasts can retain the instincts they had in life to form into packs, and so the adventurers' guild recommends that any combat against them is performed in parties.

Kobolt King

A rank 5 monster that can be reached by a rank 4 kobolt after awakening to a powerful urge to lead the pack. It has a physique almost identical to that of an adult human and is imposing enough to give humans a real scare.

A powerful monster even on its own, it can also generally be found leading dozens of other lesser kobolts. It possesses the skill Enhance Brethren, further boosting the strength of those pack members, and making it a serious threat from the instant it appears. Leaving it unchecked means it can expand its pack to over a thousand kobolts. Kobolt Kings are treated like natural disasters, with its subjugation stipulated for a party of adventurers grade C or higher with at least twenty members.

The bounty part is the right ear. Materials for weapons and armor are the pelt from the body, the teeth, claws, and bones, and the internal organs are materials used for alchemy. Bounties for defeating one are often worth a small fortune.

In the case of Gyahn, it hadn't been long since he became a Kobolt King, and his pack was still small, so defeating him was relatively easy.

Spirit Body

A skill that allows things like souls and spirits, usually without a physical form, to manifest semi-corporeal matter. The manifested spirit body can be seen and touched. Physical attacks against it are not completely negated, but more than two thirds of them are. Attacks by magic items or blessed weapons retain their efficiency.

There are varied uses for the manifested spirit body. At the lowest levels, it provides the muscles and cartilage to hold the bones together for monsters such as Skeletons. Acquiring further skills can allow a Spirit Body to act as the rotted-away muscles, increasing strength, or the sloughed-away fur and scales, increasing defenses. Other examples include the Bone Bird manifesting spirit feathers in order to fly, or to use as ranged weapons, and Sam being able to manifest a horse after ranking up and so—quite literally—increasing his horsepower. The reason the Skeleton General could wear full plate armor was also due to using a Spirit Body to fill in the gaps between the armor and the bones inside.

Another application is to control the Spirit Body without manifesting it, sending a spirit inside other people's bodies or through walls.

Spirit Pollution

A skill that represents such things as psychological confusion, depth of trauma, and deep terror. It functions as a resistance skill that protects the mind from poison, curses, magic, and other elements.

However, the majority of the organizations promoting the learning of this skill have connections to the criminal underworld. In the regular world, this skill is often considered a type of disease, and there are even specialist medical facilities for treating it.

Those actually holding this skill include clinical sadists, murderers, soldiers, or adventurers who have suffered great tragedy, and assassins who no longer feel remorse or guilt over killing others. On the flip side, many renowned artists, inventors, and other successful people have also possessed it, meaning simply having this skill is not strictly binding when it comes to personality.

Cooperation

When those holding this skill cooperate together, the efficiency and results of the endeavor receive a positive modifier. In the case of construction work, for example, errors will be reduced and the pace of the world accelerated. In battle, attack and defense will both be increased.

The degree of the modifier depends on the skill level and the number of people holding the skill. Rather than adventurers, who tend to operate in smaller groups, this skill is more suited to soldiers or construction crews who work in larger numbers.

In regard to monsters, even those with a tendency to form packs are unable to learn this skill without some awareness of allies or desire to cooperate, meaning goblins and orcs are unable to learn it. It is mainly learned by kobolts, ghouls, and other wolf-type monsters.